Stalker

Jack Adams

Atlas Productions

Stalker

First published 2021 by Atlas Productions.
Web: www.atlasproductions.com.au
Copyright © Jack Adams and Helen Goltz
All rights reserved

Proofread by Jessica Lucci.
Cover design by Atlas Productions.
Images: Man and background image by Lorraine Cormier from Pixabay; boys on their bikes image by Venera Salman, Shutterstock.

A catalogue record for this book is available from the National Library of Australia

ISBN: 978-0-6452429-3-5

PLEASE NOTE: This book is written in British- Australian English.

Remembering fondly

Donna-Maree, Fiona and Kathryn

Chapter 1

Then...

Adam Murphy wasn't the only boy at his private school to have his own security detail, but he was the only one whose guard had to sit in the backseat while Adam's grandmother, Audrey, drove the school route in her classic, regency red, Jaguar XJ6.

Except on a Wednesday – Audrey's bridge day and the one day of the week that she handed the keys to Tom Hartigan and stayed at home to get ready. Tom – a former member of Australia's Special Air Service Regiment, fondly known as the SAS – loved having the keys in his hand, the pedal under his foot. He prayed if anything bad was going to happen, it would happen on a Wednesday. Not that Audrey was a conservative driver for her age; he wished she was. She drove too fast, changed routes on a whim and listened attentively to the talkback radio when Tom would have preferred her attention was on the drive. She was an interesting old girl; probably smoked too much of the good stuff in her younger years, and never quite stopped rebelling against the system.

The car was a wedding anniversary present from Audrey's husband, Adam's grandfather, because steel was the theme of their marriage that year and he had made his considerable fortune in steel. Audrey was widowed the following year. The Jag had only ever had one owner. Tom gave thanks that at least it had four doors and he wouldn't have to clamber over them if anything should happen on the school route with Audrey at the wheel.

'He's there!' Adam exclaimed, pointing to a fair-haired boy standing out the front of his house, dressed in the local public-school uniform.

Tom swung the car into the curb and Adam's best friend, Nathan Delaney, jumped in the back seat. The boys were the same age but went to different schools; sometimes Nate got a lift with them, other times, he'd ride his bike if he had footy training. He always got a lift on Wednesday when Tom was behind the wheel.

'Hey Tom,' he said, and leaned forward to punch Adam in the arm.

'Master Nathanial,' Tom said, seriously, 'belt up.' He watched the skinny blonde kid strap on the seat belt before driving on.

'Can we go really fast?' Nate asked.

'No,' Tom said, and grinned. 'Maybe we could go a little faster on the back roads.'

'Yes!' Adam exclaimed, and looked back to grin at Nate.

'She purrs this fine lady,' Tom said, and ran his hand over the top of the timber steering wheel.

'That's why she's a Jaguar,' Nate agreed.

Tom grinned. 'Very good, Nate. So, lads, spill it… tell me everything that I need to know. Have you seen Uncle Allan recently?' he asked, with a glance at Adam.

'Sure, he came to our cricket game last week. He said that if I kept practising, he reckons I'd be good enough for the State side. He used to coach, so he should know,' Adam said.

'Yeah, and he said my bowling had got better too. We've got a game this weekend. You should come, Tom,' Nate said.

'Are you any good at cricket?' Adam asked, sizing up the driver.

'Am I any good?' Tom scoffed. 'I could have played for Australia but they were worried I'd be too good and show the rest of the team up.'

The boys laughed.

'Sounds like bull,' Nate said, with a grin.

'Anyway,' Tom continued, 'you know not to go anywhere with Uncle Allan until I meet him, don't you, Adam?' he said, trying not to come down too heavy. 'You'll lose me my job otherwise and then we won't get to drive alone on Wednesdays.'

He turned into a back street with a slightly industrial flavour and gave the car a burst of speed to make the proposition attractive and deliver on his word; the boys whooped with joy. A few minutes later, back in civilization, Tom pulled up outside Nate's school gate. 'See you, buddy.'

'Thanks, Tom, see you after school, Murph,' Nate grabbed his backpack and got out, slamming the door, and making Tom wince.

Tom pulled away from the curb and continued to Adam's school.

'Adam?'

'Yeah, I know,' he said, 'I won't.'

'Good,' Tom said, and breathed out. 'I've got to make an appointment to catch up with your principal... next Wednesday if he's free, I'll come in with you.'

'Why?' Adam wheeled around to look at him, concern all over his face. It was bad enough being the son of a famous model, he didn't want to be singled out any more than necessary.

'Nothing to worry about,' Tom said, with a smile and an attempt to relax the slight boy who was the spitting image of his father. He was also the spitting image of the former prime minister who was alleged to have had an affair with Adam's mother and model, Winsome Keeley, the *IT* girl.

Tom explained. 'The principal's an old friend of my brother, and I said I'd drop in and say hi,' he lied.

'Oh, cool,' Adam said, and visibly relaxed.

'Nope, all is fine,' Tom assured him, and glanced again in the rear-view and side mirrors.

Nothing was fine.

Adam didn't have an Uncle Allan.

Chapter 2

Now...

Nathan Delaney did his best not to be judgmental, but some days you had to call a spade a spade. He'd seen and met all types and he wasn't bad at typecasting; picking the criminals from the mislead or the downright stupid. He had to work at being tolerant when his instincts told him upfront that he was dealing with a no-hoper.

His childhood best friend, Adam Murphy, who shared his office space, was much more understanding and tolerant – it was probably why he was a psychologist. Nate was pretty sure that Adam wouldn't be looking at the craggy woman sitting opposite him and thinking how ugly she was. She'd tried her best with a floral scarf around her neck to match the pastel shift she was wearing. The make-up was packed on, but nothing would soften that face, he thought.

'Do you think you can find him, find my son?' she asked, with a voice gravelled from years of smoking.

Nate cleared his throat and leaned forward. 'Mrs Tatum, I'm wary of raising false hope but I assure you, if he can be found, we'll find him.'

She breathed out, relieved. Then, her eyes narrowed, she studied him for a few moments, nodded and said, 'Right. Let's do it then, hey?'

Folks up north say 'hey' a lot, Nate thought. He wondered if that's where she hailed from; might have had her edges roughed up living a bush life. He took the photo she offered him and studied the gangly man; he was no oil painting either. Poor bastard had little hope with the gene pool in front of him, Nate thought.

'Sorry. It's about ten years old that photo and I don't have a recent one.'

'That's fine, it gives me something to go with.'

'He goes under a different surname from mine. I've remarried,' she said. 'He's a Sabel.'

'Got it, Aden Sabel,' Nate said, scribbling the name on his pad. 'You say he's had a few problems?'

She nodded, then tugged at her shoulder-length, obviously dyed brown hair. 'He's a junkie, there's no kinder word for it,' she said. 'You name it, he's sniffed, snorted or drunk it. But you know, a mother's love can look past that.'

'Yes, apparently,' Nate said, looking at the photo. 'I have a partner who might be of help on this case too.'

'The shrink? I saw his name on the door,' she said. 'Guess it can't hurt but I can't afford to pay double.'

'No, we don't work like that,' Nate assured her. 'Can I keep this for now?' he said, waving the photo in her direction.

'Sure, it's a copy. I've seen enough crime TV shows to know you'd need one.'

'Thanks, I appreciate that,' Nate said, throwing her a bone. 'So, about my partner, Dr Adam Murphy, I bring him in to share his insights; he knows people, he reads them well. He might know where your son could go to avoid the doctors, or to get help or supplies on the quiet, if you know what I mean?'

She nodded and sighed. He softened, feeling sorry for the woman who clearly hadn't had it easy of late, maybe ever.

Nate continued: 'At the end of the day, your son is an adult now and you've done your best.'

'Yeah, I still feel like I didn't get it right though,' she said. 'I know he's not a kid anymore, but he's lived in the granny flat out the back for the past decade and he doesn't go out much. So, this is out of character. My gut tells me something's happened to him. He's got no job, no girlfriend, so where the hell has he been sleeping for the past week?'

Nate nodded.

'Got in with the wrong crowd he did, when he was young. It wasn't so bad when he was just smoking, but that stuff got much more serious. Might have helped if his father stuck around. A boy needs a role model, don't you think?'

'It helps for sure if they are a good role model,' Nate added. 'But you know, I'm no psychologist,' he said with a shrug. 'I'm a former cop and I've seen kids from terrible homes do great things, and kids from privileged homes go off the rails.'

At least it wasn't a cheating husband case, Nate thought, she'd be ripe for that. He scolded himself again for being judgmental and, putting the photo and pen down, glanced over the notes he'd made. Rising, Nate indicated the meeting was over and he'd get to finding her son. He handed her a page with the price, terms and conditions and told Mrs Tatum that Jessica at reception could fix her up.

'How often can I expect to hear from you?' she asked, rising in an ungainly manner. If he hadn't risen first, he was pretty sure she would have flashed him. The thought made him shudder.

'If I have any news, I'll be in touch right away, otherwise,

every few days. But call me anytime you have a concern.'
Nate opened the door and shook her hand.

'Thanks, I appreciate it, Mr Delaney. Don't need the
stress... that boy has caused me nothing but pain,' she said,
placing her hand against her heart as she said the words.

Poor old battler, Nate thought.

'Call me Nate, and it will be my priority,' he assured her.
He guided her back to Jessica at reception to sort out the
finer details and returned to his office. Christ, he thought,
I hope her son wants to be found. He sat at the desk and
put in a call to his cop mate, Sergeant Matt Burns. They
had a loose arrangement – Nate would share any relevant
information that came his way and Matt would run the
occasional search for Nate.

'You're not pulling out of the game, are you?' Matt asked.

'You kidding? State of origin, your shout at the bar since
you lost the last one... I've got the maroon scarf ironed.'

Matt laughed. 'Yeah, good luck with that. So, what's up?'

'Got a missing person case. Mother's just been in and is
looking for her adult son, Aden Sabel. Is he on your radar?'
Nate asked.

'Stand by,' Matt said. Nate could hear him tapping on the
keyboard. 'I've got a few Aden Sabels in the system... how
old is he?'

'Thirty, been missing a week.'

'No-one in the system in that age group; she hasn't been
in here yet to file a missing person's report,' Matt said.

'Yeah, well, he's probably not missing, just in a gutter
somewhere,' Nate said. 'He's been on the drug scene for a
while. She might not want to bring him to your attention if
you can forget I asked?'

'Right then, he's off my radar. But no priors either, so he
can't be too bad.'

'Thanks. See you tonight,' Nate said and hung up. He waited until he heard Mrs Tatum leave before heading out to see if Jessica had got the deposit secured.

*****

Adam Murphy came out of his office just in time to see Mrs Tatum departing. She greeted him with suspicion, took her receipt from Jessica and departed. Adam frowned; he knew that face, but couldn't place where he knew it from. Nate surfaced from his office.

'Hard life, that one?' Adam asked in a hushed voice.

'You can say that again,' Nate agreed. 'A real rough head. Although I never thought you'd call it.'

'Yeah, sharing offices with you is clearly rubbing off on me... you're a bad influence.' Adam agreed, leaning against the reception desk.

Jessica stood up, crossed her arms, and looked from one to the other. She came up to their shoulders but tried for a formidable presence in the middle of the two men in their suits.

'You two are horrible. Life's not a beauty contest!'

'It isn't?' Nate said, and catching his reflection in the small mirror on the wall behind Jessica, ran his hand through his blonde hair. He turned his green eyes to Adam, a carbon copy opposite with blue eyes and dark hair. 'So, we won the genetic lottery then?'

Adam laughed as Jessica smirked at the pair of them.

'I hate to think what you say about me when I'm not here,' she said.

'We say you're gorgeous and too good for us and our office,' Nate said.

'That's the gist of it,' Adam agreed.

'Hmm,' she sniffed unceremoniously, but couldn't help but smile. She was secretly thrilled, and gave it away with her body language, pushing a strand of brunette hair behind her ear.

Nate turned his attention to Adam. 'I might need your help with that client,' he said, with a nod to the door where Mrs Tatum just exited. 'Her son's been missing for a week... a druggie. Got any ideas where I should start checking out the scene?'

'Sure,' Adam said. 'Sadly, I know all the best hang-outs.'

Jessica looked surprised. 'You've been to some of them?'

'Pretty regularly over the years. I've had to try and save a few clients who fell back into old habits,' he admitted. 'Not pretty.'

'Really?' Jessica said. 'I wouldn't know where to start if I wanted to score.'

'Depends who you are and what you want. There's a hierarchy of respectability amongst drug users,' Adam explained. 'There's the homeless who usually just stick to alcohol, the cheaper the better. Then there are the party poppers taking pills or cocaine. They don't see themselves as anything like those users who inject. But, it's a slippery slope... they start occasionally smoking crystal meth and the next minute they're addicted.'

'That'll be you if you're not careful, Nate,' Jessica said and smiled at his wry expression. She grabbed Mrs Tatum's file and put it in her compendium. 'How do they get it?' she asked Adam.

'There are regular street corners where you can get pretty much anything you need or want if you're carrying cash,' he told Jessica.

'By the sounds of it, I think Mrs Tatum's son might be the type who has to have his supply at any price and he'll steal, beg and borrow to get it… that's an ugly scene,' Nate said.

Adam nodded. 'I had a client who sold his mother's furniture regularly to feed his habit, and she'd go down and buy it back each time. Heartbreaking stuff.'

Nate frowned. 'I'm just a little freaked out by how much you know about this. But then, again, any chance of some hash?'

'Nate!' Jessica exclaimed.

'Just kidding,' Nate said, and gave Adam a look that said he wasn't.

'I saw that look,' Jessica told him.

'God, imagine having to be worried about your adult kid. It would feel like it never ends.' Adam shook his head.

'He's old enough to know better,' Nate said. 'His mother, Mrs Tatum, looked familiar.' He thought for a moment, then gave a slight shrug.

'I thought so too,' Adam said.

'Maybe we're getting older. Everyone's looking familiar,' Jessica suggested.

'Yeah. You're good with faces, though, Nate. Maybe you've ingested too many mug shots,' Adam suggested.

'You'd remember a face like that, surely,' Jessica said and they both turned to her. 'See, you're rubbing off on me, Nate. You're a bad influence.'

'I've been telling him that for years,' Adam said.

'So have his parents,' Nate joked. 'Speaking of which, how are the wedding plans coming along?'

'Ooh, yes, how exciting,' Jessica's said, her face lit up with the glamour of the pending nuptials.

Adam sighed and moved to sit on a chair in their waiting

area. He placed his hands along the back of the chairs beside him. 'It's a circus.'

Jessica laughed, then sobered. 'Sorry, I was picturing a wedding with several clowns in the wedding party and a trapeze. Sorry... carry on.'

Adam smiled. 'That'd be better. Mum's sold the rights to some women's magazine and now Stephanie's trying to get me to sign a waiver that I won't speak with anyone except the sponsor. For the love of God,' he said and rolled his eyes. 'I wish Mum would get a new publicist and drop my ex. Better still, I wish she'd bloody elope with Jack. It's not like they're newlyweds, go to Vegas or something.'

'No, that's no fun. The wedding of Winsome Keeley, the *IT girl* with Jack Bernham, the *Voice of the Nation*, so exciting,' Jessica said, then seeing their faces added, 'well for some of us who aren't cranky or only interested in football.'

The office door opened, and they all froze as if caught in the act of doing nothing, which they were. They breathed a sigh of relief at seeing the mature aged man at the door.

'Ah-ha, so this is what you do when I'm not here,' Robert Ware said, looking at the laid-back group.

Adam pointed at a chair, welcoming his part-time psychologist colleague and former mentor to take a seat.

'Don't mind if I do.' He dropped near Adam and sighed.

'We've got no appointments for an hour or so. I'll get some coffee,' Jessica suggested, slipping into the small office kitchen.

'Was that a new client I just saw on the way out?' Rob asked. 'She looked familiar.'

'Yes!' Nate said, 'I haven't lost it! I thought the same thing.'

'Is she your client or Adam's?' Rob asked Nate.

'Mine, but maybe both,' Nate said. 'She's looking for her

adult son who hasn't come home for a week. She doesn't want to go to the police… he's a druggie.'

'Ah, right,' Rob said. 'What's his name? Maybe we know her from her son.' He accepted a coffee and thanked Jessica.

Nate searched his memory. 'Different name to his mother who remarried… she's Tatum, the son is…' He clicked his fingers, remembering, 'Aden Sabel.'

Rob frowned and sipped his coffee. Adam glanced his way, studying his friend and mentor. He knew his mannerisms well from the years under Rob's tutelage.

'What are you thinking?' Adam asked.

'Nuh, don't know that name.'

'Well, you're a big help,' Nate said and took a biscuit from the packet Jessica offered and thanked her. 'He's in his thirties but he's never been missing for this long,' Nate said with a mouthful of biscuit.

'Hmm,' Rob said. 'Missing kids, even if they are adults now, must be every parent's nightmare. Remember that young boy who went missing when you two were about 10 or so? My boy was about 13 at the time, scared the hell out of me.'

'No, who was that?' Adam asked, helping himself to a second biscuit.

'His name was Dean, something… I can't remember. A stranger picked him up from his swimming meet,' Rob said.

Jessica shuddered. 'How frightening. That must have worried your folks, Adam, given your mum's profile.'

Nate looked at Adam. 'When we were 10, you still had Tom, the SAS security guard then.'

Jessica laughed. 'How weird to be a kid with your own security guy.'

'He was cool though,' Nate said with a smile. 'Especially when Audrey let him drive the Jag.'

Adam agreed. 'That car rarely got up to top speed.' He turned back to Rob. 'So, what happened? Did the family pay up and Dean came home?'

Rob shook his head. 'The family paid and Dean was never seen or heard from again, declared dead after several bloodied items of his clothing were found. His murderer never told where Dean's body was buried.'

'That's a terrible story,' Jessica said, 'his poor parents, what anguish.'

Nate sighed. 'Sad reality – one kid never saw past ten, the other – Mrs Tatum's son – can't get out of his own way to make the most of the life he is given.' It bugged him, though. He knew her face, and it didn't come attached to a happy memory.

Chapter 3

Then…

Ten-year-old Adam Murphy raced from the cricket pitch to the boundary as soon as the final cheer went up, the cricket bat wedged under his arm.

'Uncle Allan, you made it!' he said, his grin wide, his dark hair tousled, and his eyes alive with excitement. No one ever came to watch him play, not like the other boys' dads who coached from the sidelines.

'Wouldn't miss it,' Allan Sheffield said and scuffed the young boy affectionately around the shoulders. 'You did well today.'

'We lost though,' Adam said.

'But you played well. That's cricket,' Allan said with a shrug. 'Ah, here he is now.'

Both heads turned to see Adam's best friend, Nate, heading towards them.

'Good game, young Nate,' Allan said.

'Thank you, Uncle Allan,' he said, using the name he was invited to use, even though Allan was not Nate's uncle. He wasn't Adam's either.

'Did you see me bowl out that last guy?' Nate asked.

'It was excellent,' Allan said, grinning at the enthusiastic lads, 'and that boundary shot of yours was terrific too, Adam.'

'It would have been a six if Nate's team hadn't caught it out.'

'Yeah, probably a four,' Nate said, stirring his friend.

'Where's your hat?' Allan asked Nate, hoping to send him off to find it while he had a moment alone with Adam.

'I've lost it somewhere. Mum says I manage to lose everything eventually. I lost my cricket gloves, too. That's why I'm a bowler now instead of a catcher.'

'You need a manager,' Allan said, and grinned. 'That's what I do. I manage to get very important people to where they have to be and return their items when most of them lose them, too. Maybe you are going to be very important Nate, and people can run after you bringing you your things.'

'I definitely will be,' Nate agreed.

Allan sighed. 'Well, I'd best run boys. I've got to get back to work. Would you like a lift home?' he asked, trying another angle to get Adam alone, intending to drop Nate off first.

'Can't, but thanks, Uncle Allan,' Adam said.

'We're going to practice for a while,' Nate explained. Then his eyes widened as he glanced at the car park. 'Is that your car?'

The three looked to the nearby parking lot behind a white timber rail where half a dozen cars were parked, including a limousine.

'It is, that's my job. I take very important people where they need to go,' Allan said.

'Has it got a fridge inside? I saw one once with a fridge and a window that goes up and down behind the driver.'

Adam pushed his cap back off his forehead to look up at Allan.

'It has both of those,' Allan said.

'Wow,' the boys said in awe.

'A lift next time I make it to one of your games then?'

'Sure, thanks,' Nate said. The boys were still staring at the car, tempted to take the ride.

'That'd be great,' Adam said. 'Thanks, Uncle Allan.'

'Anything for my favourite nephew and his best mate,' he grinned and took the keys from his pocket, threw them in the air, caught them and with a wink, headed off, already planning his return.

Climbing into the car, he watched the boys run back onto the field. He ran his hand along the dashboard of the expensive leased car. He had a plan; no, he had two plans, and they were both good. One was bound to work.

Driving for VIP Private Taxis hadn't always been his job. He'd had a job with the Electrical Generating Board before they sacked a hundred workers. With the strikes that followed, the daily blackouts, the money drying up, he gave up hoping to be back on the floor and looked elsewhere for a job. Fortunately, or unfortunately, depending on which side of the family you belonged to, his father-in-law died that same year and his wife got a small inheritance. They leased an upmarket, prestige sedan. He did a chauffeur driving course and got a job with VIP Private Taxis and was given his uniform. The tips were good; he had his favourite and regular clients.

He knew he was lucky – his school sweetheart-now-wife, Melissa – Millie – and his mother both thought the sun shone out of him. And that was enough to want to make them happy. But as Allan reflected, life was shit sometimes, and as it turned out, it was shit for a few years in a row. Not for all people though… some folk just seemed to have it all – money, power, looks, good fortune.

He thought about the two years gone by; when he lost his job and his wife miscarried. They hadn't been able to get pregnant since, and it was all she ever wanted. Being a hard-working family man didn't amount too much when he couldn't bring home an income or give Millie a family. He had to step up; he was 27 and not getting any younger. They put their name down to adopt, but there was a new treatment… IVF. Allan didn't know what it stood for, but Millie did. She knew all about the procedure; it was her great shiny hope. It cost a lot of money.

Allan drew a deep breath; he was going to make it happen. The plan… forget about the large tips. He had a much bigger vision than that, and he was grooming relationships with just the right clientele to make it happen.

Chapter 4

Now…

Jessica rolled her eyes and tapped her watch at Nate, as he finished up on the phone and came out of his office.

'Adam's been waiting for you for about fifteen minutes. He's got a client in two hours, that's as long as you can have him for this morning.'

'Fine bossy boots. I've lost my keys,' Nate said, patting down his pockets. He looked over her reception desk as if they would be sitting there.

'You need a manager,' Adam said, coming from his office and overhearing the conversation. 'Someone who can get you to places on time and find the thing you lose.'

Nate stopped, then laughed. Adam joined in.

'You know you two do that often,' Jessica said and explained when they both gave her a blank look. 'One of you will say something not funny, but then you both find it amusing or profound. I'd love to read your minds.'

'That'd be scary,' Adam assured her, 'especially Nate's.'

Nate gave his best friend a smirk and then shook his head at their childhood memory. 'Good old Uncle Allan with the flash limo service.'

'Yeah,' Adam said cynically. 'I wonder where that nutter is now.'

Jessica laughed. 'It's not like you to call someone a nutter, Adam Murphy! I've heard it all now. If your patients hear you say that...'

'Trust me, Uncle Allan deserved the title,' Nate said, defending Adam. 'We might have to take your car.'

Adam groaned. He wasn't keen on taking his Mercedes – a birthday present from his mother – into some of the shadier areas, besides it was Nate's client they were trying to find.

'So, whose side of the family was Uncle Allan from?' Jessica asked.

'Neither, as it turns out, but he tried to convince us he was Adam's uncle,' Nate called back.

'That's a worry,' Jessica said and looked at Adam for an explanation. He didn't offer it.

'Ah-ha!' Nate exclaimed and leapt on seeing a set of keys near the photocopier. 'Got them. Let's go.'

They bid Jessica farewell, Adam promising to return on time.

'Got the photo?' Adam asked as they ran down the stairs to the car park.

'Damn,' Nate grumbled, threw the keys to Adam and turned to run back upstairs. 'Pick me up out the front.'

'Yes Sir,' Adam called back.

Nate rushed back upstairs, startling Jessica as he entered and noting the momentary look of panic on her face. He ran in, grabbed the photo of Aden Sabel and gave her another wave goodbye. He raced down the front entrance and into his waiting car. 'Thanks driver, onward.'

Adam chuckled. 'I wish there was an eject button for the passenger seat.'

'We should think about getting a buzzer system on the door, so Jessica only lets in people with appointments and can talk to them safely if they haven't got one. What do you think?'

'Brilliant. Why, did she say she was nervous?' Adam glanced over at Nate, then back to the road.

'No, but she sure as shit looked it when I just raced back in there and scared the hell out of her. You know she left the city job because she didn't like the idea of being trapped in a building if there was an attack or something.'

Adam nodded. 'Yeah, a lot of people felt that after that last spate of terrorist attacks.'

Nate sat back and looked at the photo of Aden Sabel. 'So, which shady location are you taking me to first?'

'Under the bridge on the banks, there's an area where a lot of the down-and-out hang out. We can show the photo around; I've got a few contacts there.'

'I bet you have,' Nate joked.

Adam turned into a service station and Nate leaned over and looked at his full petrol tank.

'Sandwiches,' Adam explained.

'Can't we eat later?'

'Not for us, you dope.' Adam left the ignition running and headed into the servo, returning minutes later with a plastic bag full of packaged sandwiches. Nate had moved into the driver's seat, so he slid into the evacuated passenger seat beside Nate.

'Aren't you the nicest guest?' Nate joked. 'Good manners not to drop in empty-handed.'

'That's me, well-bred. Some of them haven't eaten for days, some have one meal a day when the charity van rocks up, and others will only talk if there's an offering.'

They drove on and Adam directed Nate to park in a spot he'd frequented before.

'Best leave your jacket and tie in the car,' Adam said removing his. He grabbed the bag of sandwiches while Nate carried the photo.

The smell of the mangroves was the first assault on their senses – the rotten egg smell that permeated the area on the banks of the river. As they moved closer to the darker areas under the bridge and near the tunnels, the smell of rubbish, sweat and unwashed bodies joined the blend.

Nate fell behind Adam, who searched for the faces he knew, and the ones that might welcome him. He approached an old man with grey tufts of hair and whiskers. He smelled of a cheap spirit but smiled at seeing Adam.

'Frank, here you are. How are you?' Adam said, squatting down.

'Good my boy, good. Ah, but you're not looking the best. Thin and tired, work will do that to you young fellow,' he said, studying Adam.

'That's the truth of it,' Adam said. 'Meet my friend, Nate.' Adam looked up at Nate. 'Nate, this is Mr Frank Vaughan.'

'Gidday, son.'

'Hi Mr Vaughan,' Nate said.

'Call me Frank, everyone does, but I appreciate your manners, Son. Your mum would be proud.'

'Have you eaten today?' Adam asked.

'Not as yet, but it's early,' Frank said. 'I've had a nudge though,' he said with a glance to the bottle. 'Just to fortify myself for the day.'

'Right, well it's not bribery,' he said, offering a sandwich, 'but I'm looking for a man. His mum is looking for him, actually. He hasn't been home for a week.' Adam glanced at Nate, who leaned down with the photo.

'His name is Aden,' Nate said. 'Any chance he's been around?'

'No, I'd remember that ugly mug,' Frank joked and Nate laughed.

'No oil painting, not like we three,' Nate agreed and made Frank laugh.

Adam grabbed two pre-packed sandwiches. 'Can you manage egg and lettuce, and chicken and mayo?'

'I'll do my best son, and thank yer.'

'I'll be seeing you soon, Frank. You've got my card still if you need something?'

Frank patted his coat pocket. The card was long gone.

The men shook hands. Adam rose and with Nate, they moved on, repeating the process further along, before moving to a new location. After four stops and exhaustion of their sandwich supply, Nate called it.

'I'd say Aden is not hanging around the homeless and druggies of the city.'

'I'm with you on that. What next then?'

Nate sighed. 'I'll get Danielle to visit the hospitals and morgues. And you?'

'Hungry girl, as Jessica calls her. I wish we had some sandwiches left.'

Chapter 5

Then...

Adam's security detail, Tom Hartigan, rapped on the principal's office door and entered when beckoned. The man behind the desk rose and extended his hand.

'Mr Hartigan, please come in. I'm sorry there's no receptionist to greet you. Wednesday is her late day,' the principal, David Rodwell said.

'No problem. Please call me Tom,' he said, taking the offered seat at a small boardroom table in the principal's office.

'I don't want to make you sit opposite me at the desk. Might bring back bad memories,' he joked and Tom dutifully laughed. He wondered how many times David Rodwell had successfully delivered that line.

Tom sized him up as he always did – it was his job and his training. Rodwell was a typical bureaucrat in Tom's experience. Round around the middle, not fat, not thin, not fit. His hair was thinning, he was closer to fifty than forty, but his suit was expensive, as expected for a private school principal dealing with parents who had money.

'Thank you for seeing me concerning Adam Murphy. I need to speak with you about security on your sports' days,' Tom began.

Rodwell's eyes widened. 'Has there been a threat?'

'No, not at all,' Tom said and saw the principal visibly deflate.

'We hire security every year for the annual art exhibition, but otherwise, we haven't greatly needed to do so. Some boys have their own protection, like young Adam,' Rodwell said.

Tom nodded. 'Adam mentioned a man was coming to cricket practice and watching him play. He identified himself as Allan but he's not on your staff I believe.' Tom said and withheld that Adam was calling the man Uncle Allan. Tom's training also taught him to give as few details as possible to those who don't need it.

Rodwell grimaced. 'Ah, yes, it is a little hard to monitor who attends the external sports outings. By that I mean the sports we play against other schools and often in public spaces. The public can watch, relatives and family can come along, and often the boys will stay after and play on with their friends, not necessarily from our school.'

Tom knew this as Nate had also been joining Adam.

'You could easily be there yourself or have someone there to watch over Adam if you were concerned, but we definitely don't have a staff member by the name of Allan.'

'Thank you. I'll do that then,' Tom said. 'I might alert your sports master, however, if you have no objections?'

'Leave that with me,' the principal said. 'I'll raise it with him today.'

Tom rose and offered his hand to shake. He expected the meeting would be futile, and he was right, but if nothing else, he had flagged that someone unsavoury was hanging around. If the principal was worth his pay packet and for the safety of the other boys, he'd get all his staff on alert as well, but somehow, he doubted that would happen. Tom doubted Rodwell would even give the sports master the heads-up.

He returned to his car, annoyed at what he considered was a waste of time. If Adam's parents were ever around, the kid might ask them about his Uncle Allan, but there was even less chance of that. Poor little bugger, he thought.

Chapter 6

Now…

Audrey Murphy often looked out of place, and today was no exception. The tall, graceful woman who regularly forgot she was a septuagenarian came through the office door of *Delaney and Murphy* and looked around the empty waiting room as if expecting someone. Dressed to the nines and with a grey bun highlighting a long swan-like neck, she looked lost for the opera. Behind closed doors, Nate was on the phone in his office and Adam was with a client that Jessica had labelled 'Goth-girl' in her head – it was one way of ensuring privacy when identifying the clients, should anyone be around to overhear.

Jessica smiled at Audrey and finishing on the phone, rose from behind her desk to greet the visitor. This was a client for Nate – she was probably looking for her stolen pearls.

'Good morning, may I help you?' Jessica asked.

'Good morning.' Audrey crossed to the desk before speaking. 'I am Audrey Murphy, I am seeking my grandson, Adam.'

'Mrs Murphy! How lovely to meet you, I'm Jessica Johnson.'

'Hello Miss Johnson,' Audrey offered her hand, and the ladies shook.

'Please call me Jessica.'

'Please call me Audrey. I believe the name has become somewhat popular again, along with Florence. Who would have thought?'

Jessica laughed. 'It's a timeless name... like Audrey Hepburn, so beautiful. But yes, Adam,' she glanced at his door. 'He is just about to finish with a client, five minutes no more, if you can wait? Can I offer you a chair and a cup of tea?'

'Darling, at my age I believe it is important to be vertical as much as possible for as long as possible,' she said with a smile.

The door to Nate's office opened, and he stormed out.

'I knew the voice! Audrey!'

'Darling Nathaniel,' she held open her arms, and the two held each for some time before he stepped back smiling. 'My, you were always a handsome young man, but look at you now. Quite the catch.'

Jessica could not believe that Nate reddened. He shot back: 'You say that every time you see me,' he said. 'I haven't changed that much since last month.'

Audrey laughed.

'You are back from walking the Camino. How was it?' he asked, interested.

'Adam's mother was right... not enough wine bars, but interesting nevertheless. All that time in one's head thinking as you walked, it can't be good to think that much,' she said, and Jessica laughed again.

'And your grandson makes a living from it.' Nate shook his head.

Jessica decided she liked the dry old girl, but noticed Audrey did not call her daughter-in-law, Winsome by name, but rather Adam's mother.

At the mention of Adam, his office door opened, and he stood aside to allow a girl dressed all in black with black dyed hair and dark kohl eyes to exit. Adam walked a few steps with her before his eyes widened at seeing Audrey. He grinned and quickly sobered when Goth-girl looked at him. He said goodbye to her at the exit and closed the door behind him.

'Hello, darling boy! You took my breath away then, you looked so much like your father.' She put her hand on her heart. 'I'm back.'

'You are,' he said enveloping his tall, but not as tall as himself, grandmother in his arms. 'I've missed you. You'll take tea?'

'Have you time?' she asked, looking at the empty waiting room and then giving Adam a sly grin. 'I've come to talk to you about the wedding.'

Adam groaned, then checked himself. 'Sorry, I want Mum to be happy and Jack's great.'

'No, it's my first reaction too,' she assured him and accepted a tea. 'Only if it is a herbal variety.'

Adam looked at Jessica, doubtful of having anything herbal on the premises.

'Peppermint or chamomile?' Jessica offered and received a grateful smile from Adam.

'Peppermint is perfect, Jessica darling, thank you.' Audrey turned to Nate. 'Nathaniel dear, join us if you have time, as this affects you too.'

'Uh oh,' Nate said and moved to seat himself at the table with Adam and Audrey.

'Your mother wants to hire extra security for the wedding for you, Adam, and for anyone at your table, which will be you, Nathaniel,' Audrey said.

'What the hell for?' Adam asked, perplexed. 'Seriously, it never ends. Last month was the anniversary of her affair with the prime minister which Stephanie played up in the media and I had to cancel appointments for a week. Then Mum announces the wedding, and every idiot in the media called the office non-stop wanting a comment. Poor Jess was exhausted. Now Mum wants to put security around the place like a prison, for the love of God!'

Adam closed his eyes momentarily and took a deep breath.

Audrey patted his hand and said calmly, 'I know, my boy. Some things never change. Can I talk openly?' she asked discreetly, and Adam nodded as Jessica delivered tea and a plate of shortbread to the table, plus coffee for the boys. Adam invited her to join them.

'Thanks, but I'll keep working,' she said, intending to listen in from her nearby desk.

'Where have you been hiding these biscuits?' Nate said, 'I haven't seen them before.'

'Hiding is right,' Jessica told him. 'They are for guests, not for private detectives.'

He gave her a smirk.

'Well done, young lady. You clearly have Nathaniel under control and he is the hardest of the two to manage,' she said, teasing her grandson's best friend.

'No mean feat,' Adam agreed.

'It hasn't been easy,' Jessica admitted.

'Hello, I'm sitting here,' Nate said and brought on a round of laughs.

'But seriously, we need to speak of the former prime minister,' Audrey explained.

'He's not coming to the wedding, is he?' Nate asked, shocked, biscuit suspended on his lips.

'No, it's about DNA,' Adam answered without having to be told, and Jessica gasped. Audrey sipped her peppermint tea and nodded.

'No. At your mother's wedding? Would someone try to get your DNA?' Jessica asked.

'People suck,' Nate responded. 'They'd earn a good price on that story if they could get an item from the former prime minister or a relative and match it to Adam's DNA. The *IT* girl and the Prime Minister's love child.'

Adam winced, even though he'd heard it all before. He turned his attention to his grandmother. 'What is Mum proposing?'

Audrey sat back. 'Your table will have a dedicated waiter and concierge service.'

Adam shook his head. 'This is just too much.'

Audrey continued. 'Apparently, every item you use from the reception to dinner – cutlery, glasses, plates – even if you touch a towel in the bathrooms, to avoid touch evidence will all be collected and professionally cleaned or destroyed.'

'But why hasn't someone done that before now?' Jessica asked.

'Because no one cares,' Adam said with a shrug. 'Mum just likes to be dramatic. She thinks because she is in the spotlight again for a minute, that the media are going to go to all that trouble to dig up an old story.'

'It'd be a good story,' Jessica said, and then shrugged. 'I'm sorry, I don't mean to be a fan-girl, but I still think it has relevancy.'

'Really?' Adam frowned. 'I don't get it.'

'That's because it is all you've ever known,' Nate said. 'But not everyone knows a celebrity or gets to call them Mum.'

'Mum and I can't believe the *IT* girl is your mum – Winsome is so beautiful – and that Jack Bernham is your godfather is too much!' She turned to Audrey, 'we've been to several of his concerts.'

Audrey smiled politely at Jessica and turned to Adam. 'Jessica's right, people are interested and you'll just have to play the game, darling boy, I'm sorry.'

Adam narrowed his eyes. 'How come you know about this and I don't?'

'Because your mother's assistant rang me and said your mother thought it best coming from me.'

Adam sighed. 'Righto, whatever, let's just get it done.'

'Well done, Adam, that's the spirit darling,' Audrey said. 'Besides, we don't want your dear late father dishonoured.'

'Definitely not,' Adam added, remembering it also affected his paternal grandmother seated by his side.

'There's one more thing,' Audrey said.

Nate laughed at seeing Adam's pained expression.

'She wants the Merc back?' Nate asked.

'Not yet,' Audrey said with a chuckle. 'Your mother has hired you some personal security—' Audrey held her hand up to cut in before Adam went off on a tangent again. '— you boys will remember him… Tom Hartigan.'

Adam and Nate momentarily froze and then looked at each other.

'SAS Tom?' Nate asked. 'Is he still doing the job?'

'Apparently so,' Audrey answered.

Adam grimaced. 'It didn't end well last time.'

'You were a boy. If it didn't end well, my darling, it is

entirely his fault. Personally, I didn't like the way he drove my Jaguar.'

Adam smiled, and Nate grinned.

'We did,' Nate added.

'Hmm,' Audrey said, unimpressed. 'Well, I believe he'll be in touch.'

Jessica couldn't read Adam that well, but from the look on his face, there was more than just the wedding at stake. History had resurfaced.

Chapter 7

Then...

Tom Hartigan sat as close as he could to the middle of the back seat of the Jaguar without blocking Audrey's view in the rear-view mirror. His eyes took in everything around him, but his body remained composed, like a duck – calm on the surface, furiously paddling underneath. Now and then she gave her opinion on a story aired on talkback radio, but Tom was short on conversation. He didn't like to make small talk when he was on the job.

'What do you think, Adam?' Audrey asked.

'I agree with you, Audrey.'

'But why?' she challenged him. 'A well-rounded person should be able to talk on any subject, and if you can't, what do you do?'

'Ask questions,' Adam said and behind him, he caught sight of Tom mouthing the words with him, making Adam grin.

Tom knew Audrey saw him too, but she indulged him so he could build a relationship of trust with the boy. She gave him a small smile when he caught her eye in the mirror.

'Exactly, ask questions,' she responded. 'So why do you

agree with me, even though that's the right answer,' she said to her grandson who wasn't allowed to call her 'Grandma' and not because it made her feel one hundred years old, she had explained, but because she wanted Adam to know he was her equal.

'Because change is good, I think. So, a change in government will give us fresh ideas,' Adam said and looked to his grandmother for a reaction.

'Excellent, I couldn't agree more,' she said and with a nod of approval in Adam's direction, returned to listening to the radio.

Tom disagreed. The last thing Adam needed was change. From studying the kid, he knew Adam needed all the security he could get. If his parents weren't around, there was nothing like a grandma, grandpa, uncle or aunt, to provide a sense of family. Even a sibling. Both Adam and Nate were the only child, no doubt it strengthened their bond, Tom thought. Speaking of which, Tom leaned forward between the seats. 'When is your next cricket game, Adam?'

Adam shrugged. 'Not sure. There's some inter-school sport on for a while.'

Tom sat back, not convinced. He sensed Adam wanted to keep Uncle Allan to himself, his secret. He'd have to get it out of Nate or call the school directly. The kid was smart and didn't want Tom pushing his new-found uncle away. Tom didn't like it, not one bit.

'What are your motives?' he mumbled, watching any car that got too close.

Adam turned to face him. 'Huh? What was that, Tom?'

'Just talking to myself young Adam, ignore me,' he said. 'So, have you seen Uncle Allan lately?' he cut to the chase and the speed at which Adam's eyes went to his grandmother and back to Tom confirmed his theory. Adam had told no one and didn't want to.

Why?

Had this Uncle Allan person told Adam not to mention him, or was it feeding Adam's insecurity to have someone who cared about him other than Audrey and Nate?

Adam shook his head in the negative and turned back quickly, grabbing his bag as the school came into view.

'Thanks, Audrey,' he said, leaning over and giving her the expected kiss on the cheek.

'Enjoy your day of learning and fun, my darling,' she said, and Adam was out of the car in a minute. Tom was faster. His job was to see Adam in through the school gates, but he knew better than to escort him. Adam was too old now at 10-years for that, it was just uncool, so he leaned back against the car's exterior, watching Adam and everyone around the boy.

'See ya, Tom,' Adam called back.

'See you, mate.' He waited until Adam was out of sight, opened the car door and asked: 'Can you give me a few minutes, Mrs Murphy? I just need to check something.'

'Of course, Mr Hartigan, take your time,' she said and turned the car off.

Tom headed to the school reception desk and was pleased to see an administrator present. Five minutes later, he was back in the car with Audrey, and the cricket roster for Adam's year. Adam had a game this very afternoon and Tom intended to be there. He might just meet this Uncle Allan for himself.

Chapter 8

Now…

Danielle always took the stairs two or three at a time, even in her high heels. She arrived at the office of *Delaney and Murphy* and barged in, startling Jessica at her desk.

'Sorry, Jess,' Dan smiled. 'Everyone's so jumpy of late.'

'It comes with working with strange people,' Jessica said, rising from her chair to stretch.

'Nate and Adam are weird, but I've known odder folk,' Danielle said.

'Not them, their patients or clients.' Jessica laughed before contemplating what Dan said. 'But then again, you might be onto something there. Like attracts like.'

Nate stuck his head out of his office. He hated to be left out and could hear the girls talking. He brightened at seeing his researcher in the flesh.

'Dan, you're here. What's happening?' he asked.

Jessica gave them the quiet signal and indicated Adam's office. 'He's got a patient in there.'

'Anyone interesting?' Danielle asked.

'Are any of them?' Nate added. 'C'mon.'

Danielle gave Jessica a wave and followed Nate into his

office, plonking herself down in a chair opposite his desk. 'No luck, I'm sorry to say.'

'Damn,' Nate said with a sigh.

'Your Aden Sabel is not in any hospitals, health centres or morgues in the city's boundaries,' she said and sat back. Nate joined her in sitting back and rocking in his chair.

'Where the hell is he? Probably six feet under,' he muttered.

'Well, you'll have no chance of finding him then,' she said. 'What if I did some surveillance on his mother's house?'

'Why?' Nate asked.

'We only have her word for the fact he's missing. What if she's been mistreating him and he's escaped? Should we be finding him? He is an adult after all. He might sneak back for clothes or money when she leaves the house.'

Nate frowned as he thought about it. They heard the office door open and close, and Adam talking with Jessica after seeing his client out.

Nate refocused on Danielle. 'It's a bit out there, and yeah, he is an adult. But Mrs Tatum paid a reasonable fee to find him… would most parents do that when they've got a son who has only been missing a week and is a druggie by nature?'

'It might depend on the level of co-dependency,' Adam said overhearing and stopping in Nate's office door.

'Thank you, Dr Murphy. Spoken like a true psychologist,' Nate said with a grin.

Danielle rose and hugged Adam. She always did, and he always found it confronting, which is why she continued to do it.

'How's your new girlfriend?' Danielle asked.

'Great. Away at a library conference,' Adam said. He moved out of the doorway to allow Jessica to join them.

'A library conference!' Danielle said and glanced at Nate and Jessica. No one said a word.

Adam rolled his eyes. 'Go on, you're dying to.'

'We are so not,' Jessica said, defending the three of them as they exchanged smiles. 'How long does it go for?'

'I'm not telling,' Adam said. 'None of you need any encouragement.'

'What if it never finishes?' Nate asked dramatically. 'If they keep reading between the lines!' Everyone broke up.

'That's very good, Nathaniel,' Adam said with a smirk. 'It ends. Four days, she'll be home on the weekend.'

'I hope no one will be checking her out,' Danielle said with a wink to Adam and he rolled his eyes. He turned to Jessica. 'Do you want to have your turn before I leave?'

'Definitely not. Unlike the other two, I can help my shelf, I mean self,' she said and gave him a grin as the others groaned.

Adam shook his head.

'I'm just kidding,' Jessica added quickly, not yet as confident in Adam's company – as she was with Nate – to tease him too much. 'I love my library and can't imagine life without it.'

He gave her a conciliatory look and looked at Nate and Danielle. 'You two would be better for a bit of reading.'

'Sure we would,' Nate agreed.

'And not comics,' Adam added as a departing shot, but Nate called him back.

'By the way, there's no sign of Mrs Tatum's beloved son. Want to pay a house visit with me?' he asked.

'Why? Can't Dan go with you?' Adam asked, with a glance at Danielle sitting with her boots on Nate's desk.

'I want you to read the situation,' Nate said, sitting forward in his chair. 'Dan thinks it might not be legitimate. Tell him why,' Nate said, handballing the discussion to Danielle, who filled Adam in on her theory.

'He's nowhere to be found, and I mean nowhere. I'm guessing that household is probably surviving on two welfare checks so she needs him to come home… maybe she's found him and is not telling us. I think we should check her out, as well as look for the son.'

'Okay, a bit out there…'

'That's what I said,' Nate agreed. 'God, we're thinking alike.'

Adam glanced towards Rob, his fellow psychologist's office. 'I'll book myself in for treatment,' he said and looked back to catch Nate's wry look.

'If you don't think it is plausible, I'll just go sus it out myself,' Danielle said. 'Woman's intuition… but whatever.'

'No, we'll go,' Nate said. 'I've got to talk with Mrs Tatum anyway and give her an update, so Adam can read her at the same time.'

'Just check with Jessica and I'll find time for you in my very busy diary,' he said smugly.

'I knew I'd pay for those jokes,' Nate said with a sigh, and Adam gave him a grin as he departed.

'I've still got a good half dozen library puns up my sleeve,' Danielle said, loud enough for Adam to hear as he departed.

Chapter 9

Then…

It had been a brilliant day; Adam couldn't remember the last time he had been this happy… except maybe the day that he and Nate both caught a fish in the creek and his was bigger. He had batted a good score of 46, and caught two players out, and Uncle Allan saw it all. He was on the boundary, watching the whole game. Adam didn't recognise him at first; Uncle Allan didn't arrive in his limo and didn't have his uniform on. But that didn't matter, he was here like he promised. Adam's dad still hadn't shown; it wasn't important in his world.

The private boys' school was playing another private school, so Nate wasn't around, but Adam would catch him later on their bikes after school. There were several dozen parents and supporters around the playing field, some yelling advice. Uncle Allan never did that, he just cheered and Adam liked that.

'Howzat?' his team bowler, Stuart, yelled out, and up went the umpire's finger into the air. Adam and his teammates cheered; the game was their victory. The boys lined up to shake hands with their opponents, and afterwards, headed to the boundary to make their way to the school bus or waiting parents.

'Uncle Allan!' Adam said, rushing to his side at the boundary.

Uncle Allan threw his arms around Adam in a fatherly embrace, then pulled away to praise him.

'What an exciting game. You played really well,' he said.

'Yeah? Thanks, Uncle Allan. So did the rest of the team. Stuart had five out for sixty!'

'Amazing,' Uncle Allan agreed. 'Do you need to rush to catch your school bus or would you like me to drop you home?'

'Could you? That'd be great! You're not in your work uniform today?' Adam noticed.

'No. I finished early to get to the game, but I've got one of the fleet cars,' he said.

'What's a fleet car?'

'My business has several cars we use depending on the client and what their needs are, so I picked one with a lot of power to pick you up in.'

'Cool,' Adam said, scanning the car park but not seeing anything that looked more powerful than Audrey's Jaguar with Tom behind the wheel. 'I'll grab my bag and tell the teacher I'm okay for a lift,' Adam said rushing off. He glanced back and Uncle Allan was still there, waiting. He gave him a grin and ran to grab his belongings.

*****

Tom Hartigan swore and hit the steering wheel of his Holden VN Commodore. He loved this car, selected for power and safety... he needed both for his work. This car beat the BMW 5 Series for performance according to the *Wheels' Car of the Year* report, and that was good enough for him. At the moment though, it wasn't the car's fault for delaying him, but every idiot on the road around him.

He glanced at the console clock again. The game would be over by the time he got there and if Uncle Allan had been there, or coerced Adam away, he'd... well he didn't know what he'd do, but killing was involved. The bloody cricket roster that the school had given him had the wrong venue, and he had gone to the other side of town.

Tom's heart was beating like a drum, and finally the cricket oval and grounds came into sight. The relief of seeing it was palpable. He steadied himself to prepare for any situation. Saying the mantras in his head that he would need.

Stay low... keep calm... read the situation...

He turned the car into the car park, relieved when he saw the school bus; he had the right location. Tom had no idea what Uncle Allan looked like or what he drove, but he was going to find out right now.

For the last ten minutes he had glanced at every car passing him and now he checked out the cars coming out of the cricket ground. Adam was not in the passenger seat of any of them. Pulling up, he leapt from the car, locking it and raced over to the school bus. He passed a mother and son walking toward the car park.

'All over?' he asked.

'Yeah, you missed it,' the kid said to him, and the mother gave him a sympathetic look.

'Bummer,' Tom said.

Within seconds, he was at the bus and accosted another kid.

'Is Adam in there, mate?'

The kid looked in, checked out the seated players and announced, 'nope.'

'Thanks, buddy,' Tom said. He ran around to the changing sheds where the last of the team was packing up and the coach – one of the older male teachers – was hurrying them along. He interrupted, no time for niceties.

'Tom Hartigan, looking for Adam Murphy, have you seen him?'

The coach looked up. 'No, he might be on the bus.'

'No, he isn't. Did he come here on the bus?'

'He did, they all did. Check with the other team. Some boys went over to say gidday to a few of their friends,' he said. 'Tell them to move along, will you? We're leaving.'

Tom nodded and gave him a less than pleased look. The guy had no idea who Tom was and why he was asking after one of the students. The visit to the principal had clearly been a waste of time, as the teachers were not on alert for stranger danger.

He arrived at the rival team's side and called out: 'St Joseph boys, back on the bus, by order of the coach.' All the faces turned to look at him. He scanned the group as they walked past him to return to the bus.

'Anyone seen Adam? Adam Murphy?' he asked loudly to be heard over the boys' talking.

'Yeah,' Stuart, the bowler responsible for the day's heroics, spoke up as he passed Tom. 'He just left with his uncle, like about a minute ago.'

'Did you see the car?' Tom pushed.

'No, sorry.'

'That's okay, buddy. Did you see which way they went?' He knew he was speaking quickly, which was not a great way to get an answer from a kid. It confused them and they'd freeze for fear of giving the wrong answer. He tried to keep his countenance relaxed, but inside he was yelling.

Stuart shook his head again. 'He said they were going to McDonald's.'

'Thanks, good on you,' Tom said and ran off. No car had passed him in the last ten minutes with Adam in the passenger seat, so they must have gone the other way. He was at the car park and in his car in seconds, flying out of the grounds – sand, dust and pebbles spraying behind him. Onto the street, he headed the opposite way to which he just came, his eyes darted back, forward and to the sides should anyone have pulled off the road.

Is this guy really going to stop at a McDonald's? Could I be so bloody lucky?

Is there a chance Adam is in the car and not in the passenger seat... could he be in the car's boot?

He felt sick at the thought, the end of everything. He dismissed it... *stay focused, stay tough.*

Chapter 10

Now…

'Good of you to find time in your diary for me,' Nate ragged his best friend, as they headed off to visit Mrs Tatum in Adam's Mercedes.

'Don't mention it,' Adam joked and then sobered up. 'I thought I could read your client and read you at the same time.' He glanced at his best friend.

Nate groaned. 'Don't do that.'

'Too late.'

'I'm not paying.'

'Have you ever? When have you next got Matilda staying over?' he asked after Nate's five-year-old daughter.

'Not for two weeks. It's the school holidays. They've gone to the coast, to Erin's parents.'

Adam nodded.

'I'm doing better,' Nate offered.

'I know.'

'Dan's going to move in for a month, and stay at her friend's place when Matilda's over for the rostered weekends. She's in between flats.'

'That's a good thing, isn't it? Would you let her stay on and rent with you?' Adam asked.

'I'm not sure she wants to, but we'll see how the month goes.' He shrugged. 'I suspect that's her motive without asking up front.'

Adam didn't push it but he was pleased Nate would have a distraction, and not come home to an empty house. Danielle was always switched on – keen to go out, keen to party. She would be perfect as his housemate.

Adam let his mind drift; he loved driving his car, his favourite possession, and he didn't have many – it wasn't his thing. But he liked to drive and since driving with Nate behind the wheel was like being at the speedway, he usually insisted on bringing his car. The Mercedes was a thirtieth birthday present from his mother.

'I love this car,' he said breaking the silence and to let Nate know he wasn't putting pressure on him to reveal his soul any further.

'I got a gift card from the hardware store for my thirtieth,' Nate said as he adjusted the air-conditioning on the passenger side.

Adam grinned. 'Yeah, well that's thoughtful of your folks. They gave me a bottle of vodka which I'm well into. Fair to say it won't see my thirty-first.'

'They know you so well,' Nate teased. 'Yet, your mum gave me nothing after all the years I've spent keeping an eye on her son.'

Adam scoffed and then frowned. 'Actually, that's not technically true.'

'I'm pretty sure I had your back a lot.'

'Not that part. Lord knows you led me into trouble a lot. The part about sending you a gift is not quite true.'

Nate turned to look at his friend, and Adam continued. 'Mum wanted me to get you a gift from her.'

'And where is it?' Nate asked, looking around and over Adam's shoulder into the back seat of the Merc.

Adam laughed and gave a small shrug. 'I figured if she didn't have time to find out what you might like from me, sign a card and get her assistant to send it, then frankly...' he let his voice trail off. His entire life had comprised presents organised by assistants and absent parents. If it hadn't been for his grandmother and Nate's family, he would think that was normal.

'So instead, she thinks you've given me something and I haven't thanked her,' Nate said. 'No wonder I'm not her favourite.'

'No. I gave her some suggestions and told her she should send it herself.'

'It hasn't arrived,' Nate said drily, and Adam chuckled and gave a shrug.

'You might get it by your fortieth,' Adam suggested.

'Guess it's the thought that counts,' Nate said and sighed.

'Am I going the right way?' Adam asked, changing the subject.

Nate checked Mrs Tatum's address again and the directions on his phone. 'Yep, just head to the southern end of the Kurilpa Bridge, I'll direct you from there. It's a small street, a dead-end.'

They drove a little while in silence and then Nate asked. 'What were your suggestions?'

Adam gave him a confused glance.

'For my birthday gift.'

'Oh that. I told Mum you'd had a drive in the latest Audi but used the inheritance you just got from Joe paying off some of your mortgage instead.'

Nate sighed. 'I'm so sensible it's sickening. I put the bulk of it away for Matilda's schooling. Joe would be proud,' he said, thinking of their friend from the asylum they had met in their childhood, who had left both of them a sizeable gift in his will.

'So, I told Mum you'd like one of those, the Audi, in pink,' Adam continued, and Nate gave him a smirk. 'I also suggested a rum distillery, Cluedo the board game as you were missing the police service, or a hardware store gift card.'

'You're hilarious,' Nate said drily.

The phone rang, startling them both. Adam answered it hands-free.

'Jess?'

'There's a locksmith security guy here,' she said. 'Has he got the wrong offices?'

'No, sorry I forgot to mention that. Tom gave us some basic security things to start doing, like putting in a buzzer and screen system for admission. Nate and I agreed with him, which is weird in itself, but that's beside the point,' Adam said, making Nate and Jessica laugh.

Nate continued: 'So you can let these guys in, but from now on if anyone arrives and they don't have an appointment, don't let them in, unless you can see their I.D. on the screen, or you know them.'

'Okay,' she said suspiciously. 'That'll stop the cold callers, at least. Why now?'

Adam looked at Nate and then back to the road. He'd let him answer.

'Some of our cases are getting hairy, that's all,' Nate said, keeping it relaxed. He knew Jessica was the nervy type at the best of times. He continued: 'Plus, with Winsome's wedding coming, we're bound to get some nutters trying to get a

49

photo of Adam. We should just get him to sign a pile and we'll hand them out.'

Jessica laughed.

'So not funny,' Adam said, wearily.

Nate nudged him. 'Of course it is. We'd get your best angle.'

'They're all good, it'd be hard to choose,' Adam retorted.

'Thanks, guys,' Jessica interrupted them. 'I'll think about whether I give you both the code to get in when you get back.' She hung up.

Nate gave Adam an update on directions and looked out at the area. 'It's not in this upmarket pocket, there are some streets behind...'

'Yeah, I know them,' Adam said. 'So, you're going to tell Mrs Tatum that you've had no joy finding her son, see what she wants to do next, and catch her reaction?'

'Yep, while you watch her, glance around, see if you can see any signs of life that the son exists or isn't locked in the basement.'

'God, people,' Adam said and shook his head. 'The son... what was his name?'

'Aden.'

'Right. Aden's probably high under some rock with no idea of what he's putting his mother through.'

'Poor old girl,' Nate agreed. 'No wonder she looks hard, the son has sapped the life out of her. Having said that, I suspect she wasn't a great beauty to begin with... it'd take some imagination.'

Adam shook his head and smiled.

'That's the street there,' Nate said and pointed.

Adam turned his car into the narrow street with the older streetscape. It was lined with small cottages, most dilapidated. Some house-proud residents had beautiful gardens, but could not maintain the house.

Nate returned a wave to an old guy watering his garden. 'That'll be me someday. Waving to the young guns as I water the plants and think back on my brilliant career.'

Adam burst out laughing. 'You don't even mow your own lawn now, do you?'

'Look, if the kid next door wants to do it for a few dollars, who am I to hold back ambition.'

'Sure, boss. What number?' Adam asked again.

'Sixty-two. It's on your side.'

The two men counted down the houses. The last house at the end of the street had the number 48 etched on its letterbox.

'Hang on,' Nate said and rang Jessica. When she answered he asked: 'Can you check Mrs Tatum's address for me again? Uh, huh, definitely 62? Thanks.'

Adam pulled over. 'Let's door-knock, see if anyone knows a Mrs Tatum. I'll do the left side.'

Nate sighed and followed him out of the car. 'I've got a funny feeling Mrs Tatum gave me a false address.'

Fifteen minutes later, with over half a dozen houses door-knocked each, and no joy… not even name recognition from the long-term residents, the two men took to the car, belted up and left the area.

'Why?' Nate said.

'More importantly, who is Mrs Tatum?' Adam asked.

Chapter 11

Then...

Tom Hartigan knew he had stuffed up. If he had been a religious man, he might have started bargaining with God to help him on this one, and he'd lift his game. But he lost that connection on a particularly bad mission some time ago.

All the training to get into the SAS, ten years in the game, the *Resistance to Interrogation* training, which was the worst three days of his life, and now, he couldn't even protect a kid. He had resented having to take the Murphy security job. It seemed like a dramatic fall from grace when he was still fit and able to contribute, but rules were rules and no SAS management team was going to send him on a mission with the limp he'd gained – he was deemed more prone to capture, apparently.

But with Adam missing, the potential of a young boy dying and a community outraged, wasn't that – on some level – what he signed up to do when he joined the SAS – to protect? And here he was assigned to look after the model, Winsome Keeley's son, and he couldn't even handle one

10-year-old school boy. Guilt, disgust, and anger clouded his emotions.

He put his foot down on the pedal and the car surged forward. If he got pulled over by the cops it would be a blessing. They could help. As long as he didn't kill anyone in pursuit. He came up behind a white sedan and shot past – nope, the driver was a young guy with 'P' plates. Next, a red hatchback with a young girl at the wheel. He overtook her at an irresponsible speed.

He knew if Uncle Allan was cunning, he wouldn't stay on the main road. He'd take a back road where no one could find him or recognise him or the car. No sooner had Tom had the thought, a split in the road presented itself.

'Christ, decision, quick, now!' He took it, the road less travelled and raced along it, well over the speed limit. A car was coming towards him and the driver glared at him like Tom was an idiotic hoon. Today, he was.

Then, up ahead, he saw a large black sedan, similar to a VIP taxi. Could that be him? He got his answer the moment the sedan picked up speed.

'Got you, you bastard,' Tom hissed and raced ahead, the Commodore surging. As he got closer, he could see the passenger was small, a child – his head barely showing between the top of the seat and the headrest. Hopefully, it was a boy – Adam.

The driver was speeding now, and so was Tom. He swore as the black car in front took the corner at a speed that could have written off both of the inhabitants. He didn't care if the driver wiped himself out, but he couldn't let Adam be injured. Tom had to put an end to it.

He surged ahead, the speedometer rising, clicking up and up, and then driving aside the sedan, he forced the driver off the road. Gravel flew from both cars, smoke rising from screaming tyres as Tom screeched to a halt further up the road, blocking it and the black sedan came to a dead stop.

He jumped out the moment his car jerked to a stop and ran to the sedan. He could only just make out the driver through the glare of the windscreen and side window. The driver was wearing a white shirt and black sunglasses. Next to him was Adam; his mouth opened in shock, his blue eyes wide and panicked.

Tom ran to the driver's door, yanked it open, and pulled the driver out. His fist hit Allan's face with a satisfying crunch that made Tom feel better. Allan hit back – a wild swing quickly defeated.

Adam raced around from the passenger side, screaming and yelling at Tom.

'No, it's Uncle Allan. He's driving me home, no Tom. No!' He was beating his little fists against Tom, watching in terror as his Uncle Allan took blow after blow, blood streaming down his face.

'Adam, wait in my car,' Tom yelled at him as Allan continued to fight. 'This is not your uncle!'

And then Adam took off. Running as fast as he could in the opposite direction.

Tom's eyes widened. 'Adam! Get back here.' Fuck, no, he couldn't let the kid just disappear. 'Fuck!' he swore. 'Adam, get back here now!'

The kid was fast and heading into the bush on the side of the road. Tom pushed Allan down onto the road and took off after Adam. He had no choice – his mission was to never the let kid out of his sight, and one thing he knew how to do was to be true to a mission.

It didn't matter how fast Adam was, Tom's legs were longer,

the kid didn't stand a chance, and Tom was fit – the limp barely noticeable when his legs were warmed up. Within moments, he was in reach of Adam, his hand grabbing at the boy's shirt.

'Stop!' he yelled at Adam, 'he's not your uncle.'

Then it hit Tom why Adam didn't turn or respond, he was running because he thought Tom was the bad guy. His hand grabbed Adam, and they tumbled to the ground.

Tom was up in a second, pulling Adam against him, facing away, his arms around the boy's waist and chest as Adam fought to break free.

'For fuck's sake, stop!' Tom bellowed in his ear.

'Let me go,' Adam hit back with his fist and feet, kicking with impressive strength given he'd just run a fast marathon.

Tom held him tighter until the fight was gone, grateful the road was unused and he didn't have to explain his actions to a passing driver.

He could only see the back of the kid's head, but he said in a low voice near Adam's ear: 'That is not your uncle. Your dad and your mum don't have brothers. So, he can't be your uncle. There is no Uncle Allan.'

Adam breathed heavily but said nothing.

'He was taking you somewhere he shouldn't be, that's why you went down that road. I bet it is a road you have never been down before.' He was trying to break through, even if it created a sense of fear in the boy.

Again, he waited as Adam's breath steadied, but the boy said nothing. Tom tried again.

'Can I release you now, Adam? Are you going to calm down and come with me?'

Adam remained silent.

'Adam?'

The kid nodded, not saying a word. Tom studied him… was the boy in shock? He tried again.

'Do you understand? Are you going to come with me, home? Audrey will be expecting you,' Tom said in a slow and controlled voice.

Adam gave a definite nod. He released the boy an inch or two and waited for a reaction. There was none, so he released him a little more, and then dropped his arms and stood back, enough to give Adam his freedom. Adam looked past him.

Tom whirled around, remembering Allan, but as expected, Allan Sheffield and the car were gone. All that remained on the road were the skid marks where he had stopped.

'Damn,' he swore and looked back at Adam. 'Come on, we've got to go. I've got to call this into the police,' he reached a hand to Adam's shoulder and the kid flinched.

'I'm not going to hurt you, buddy,' he said and tried again, but Adam moved further away, walking towards the car but keeping his distance.

Tom sighed. He had stuffed this up. He should have been Uncle Allan. He should have built up trust in his young charge, become the boy's friend and mentor so that Adam would believe what he said and trust in him. He might have even enjoyed his work more if he'd thrown himself into it. Now all he'd done was show Adam how good he was with his fists and taken from him the uncle he thought he loved.

Yep, a good day's work all round. But it would get worse. The kid never spoke to him again. Not one word.

Chapter 12

Now...

The message came in on his phone and Adam smiled as he got out of his car and departed the garage.

'*Two more sleeps and I'll be back*,' Kelsey, his girlfriend wrote.

He messaged back. '*Who's sleeping? Missing you.*' He threw in a few hearts for good measure. They had been a couple close to six months, but it felt like she had always been there, and in a way she had. They had first met when they were teenagers for a brief moment. Fifteen-year-old, beautiful, flame-haired Kelsey – sassy and independent – and the twelve-year-old boy who thought she was so beautiful, he was tongue-tied. Then he didn't see her again for almost eighteen years.

Kelsey rang. 'Forget the messaging. I had to hear your voice,' she said.

'Is everything alright?' he asked, concern lacing his voice.

'No. I miss you,' Kelsey teased him.

Adam laughed. 'Sorry, I'm in perpetual work mode expecting everything to be a drama. I miss you too. Can you go to shorter conferences in the future?' he said and enjoyed her satisfied sigh. Adam unlocked the front door of his home, pulled the keys out of the door, and noticed a package leaning against the side of the door – a long narrow box. He grabbed it, tucking it under his arm as he headed inside. 'What was your day's highlight?' he asked.

'There were two good sessions, actually. One on how to get teens to read, and another on keeping the library relevant,' she said.

'Wow, tough call on both,' he said, imagining Nate, Danielle and Jessica's jokes in his head to those sessions. None of them had probably read a book in years... except for Jessica, she seemed the type.

'And did you have any of your favourite patients today?' Kelsey asked in return.

'You mean the ones who come on time, leave early and do the exercises I set them? That'd be none then,' he said, and sighed. 'Patients, who needs them, huh?'

He dumped the box on the couch, dropped his keys on the kitchen bench and headed to the bedroom, pulling his tie off as he went. 'There's wedding news, brace yourself,' he said and told her about the security arrangements his mother was insisting on.

It always amazed Adam at how laid-back Kelsey was given her tough teenage experience in homes and institutions that few would survive. She still bore an innate fear of authority, and Winsome's extra security would not help. Adam didn't want Kelsey to pull out of going to the wedding with him. He wanted her by his side – if he was being honest; he needed her there.

So, he took a gamble on being upfront about everything and giving her time to process it. It had paid off to date, but it was early days. 'We'll be cocooned all night,' he said, finishing up.

'Are you okay with that?' she asked.

'No. But it is what it is. How do you feel about it?' he asked and held his breath.

'I think it will be okay.'

'Okay,' he said, not pushing it. They talked for a while longer and then, after hanging up, he changed to go for a run.

Returning to the lounge room he remembered the parcel on the couch and grabbed it. There was no label or card. Adam found some scissors, cut the binding, and opened the box.

Inside was a cricket bat. A bat that looked very familiar.

Eyes narrowing, Adam turned it over and saw his name scribbled on the handle in his childhood handwriting.

It was not just any cricket bat. It was the cricket bat he left in Uncle Allan's car.

Chapter 13

Then...

Tom drove the Commodore at full speed up the driveway of Adam's family home. The gates automatically opened for them and closed behind him. Adam's parents were home; they returned from interstate two days prior, their timing couldn't be better. From her cottage at the side of the property – which was in effect a larger house than most of the neighbours lived in – Audrey saw the pace at which Tom was driving and came to the door, a worried expression on her face.

'What has happened?' she asked, hurrying towards Adam as he alighted, carrying his schoolbag. 'Are you hurt?'

'He's not hurt, but there has been an incident, Mrs Murphy. I need to contact the police and speak to you and Adam's parents.'

'No police until you talk to my son,' she said, ushering them up the stairs of the main house, not removing her hands from Adam. She called out to her son as they took the stairs to his office. Adam's father, James, appeared and moments later, the family was gathered.

Winsome touched Adam's face and pulled him to sit beside her on the Chesterfield leather couch – not too close, he was still in his cricket whites and dirty.

'I'm okay, Mum,' he mumbled, as she stroked his hair and looked to James for guidance with her large doe-eyes and pale countenance. He stepped up; he always did.

'So he said he was your uncle and came to your cricket matches?' his father asked for the second time. Adam nodded. James paced as he thought.

By the window, Tom stood, arms folded, legs apart as if on parade, waiting impatiently to be told 'at ease'.

'I need to call the police,' Tom began but was cut off.

'No police!' James snapped. 'It will attract attention to Adam, where we live, and make us ripe for future kidnapping attempts.'

Adam snapped to look at his father. 'He didn't kidnap me. I like Uncle Allan, he's nice, and he thinks Nate and I are going to be really good if we keep practising our cricket.'

Audrey, sitting in a matching Chesterfield single-seat, shook her head at her son, warning him not to argue with Adam… it would only make him fearful to know too much of the truth. A small groan escaped her. 'Has Nate met him too?'

Adam realised he might have got Nate or Uncle Allan in trouble and reluctantly nodded.

'No police,' James said again. 'I need to protect the ladies as well.' Winsome and his mother smiled at him fondly. The only thing they had in common was their love for James. Audrey also firmly believed her love of her grandson, Adam, far surpassed Winsome's feelings for the son who 'ruined her figure' as she claimed.

'Did you get the car's registration? Would you recognise him?' James asked Tom.

'Yes, to both, but I'll be surprised if the registration is legitimate. I've got resources that can check out the vehicle,' Tom said.

'Let's take that path to begin with,' James said. 'And eyes on Adam every time he is in a public space.'

Tom nodded. 'I'll get onto it,' he said departing, unsatisfied. He knew the way out.

James closed the door behind Tom and went to sit on the edge of his desk. From her seat, Audrey studied Winsome as she rose and stood in the window, watching Tom leave. Extending herself so she could see out the window from where she sat, Audrey saw Tom glance up as he reached his car and he locked eyes with Winsome. Then he lowered himself into the Commodore and departed as quickly as he came.

'What are you thinking, Winsome?' Audrey asked, watching the exchange.

Winsome turned to her mother-in-law, surprised to be observed. 'I am so disappointed. I was told he was the best.' She looked at Adam. 'How did he not know that Adam had a new friend? Did he ever mention this man to you, Audrey?'

'Not a word about him,' Audrey said, 'and he had plenty of opportunities.'

'Come here, Son,' James said and Adam rose from the couch and went to his father who stayed seated on the edge of the desk and pulled Adam in between his legs, keeping his hands on the boy's shoulders.

Audrey loved to see them together, they were so similar – dark of feature, handsome, bound to be successful. Adam was so unlike Winsome, which pleased her even more.

'You're disappointed he isn't really your uncle?' James

said in a calm voice, and Adam nodded. 'I want you to learn one very valuable lesson from this, Adam. Are you listening?'

'Yes, Dad.'

'Look at me.'

Adam raised his face to lock eyes with his father.

'Trust no-one. Do you understand?'

Adam nodded.

'The exceptions are me, your mother, Audrey, Nate, Nate's parents, and that is it. Not even Tom. Do what Tom tells you to do because I pay him to protect you, but trust no one else. Yes?'

'Yes,' Adam nodded.

'Tell me who you trust?' his father challenged him. Adam was not nervous, Audrey challenged him all the time.

'I trust no one except for you, Mum, Audrey, Nate, and Mr and Mrs Delaney,' he responded with an earnest face, looking up at his father.

'Exactly. Well done,' his father said with a smile.

'Dad, I don't want Tom to be my security guy anymore.'

His father studied him. 'Why?'

'I don't trust him,' Adam said.

Audrey smiled. 'The boy has spoken, James.'

James smiled and mussed Adam's hair. 'You're a quick study, Son.'

Winsome turned from the window. 'Tom's very good, straight from the SAS. I'd trust him with my life and he's just saved yours, Adam.'

Adam shook his head. 'He didn't even know who I was with and he beat up Uncle Allan. I don't want him.'

Audrey frowned. 'I'm sorry that you had to see that, my darling,' she said.

'Well, Son, if that's your decision,' James agreed, 'you're old enough to make that call.'

Adam smiled, satisfied.

'I'll find someone else for you,' his father said.

'I can take care of that,' Winsome said.

'Why don't I take care of it?' Audrey asked. 'I have a friend quite high in the ranks of the police service. I'm sure he can assist me with the best way forward.'

James smiled at his mother, and Audrey, like Adam, basked in James's love when it was reflected upon her.

'We'll leave it in your most capable hands then, Mum,' he said. And then James pulled Adam in for a hug, a rare few moments of love expressed to a boy drowning in neglect.

Chapter 14

Now...

Nate had stewed all night and now he paced around in the waiting room of *Delaney and Murphy* like a frustrated customer. Fortunately, the waiting room was large enough for him to walk eight paces in one direction before having to turn and repeat the same. Jessica watched him from her desk.

'So, I'm now just supposed to wait until Mrs Tatum contacts me? Why did she pay if she wasn't interested in the results?' he asked, confused. He stuck his hands in the pockets of his navy suit and turned to pace the opposite way. 'Why would you?'

'It's weird,' Jessica agreed. 'But Mrs Tatum seemed so genuine at the time, so concerned. Don't you think?'

'Absolutely. Rough as guts, but I thought she was serious about wanting to find Aden. Why would she give a false address, unless she's in trouble with the law too?'

'Or she's got a meth lab at her house,' Jessica said and laughed at her own joke.

Nate thought for a moment. 'That might not be too far

from the truth.' He sighed. 'Well, the case will just have to go on hold until she contacts us.'

'At least we got an initial payment, so she has compensated you for the work done,' Jessica said, printing out Nate and Adam's appointments for the days and rising to go to the printer to collect them.

Outside the door, Nate saw Adam looking at the pin pad and trying to recall the code. He opened the door. 'You look familiar, come in.'

Adam smirked at him. 'Thanks.'

'Something you want to tell us?' Nate said, studying the cricket bat tucked under Adam's arm. 'Are you taking up the sport again? From what I remember, you weren't half bad, almost as good as me,' he said, stirring his friend.

Adam laughed. 'Yeah, you were the benchmark,' he said, ribbing Nate.

'I love cricket. But I love football more,' Jessica said. 'I don't mind baseball either.'

They both looked at her and then away.

'From memory, I was great at the sport, thanks very much,' Adam reminded him. 'And no, my cricket days are over… I'm retired from the pitch.'

He was about to blurt out about the parcel and then thought better of it in front of Jessica, in case it made her nervous. She handed them both their meeting schedule for the day.

'Thanks,' Adam said. 'I can do this electronically if you like? Save a tree and all that.'

'Excellent,' she said and smiled. 'Nate?'

He waved the list at her and she rolled her eyes. 'I'll print your meetings out for you then.'

He thanked her and the phone rang. As Jessica answered it, Adam turned to Nate and asked: 'Got a minute?'

'Sure,' Nate said, sobering on seeing Adam's expression. He followed Adam into his office.

Adam dumped the bat on his desk. 'I got a parcel last night. It wasn't mailed, it was delivered, no marking and no card.' He nodded at the bat, and Nate picked it up. 'That was inside.'

Nate looked confused. 'Who would send you a cricket bat?' He turned it over. 'Wow, this is your bat.'

'Yeah, my actual bat from primary school days.'

'That's cool,' Nate said. 'I wish I had my childhood bat.'

'I didn't keep it. I left it in Uncle Allan's car that day Tom forced us off the road and punched Uncle Allan's lights out,' he told Nate. 'I left it in his car,' he emphasised.

'Except there was no Uncle Allan,' Nates said and scoffed. He froze, realising the implication. 'And you haven't seen this bat until now?'

'No.'

'But last night it arrived at your home address?' Nate asked, his eyes widening with alarm.

'That's the gist of it.'

Nate lowered himself in a chair opposite Adam's desk and exhaled. He looked up at Adam. 'Uncle Allan's back.'

Chapter 15

Then...

Tom knew in a few minutes when he dropped Nate off at school, and he was alone with Adam in the car, the atmosphere would be icy again. A week had passed, and the kid had not uttered a word. *What the fuck was that about?*

'See you after school,' Nate said, leaning forward through the middle front seat and hitting Adam on the arm.

'I'll be on the bike,' Adam said, turning to watch his friend depart from the car at Nate's local school.

'Yeah, usual place. See you, Tom and thanks,' Nate said, and grabbing his school bag, opened the car door and alighted.

'See you next time, Buddy,' Tom said, waiting as Nate closed the door and got safely inside the school yard.

Tom drove on. 'So, where's the usual place?' he asked with a glance at Adam.

Silence.

He sighed. 'Kid, this is ridiculous. Your dad told you that Uncle Allan was a phoney, and dangerous. You can trust me; you can't trust him. So, what's the problem here?'

Silence. He couldn't even see the kid's expression as Adam stared out the window. All he could see was the back of his head, which he wanted to whack at this moment in time.

He tried a different tack. 'I wouldn't hurt anyone else like that. I just knew he was going to hurt you, that's why I went off the deep end,' he said, trying again. 'That's my training.'

Silence.

He had had enough, and unaware that Audrey was seeking a replacement for him, he said: 'Okay little buddy, this is what's going to happen. You either speak to me or I'll give your dad my resignation and you can get a new security guard.'

He expected something – maybe not a *please don't go*, but something. He pulled up at the school gate, cut the engine and got out quickly to get around to Adam's side before he bolted. Adam was fast, Tom had already experienced that, and he was out of the car like a shot. Tom grabbed the kid by his school bag on his back, pulling him back from entering the school yard. He squatted down in front of him.

'Adam?'

He couldn't read the look in the kid's eyes. Fear, distrust, hate, all three... he let Adam go, stood, and watched the young boy enter the school gates safely.

By the following Wednesday he had been dismissed, and it would be the last time he'd see the kid for twenty years.

*****

Nate tore down the embankment on his Malvern Star bicycle, Adam close behind on his bike. They were the same colour bikes, and both had an equal number of plastic clips on the spokes, clicking like motors as they sped along. Nate looked back over his shoulder to make sure his best friend was following; Adam usually followed. The boys whooped as the speed gave them a rush of excitement. They pulled to a sharp stop, skidding around the edge of the river just where it met the border of the lunatic asylum and spraying up dirt and grass.

The afternoon was perfect – a cool breeze, hot enough to swim, and shaded by the spotted gums that towered above them. This was their favourite spot near the River Park Lunatic Asylum, and a regular haunt.

'Last one in is a rotten egg,' Nate yelled and pushed his bike aside. Adam raced him, breathing down Nate's neck, refusing to be a rotten egg.

They ran into the water, ducked under and immersed at the same time.

'That was a tie,' Adam declared, and Nate laughed.

'Watch out for dead bodies,' he said, and Adam splashed water at him.

'It's true, they could be stuck in the reeds and come to the surface when we kick around,' Nate said, teasing his best friend.

'Like the one we saw before, but it was floating,' Adam said, recalling the runaway from the asylum, and the police and ambulance men dragging the body out of the river.

'You think we'll ever see Joe again?' Nate asked.

'Nuh, I think he escaped. He would have said goodbye if he was just going home.'

Nate pushed his wet hair back off his face and headed to the bank. 'Let's climb and see who's in the yard. Your girlfriend might be there.'

'She's not my girlfriend,' Adam said, half annoyed as he followed him out. He wanted her to be, though. 'I bet she's gone too.'

'She was going to wait until we hid her,' Nate said. 'She could have run away with Joe; they might have broken out together.'

They found the familiar footfalls in their favourite gum tree and climbed it quickly to the branches that let them sit and dry out in the sun, and see the full exercise yard and gardens of the asylum.

'Nope, not there,' Adam said. 'Neither of them. I bet we won't see Kelsey again.'

'And you didn't even get to give her flowers or write her a soppy love letter,' Nate teased.

'Shut up,' Adam said with a grin, 'or I'll tell Kelly Hopkins you like her.'

'Do not.'

'Sure you don't,' Adam said, pleased with himself that his threat had worked.

Nate changed the subject, an admission of defeat. 'Think you'll ever talk to Tom again?'

'Never.'

'What about on your birthday if he buys you a present?'

'Nope. I don't want his present, and I'm not talking to him. You should have seen the way he was hitting Uncle Allan.'

'Wish I had,' Nate said and sighed. 'Was he like an amazing fighter?'

Adam shrugged. He didn't want to concede that Tom had done anything good. 'He was just stronger.'

'Poor Uncle Allan,' Nate said.

'Yeah. I hope he didn't die from it. Like have internal bleeding or something like that. I saw that on a TV show.'

'I never get to watch whatever I want. Mum's like a guard dog around the TV and if Dad's home, it's just news or football. You're lucky.'

'Yeah, lucky,' Adam said, not feeling like that at all.

Chapter 16

Now...

Nate glanced at the clock. He didn't know why he was so apprehensive about Tom Hartigan coming in this morning, but it probably had something to do with the fact that Adam's eyes narrowed every time his former security detail's name was mentioned. Nate had messaged Adam's part-time partner, psychologist Robert Ware, to check he was definitely going to be in the office this morning. It was one of Rob's scheduled days and given he had once been Adam's mentor and was a successful psychologist in his own right, Nate hoped he might read heads better than himself. Rob was in Adam's office with him now. Nate couldn't hear anything emanating from there, but he heard Jessica buzz in a visitor from the foyer.

Nate came out and waited at her desk.

'Tom Hartigan's on his way up. What's going on?' Jessica asked, looking from Nate to Adam's door. 'Everyone's super tense this morning.'

'Yeah, we knew this guy when we were kids. He was Adam's security guard.'

'Wow, that's cool,' Jessica said.

'Not cool, no love lost there,' Nate assured her with a grimace.

Seeing Tom at the door, Jessica hit the green button on her desk, letting him in. Tom Hartigan walked into the reception of *Delaney and Murphy* with a confident stride. A handsome, fit man, in his late fifties, with a full head of salt and pepper hair and a few days' growth, he stopped short on seeing Nate and grinned.

Nate laughed. 'Tom Hartigan! Well, it's been a while,' he said, offering his hand.

'Jesus, look at you,' Tom said, looking at Nate eye to eye. 'You were such a troublemaker I always thought you'd end up doing something crazy, and to think you became a cop and P.I.'

'Yeah, that's crazy. You can blame my parents,' he joked. 'You're still looking after yourself, Tom.'

'I stay tidy,' Tom agreed. He laughed again. 'Wow the last time I saw you, you were 10. You've grown a bit.'

'Happens,' Nate agreed with a grin. He introduced Tom to Jessica, and then Tom swallowed and cut to the chase. 'What can I expect?' he said, folding his arms across his chest and with a nod to the only other office door that remained closed.

Nate grimaced. 'Can't say. He's hard to read sometimes, even for me. But it's been nearly twenty years... water under the bridge.' And then Adam's door opened.

*****

Tom was taken aback – it was James Murphy. He had checked Adam out online, but most of the photos were of Adam blocking his face, or speeding away in a car. The last full-length photo was at Adam's father's funeral when Adam was 16, wearing a dark suit and looking like a young male model. Now, his father may as well have walked out of his office. Tom conceded, Adam also looked like the former prime minister too – he could see why the gossip mags loved to fuel that story. To think he nearly didn't get this guy to adulthood.

Adam came towards him, another man close behind; you could hear a pin drop in the office.

'Adam, it's been a long time,' Tom said, extending the olive branch. He didn't extend his hand, leaving Adam to lead with the front foot if he chose to do so. He didn't.

Tom could sense Nate studying them both as he and Adam sized each other up. Nate cleared his throat and introduced Rob, who stepped around Adam like he was the support crew, and shook Tom's hand.

'Adam's roped Rob in to consult a few days a week,' Nate explained.

'The other days, I'm on the golf course,' Rob said.

'Yeah, so let's take a seat, hey,' Nate said, 'we're not expecting anyone for an hour or more. What do you think about some coffee, Jess?'

'I think that's a good idea,' she said, studying the faces in front of her.

Adam sat at the table and Tom sat directly opposite him. Nate and Rob threw a few comments in to cut the tension and then Tom burst out: 'You didn't say one word to me after the Uncle Allan incident, and now, twenty years later, you are still doing this silent shit. What the fuck?'

Adam looked away for a moment, his jaw locked. Rob stepped in.

'Sometimes, childhood trauma can do that if—'

Tom cut him off. 'Sorry, Rob,' he said and turned back to Adam. 'I fucked up. Is that what you want to hear?' Tom asked. 'I left the SAS because I was injured, and I didn't cope with that after years of training to get in there in the first place. I was in a bad headspace. But you're still here, aren't you? If you hadn't bullshitted to me about your cricket games or when you were next playing, that whole incident could have been avoided.'

Adam turned to face Tom and laughed with surprise at Tom's outpouring.

Nate's eyes widened at Adam's reaction, he spoke up: 'Let's just get this all out in the open now and move on, hey? Adam?' He invited his best friend to speak.

Adam studied Tom and then he said in the controlled voice he used with his patients that were on the verge of losing it: 'Does it make you feel better blaming it on a 10-year-old?'

Tom's jaw locked, but he had the good sense not to say anything.

Adam continued: 'You didn't give a fuck about your new job guarding me, even though for a while Nate and I thought the sun shone out of you,' he said. 'You didn't have to like me, but it might have occurred to you that bashing up one of the few people who were important to me, in full sight, might have freaked me out. I watched you pummel the man I thought was my uncle. Then...' Adam continued in a measured voice, 'You chased after me, forced me into the car and told me I was being kidnapped and that Uncle Allan intended to sell me for money or bury me.'

Jessica gasped from the nearby kitchen where she was listening, and Rob masked his initial shocked expression.

'Do you know how many nights I lay awake freaked out

by that? I didn't know if you or Uncle Allan were the bad guy.'

Tom gave a small nod, conceding the point and Adam continued.

'But you know, I don't care about any of that now,' he said. 'I knew why you were never where you were supposed to be… watching me anytime I was in public, like at that cricket game. Because you were too busy having an affair with my mother.'

Nate's eyes widened and a glance at Rob told him that Rob knew all about it.

'Adam… it just got a bit out of control…' Tom started.

'I saw you both, more than once. I did you a favour not telling Dad, more than you did for me.'

Tom exhaled between his teeth, the fight going from him. 'She was beautiful, your mother,' he said.

'And weak, apparently,' Adam added. 'And if Mum's hired you again to do security, you can fuck off and do that somewhere else, because I wouldn't trust you to provide any to my girlfriend, Nate or me.' Adam rose from the table.

'I need this job,' Tom blurted out. 'Hear me out, please.'

Adam froze and then, to everyone's surprise, especially Tom's, sat again. They accepted the coffee Jessica put in front of each of them, and Nate thanked her. She raised her eyebrows, enjoying the live soap opera.

After a few moments of silence, while everyone sipped their coffee and waited for Tom to start, Rob kicked it off, which was why Nate wanted to be sure he was along – he'd know what to do.

'With an outsider's perspective, if I may?' Rob said, not waiting for an answer. 'It appears to be the perfect storm,' he said, and they all looked at him. Rob continued: 'Adam, your mum hired a man physically capable but mentally not ready for the role; you were at more risk than anyone thought and you placed your faith in the wrong person, which is understandable for a young boy; and your dad was being protective of the family hence his actions in hiring security. It was a different time too.'

Tom nodded. 'Everything you said is true. I regret a lot of it, but not bashing the hell of that creep. I just wish he hadn't got away.'

Adam's jaw locked.

'I've played that scene back in my head a thousand times...' Tom admitted.

'What scene?' Nate asked, watching Tom and Adam like it was an action movie playing out in front of him. He sipped his coffee and encouraged Tom to elaborate.

Tom ran a hand over his face. 'When I couldn't find you at the cricket ground, Adam, one of your little cricket mates said you had left with your uncle just minutes before, but he couldn't tell me what your uncle looked like or what he was driving. I was sick to the stomach with stress. I tore after you and I got to a crossroad.'

'Wow,' Rob said, 'tough call.'

'Exactly,' Tom said. 'I knew if my suspicions were correct, and I was pretty confident they were, after all, what creep tells a young kid that they are his uncle and stalks him?'

'Uncle Allan, apparently,' Nate added, then realised he wasn't helping and invited Tom to continue.

'I took a gamble,' Tom said, 'an educated gamble that Allan would want to get you off the main road. I didn't know if you would go quietly, or believe whatever lies he spun you, or if you'd try to get away. I tore down that off-road like the devil was chasing me, and I have to tell you, I have seen that choice in my head thousands of times in the last twenty years.'

'Perhaps you should have got some counselling,' Adam said drily, and Nate laughed.

Tom ignored them. 'There's more, stuff you don't know about.' He glanced at Rob before continuing as if accepting he was the one who would know everyone's limits.

'Go on,' Adam said, and Rob nodded.

Tom looked at Adam. 'Was that the first time you accepted a ride from him? From Uncle Allan?'

Adam thought about it for a moment; it was twenty years ago.

'No,' Nate added. 'He took us home in his limousine once, remember?'

'Yeah, that's right,' Adam said. 'He got pulled over by the cops.' Adam smiled, and Nate laughed at the memory.

Tom didn't crack a smile. 'That cop might have saved your lives that day.'

The room sobered and Tom continued. 'Allan Sheffield, or Uncle Allan as you knew him, did twenty years for kidnapping and murder.'

Chapter 17

Then...

Allan Sheffield felt the pressure building. It was only a matter of time until one of the 'nephews' he was trying to win over would tell a relative about their new Uncle Allan. He had to act now and fast. Besides, his wife Millie was excited about the IVF. He had promised they would have the funds, and she wasn't to worry about it, she was to leave it all to him. They had their first appointment in a matter of weeks.

Allan pulled his limo into the cricket grounds' carpark, relieved that the school bus and snobby parents in their Mercs and BMWs had left. He anxiously searched the field. Allan was late but with intent – he was hoping Adam had stayed on to have a hit with his friends and Nate. It confounded him why Adam's security guy dropped him off at the school gate but let him hang around in a public park where anyone could run off with him. Anyone like him.

Allan left his car, locked it, and, tipping his cap back further on his head, he made his way to the boundary. He spotted the boy straight away – a slight, good-looking kid. He'd be a powerful young man in time to come, Allan imagined. Just like his father. Allan had seen the pictures. He knew exactly whom he was dealing with, how rich they were, and how much they could pay.

Nate spotted Allan first and waved, and Adam turned, his face filled with excitement setting eyes on his 'Uncle.' Allan sighed. He was a good kid; he hoped to have a son like him one day. Allan grinned and waved back, watching for fifteen minutes as Adam missed a catch, and took another. Then the boys packed it in and Adam and Nate raced to meet him.

'Hi Uncle Allan, we thought you weren't coming,' Adam said, hugging him.

'I had to take a client to the airport, lads, but I got here in time to see that great catch, Adam, and that boundary hit, Nate. You're both having a fine season.'

'Thanks, Uncle Allan,' Nate said. 'I like cricket but Dad says it is boring and wants me to play tennis.'

'Except you're bad at it,' Adam said and Nate punched his arm. Adam laughed.

'So would you like a ride home?' Uncle Allan asked, and the boys' eyes lit up. He didn't want to take both kids, that was just adding to the work, but he knew he had more chance of getting them in the car if they came together.

'You've got the limo!' Adam said. 'Cool.'

'Can we sit in the back and try the window between you and us?' Nate asked.

'Absolutely, and not only that, I might have put some soft drink and chips in the back seat bar.'

The boys laughed with delight.

'Grab your bags,' Allan told them, 'and I'll meet you at the car.'

*****

He was still deciding whether to drop Nate off and never drop Adam off, or take them both. It would be harder to take them both, and Nate was rowdier and stronger than his little friend. But Allan didn't want to get too close to their homes. The car was recognisable and sure, if they tracked him down, he could say he dropped Adam at his front gate, but then why the hell would he be dropping him home in the first place?

The dark screen went down again between the passenger and front seats and both boys laughed.

'That's so cool,' Nate said.

'It's good for me too,' Allan told them, looking back in his rear-view mirror. 'If I get a cranky client, and they put the screen up, I don't have to look at them. Help yourselves to a soft drink and chips, lads.'

'But what if we spill it, Uncle Allan? Audrey won't let us eat or drink in her Jaguar.'

'Understandable,' he said. He knew who Audrey was, he had done his research. 'She's very wise, your grandmother, but I'm about to get the car cleaned so don't be concerned if you spill anything.'

'Do you know Audrey?' Nate asked.

'Of course, Adam's grandmother is a lovely lady,' he said, confirming his family connection. He had never met her. 'Speaking of lovely ladies, do either of you have a girlfriend?'

Nate grinned and Adam reddened.

'Adam's in love with a girl from the madhouse.'

'She's not a lunatic,' he said, defending Kelsey. 'She said she ran away and they put her in there.'

'That's terrible,' Uncle Allan said with a glance back at Adam. 'You'll have to try and make her day brighter.'

'I said he should get her some flowers or write a love poem,' Nate joked.

'Have you got a girlfriend, Uncle Allan?' Adam asked.

'I did have. Then I gathered her up some wildflowers, went on a picnic, and asked her to marry me. Now she's my wife.'

'That's super romantic,' Adam said, and nudged Nate, daring him to comment.

'It was,' Allan agreed.

Allan was coming to the intersection now where he had to decide – go straight ahead and take Nate home or turn left onto the off-road and take both boys. Nate would be worth nothing, but trouble.

His blood froze as a siren sounded behind him. A quick look in the rear-view mirror told him it was a cop car.

He almost swore, then remembered the boys and played cool.

'Just pulling over to see what the good men from our police force want from me, lads,' he said, indicating and slowing down to pull over. 'I'll put the screen up and you two can be in hiding, but listen in. What do you think?'

'Yeah!' Adam agreed as if it were a great game. Allan hit the button to raise the screen.

He gave them a wink and a smile as he disappeared from view. He put down the passenger side window and waited. A stocky, middle-aged policeman appeared in the window.

'Good afternoon, Sir, sorry to interrupt your afternoon.'

'Not at all, officer, what can I do for you?' Allan asked, his heart racing.

'Just letting you know that you have a rear tail light out. If the traffic boys pick you up, they'll fine you, so might be worth getting it checked.'

Allan breathed again and smiled. 'That's most kind of you, thank you for that, officer.'

And then the screen between them went down and the officer's eyes widened. Allan cursed himself for not locking it.

The police officer laughed at seeing the two boys with their drinks and chips, dirtied in their cricket whites and having the time of their lives.

'Well, that's a surprise,' he said and grinned.

'My nephew and his friend,' Allan explained. 'If I pick them up from cricket, they like to be chauffeured home.'

The police officer laughed and shook his head at the boys.

'Cheeky lads. Well, enjoy the ride with your uncle.' He gave Allan a nod and, receiving Allan's thanks again, departed.

Allan put up the passenger window and told the boys they'd be home in a few minutes. There would be no attempt today.

Chapter 18

Now...

Nate rose, shocked, and paced around, his hands going behind his head before he ran them through his hair and sat down again. The impact of that day hit him.

'So, you think if we hadn't got pulled over that day...'

'Oh my God, imagine both of your parents...' Jessica said, and they all glanced her way. She gave them an apologetic look and got back to work.

Tom's lips thinned as he thought about the consequences of two families losing their boys. 'I'd say he took you both to make sure he could get Adam in the car. He may have intended to drop you home, Nate, but never Adam, or he might have taken you both. The cop sighting Allan and his car put an end to that plan.'

'Holy shit,' Nate said.

'It was a broken tail light, I think,' Adam said with a glance to Nate, who agreed.

'Yeah, we were in the back seat, behind the screen, but we put it down to surprise the cop,' Nate said.

'Good thinking, even if you didn't know it. That saved your life,' Tom said.

'Who did he kidnap then?' Adam asked. Before Tom could answer, the office buzzer went off and Jessica buzzed in the visitor.

'Danielle,' she told Nate.

'My surveillance researcher,' he informed Tom as Danielle arrived at the top of the stairs and bounded in at the sound of the buzzer.

'Hi everyone… ah, sorry, is this private? Captain Tom!' she said, her eyes lighting up as she saw Tom Hartigan sitting at the end of the table.

'You two know each other?' Nate asked suspiciously.

'Sure, I'm in the army reserve, and Captain Tom trains the recruits. He's given me grief many a time,' she said ribbing Tom.

'Private Danielle Walters,' he said and grinned. 'I've had worse to train.'

She gave him a smirk and accepted Nate's invitation to sit down.

'Winsome has hired Tom to do security before and at the wedding,' Rob explained.

'Really?' Danielle said, with a glance at Adam.

'Really,' Nate responded.

Adam continued: 'So who did Allan Sheffield kidnap that day?'

'Dean Beals,' Danielle piped in, and everyone turned to her. 'Back in the eighties?'

'Yeah. How do you know that?' Nate asked.

'True crime podcasts. I heard an excellent podcast on it a few weeks back. Must be coming up to a significant anniversary, is it?' she asked.

Tom nodded. 'Twenty years ago that Allan Sheffield, limo driver, abducted and murdered a young boy.'

Adam frowned. 'So, how long elapsed between when he tried to take us for the ride in his limo that day and then took this other kid, Dean?'

Nate saw Danielle's eyes widen and was pleased she didn't interrupt with questions – the tension in the room was bad enough and the sooner the meeting was over, the better.

Tom continued. 'It was exactly one week after he abducted you that second time alone, Adam. When we had the fallout. He must have been establishing the relationships at the same time and when you didn't work out, he took the other kid.'

'Young Dean Beals,' Rob added. 'I remember he went missing after his swimming training.'

'That's exactly what happened. At least back then I didn't tell you about Dean,' Tom said with a look to Adam. 'You remember the abduction then?' he asked Rob.

'Like it was yesterday,' Rob said. 'My son was around the same age as the boys,' he said with a nod to Nate and Adam, 'and every parent and every school stepped up security after that. We were all terrified… it's every parent's worst nightmare.' He didn't mention his own son was in prison, for white-collar crime – brilliant with numbers to the point he embezzled from his employer and got away with it for a long time, but not a lifetime. It was Rob's greatest heartache. 'The parents paid the ransom for their son, Dean, didn't they?'

'They did,' Tom said. 'But Allan Sheffield did not return the boy. Dean Beals disappeared off the face of the earth.' He glanced at Adam for a reaction.

'His mother still holds hope, though, that they'll find him and she can bury him properly,' Danielle said. 'They spoke with her on the podcast. Dean's father has passed away.'

Adam's eyes narrowed as he thought. 'Who else did they interview on the podcast?'

Danielle gave a small shrug. 'No one. Just the police detective at the time and Dean's Mum, I think her name was Yvonne. She lives interstate now. She said she didn't move for a long time; worried Dean would come home and she would be gone. But eventually, once he turned 18 – or would have if he were alive – Yvonne said she accepted he was not coming home and if he did, he was an adult and could find her. She needed to move on from the pain.'

They sobered at the thought of Dean's mother's anguish.

Danielle looked to Tom. 'You don't think he's going to come back for grown-up Adam now, do you?' she said with a look of disbelief as if the idea was crazy.

'Yeah,' Tom said, 'that's exactly what I'm thinking.'

Chapter 19

Then...

The pressure was on. Allan Sheffield had to act fast now, or it would blow his plan out of the water. He'd missed out on taking the boy, Adam, and he was counting on that being a sure thing. Bloody cops and the security guard who was good with his fists. Allan had one more iron in the fire.

He smiled when he recognised the phone number showing on his VIP taxi screen. The technology was only a year old, but worth every cent, and he'd learnt the numbers that mattered. He turned his car radio down, cleared his throat and adapted his broad Australian accent to what his mother called a 'plummy' voice.

'Allan Sheffield, at your service,' he said.

'Good morning, Allan, it's Phillip Beals calling. I know it is short notice, but any chance of a lift from the office to the airport in half an hour? My wife said she would book you, but then clean forgot.'

'Of course, Mr Beals. I'll be outside your office in thirty minutes.'

'You're a lifesaver, Allan, thank you. See you then.' The line was disconnected.

Allan couldn't resist a satisfied smirk. Twenty minutes later, he pulled up out the front of Phillip Beals's business and alighted to open the back door of his limousine for his client when he bounded down the stairs not long after.

'You're a lifesaver,' Phillip Beals said, giving Allan a grin and diving into the back seat.

Allan moved quickly to the front seat. He didn't keep businessmen waiting, and he didn't drive like he was on a Sunday picnic. Time was money and the feedback he got from his clients – the reason they came back to Allan all the time – was because he understood that.

Money, Allan mused. Great for those who have it. He also didn't speak unless invited to do so by his clients and he hoped like hell Phillip Beals would start talking. Allan had a question to ask. It was his lucky day.

'Oh damn,' Phillip muttered.

'Do we need to turn around, Sir?' Allan asked.

'No, all good. I'll need the QANTAS domestic terminal, thanks Allan,' he sighed. 'I just remembered my boy has one of his swimming finals on today. I told him I'd try to get to it.'

'I'm sure he'd understand.'

In the rear-view mirror, Allan saw Phillip glance at his watch, then sigh again. There was no chance he could make the swim meet, but Allan could.

*****

Nine-year-old Dean Beals scanned the parent's faces in the stands around the boundary of the public swimming pool. He had made it to the heat for his age group and his father had promised he would try to get there. He promised that a lot, but rarely made it.

A cheer from his schoolmates drew his attention back to the pool.

'Go Brady,' he yelled, cheering on his friend and his school house colours. Dean left the stands and got ready to swim; his race was next. He glanced once more towards the stands and his face broke into an enormous smile. Standing near the aisle row, giving Dean a wave, was Uncle Allan.

Allan Sheffield held his thumbs up to wish him luck and Dean nodded, beaming. He could win now, he had to win for Uncle Allan. He focused, ignoring the jests and comments from his friends, this was serious. Dean stood up on the numbered block when his time came, glanced once more at Uncle Allan who gave him a nod and a look of intent that said: 'You can do this.' He could, he knew it.

'Take your marks.'

Dean leant down, ready to dive. The starter gun went off and he extended his body in flight, slicing through the water. It felt good.

'Stroke, stroke, stroke,' he pumped himself along. He could do this; he would win this for Uncle Allan. Turning at the end, he risked a glance while grabbing a breath, he was in front but not by far. He pumped harder, not taking time to breathe, just pushing on and taking a quick gasp when he had to. He saw he was ahead.

His fingers touched the end of the pool and he looked up and around. He was first, he had done it. Dean heard a cheer from the stand and looked up to see Uncle Allan looking as proud as punch. Dean gave him a wave and pulled himself out of the pool, racing up to see him.

'You're here,' he said, hugging Uncle Allan, despite being wet.

'Wouldn't miss it. Well done, young Dean, you were amazing.'

'I've made the finals, I can't believe it,' Dean beamed.

'I can, of course,' Uncle Allan said. 'You're destined for big things in the pool, young man. I wouldn't be surprised if I'm buying tickets to see you swim at the Olympics!'

Dean laughed with delight.

An announcement came over the loud speaker asking all students who had completed their races to change and assemble at the school bus.

'I've got the car here, the limousine. I'll drive you home if you'd like a lift in the limo,' Allan offered.

'Yes please, better than the bus. Dad didn't make it but we can tell him all about it,' Dean said, angry at his father but not wanting to ruin his moment of happiness.

'Your Dad rang me,' Uncle Allan said, speaking the truth. 'He had to get away quickly on business and asked me to tell you he's so sorry to miss your race.'

'He's always sorry for missing stuff; Dad doesn't care,' Dean said, with a shrug.

'Hey, of course he does. I'm sure he is as proud of you as I am at this very moment.' Allan patted the young boy on the back. 'Go grab your gear and we'll go.'

Dean gave him another quick hug and raced off to change and get his schoolbag. Excited to drive in the limo, ten minutes later, they left the pool car parking grounds and Dean disappeared.

Chapter 20

Now...

Nate was enjoying the catch-up even if Adam continued to look pained. Nate and Adam were too young to remember the Dean Beals crime, but there's nothing he liked better than a mystery – it was the cop in him – and cold cases were as mysterious as they came. He already had a missing client – Mrs Tatum who was not supposed to be missing, her son was the missing one after all. Now he couldn't find either of them. He sighed at the thought, then tapped back into the conversation playing out in front of him.

'If I had gone to the police, they might have prevented it,' Tom was saying. 'I was going to tell them about Allan, but your dad forbade it.' Tom ran a hand over his jaw and Nate inhaled, waiting for Adam's reaction to that.

'Christ,' Rob said and looked at Adam. 'If you ever had nightmares about being kidnapped, Dean's story is not one you need to hear.'

Adam shook his head at Tom. 'So, it's my fault that you weren't across the Uncle Allan relationship and lost your job, Dad's fault Dean was taken. Anything your fault?'

Tom gave Adam a smirk. Yep, no love lost there.

'Poor kid,' Nate said, refocusing the discussion. 'I wonder what became of him? If he was killed and buried somewhere or if there was a chance he was still alive?'

Tom shrugged. 'It took little for them to trace it to Allan Sheffield. Your father, at least, put the cops in the right direction.'

'Did he?' Adam asked, surprised. 'So, he is only half to blame?'

Rob cleared his throat, a signal to Adam to rein it in. Adam sat back and gave a small nod, without looking at his mentor and supervisor.

Tom continued. 'Your father wouldn't let me mention the abduction attempt for fear of reprisal, but he allowed me to tell them that Allan had been hanging around and calling himself Uncle Allan, and that he was the driver for Dean's father and your father when needed. It's how he came to target you two boys. It was enough for the police to go on.'

'The cops never spoke to me, or you, did they?' Adam asked Nate, who shook his head.

'Your father wouldn't allow it,' Tom said. 'Nate's name was never mentioned.'

Adam looked at Tom. 'So why now? Why are you back on the scene? Have you stayed in touch with Mum the whole time?'

'No. I saw the announcement of your mum's engagement to Jack, and I saw the photo of you trying to avoid the media. I contacted her and sent her my congratulations… we emailed and she mentioned the job to me,' he said and shrugged. 'That's it. I'm sorry for how it went down. I can't change that now. But I need this job, financially.' He threw up his hands and sat back in the chair.

Adam exhaled and thought for a moment. No one said anything. 'Okay.'

'Okay?' Tom said, his eyes wide with surprise.

'Really, okay?' Nate asked, confused.

Adam shrugged. 'It was a long time ago and if you need the work.'

Nate looked at Rob, confused, and Rob gave him a small shrug, his brow furrowed.

'I'm not sure what the scope of your contract is, Tom, but there's something you should know,' Rob said and gave Adam a nudge. Adam rose and went to his office.

'Is that it?' Tom asked, confused, watching Adam walk away.

'No, hold up,' Nate said, and Adam returned with a cricket bat. He handed it to Tom and sat back down.

Tom looked confused and then turned it over and saw the small signature. His eyes widened, and he looked up at Adam. 'You lost this on that day. You left it in Sheffield's car with your schoolbag.'

'I know. It arrived outside my house last night. No note, nothing.'

Tom inhaled sharply. 'Now? You've just got this back now?'

Adam nodded.

'What's going on?' Nate asked Tom, sensing he knew more from his reaction.

Tom looked at the men and placed the bat in the middle of the table. 'Allan Sheffield was released from prison last week.'

Chapter 21

Then...

Charlotte Duffy – who only answered to the name Charlie – was behind the wheel of Audrey's Jaguar. It was Wednesday and Audrey trusted the young woman to drive her beloved grandson and his best friend to school while she prepared for her weekly bridge game. Charlie was, after all, recommended by the commissioner of police, Audrey's dear friend. Beside Charlie sat Adam, a little uncomfortable in the presence of his new security detail, and in the back seat was Nate, not at all uncomfortable and falling in love.

'Have you driven a Jaguar before, Charlie?' Nate asked.

'No, but I've driven a tank,' she said.

'Wow, bet it wasn't fast but it could crush every car it saw,' Adam added.

'That's exactly right, Adam,' Charlie said, 'but I can't say I got to crush any cars, most disappointingly.'

'But you were in the tank to fight the enemy?' Nate asked.

'For training to fight the enemy if needed,' Charlie said. 'I was in the army for twelve years. Now I do special projects. But if we go to war, I'll be ready. In the meantime, Mr Murphy and Mr Delaney, I will fight to keep you both safe,' she said with a smile.

'So, we're special projects?' Nate asked.

'Yeah, I'm special, you're the project,' Adam said and laughed at his own joke.

'That's what Mum calls the people at the loony bin – special,' Nate said with a grin.

Charlie enjoyed their banter and, pulling the Jaguar kerbside at Nate's school, wished him a good day.

'See you tomorrow,' she said.

'I only come when Audrey's not driving,' Nate said. 'Otherwise, she listens to the radio and makes us listen and answer questions.'

Adam nodded. 'It's hard work.'

'See you, Charlie. Catch you on your bike, Murph,' he said, punching Adam's arm through the front seat gap.

'Have you been friends for long?' Charlie asked as they drove off.

'Since we moved into this area. He's my best friend,' Adam said.

They drove along for a while listening to the music that Adam had selected. Audrey allowed it as long as he put it back on her station before she next drove.

'You don't have to walk me in,' Adam said pre-empting their arrival at the school.

'I am walking you to the gate, Mr Murphy,' she teased. 'If that embarrasses you, you can pretend I'm your big sister, cousin, aunty, girlfriend, whatever. I'll even kiss you on the cheek if that helps when I wave you off.'

Adam laughed at the idea but wasn't totally against it.

'Is it exciting having a mum who is so famous and beautiful?' Charlie asked with a glance at Adam.

'Nope.'

She smiled. 'Yeah, I get that.'

He looked across at her and Charlie explained.

'When I was a kid, we were a military family, so we grew up in military residences and went to elite schools. My father was high up, like at one stage we were living in the governor's house. Everyone was either really careful around me or kissing my butt. I never liked it.'

Adam grinned as he watched and listened to her.

'Me either. I hate it.'

'Some people like that sort of thing,' she said and shrugged.

'Not us,' Adam said.

'Nope, that's for sure.'

*****

Later that afternoon, with school done for the day and dusk some hours away, Nate was cruising along the wide street, Adam riding beside him. They turned their bikes off onto the dirt track that led to the creek.

'She's like Sarah O'Connor in the *Terminator*,' Nate said.

'I know, just like her. She's really muscly and super fit.'

'She even looks like her,' Nate said. 'She could do that body double stuff for her in the movies.'

'You like her,' Adam teased.

'Yeah.'

Adam hadn't expected that, he thought Nate would deny it.

'If I was older, I'd ask her out. Unless you want to ask her out. She's your bodyguard,' Nate said generously.

'Thanks. I like her but not like a girlfriend.'

Nate visibly relaxed and smiled at his best friend. 'Do you reckon she'd beat Tom in a fight?'

'She's smaller, but she'd be faster. We should get the *Terminator* movie and watch it again! I'll tell Mum I want it,' Adam said.

'Will you have to wait for your birthday?'

'Nah.'

'Beat you to the bottom,' Nate said with a head start as they skidded down the dirt hill towards the creek.

Nate won. They threw their bikes on the ground and stripped to their shorts for a swim.

'Think we'll see your Uncle Allan again, ever?' Nate asked.

Adam shook his head. 'Nuh, no way. Tom nearly killed him. He probably hates me now and won't come back. Adults never stick around for long.'

Chapter 22

Now...

Nate huffed out with frustration. Out there somewhere was the man who called himself Uncle Allan, who killed a boy and now left a cricket bat memento at Adam's house. Add to this, he had not heard a word from Mrs Tatum or her missing son. Who pays to find a relative and then disappears themselves? He stopped short. Maybe that's what's happened... maybe she's disappeared as well.

He grabbed his phone and rang his police mate, Burnsy, again.

'Someone dead or missing?' Burnsy asked on answering.

'Not me, you'll be pleased to know,' Nate said and heard his mate chuckle. 'You know that missing guy I asked you to check up on last week?'

'Yeah, Aden someone or other,' Burnsy said.

'Aden Sabel. Now I can't find his mum.'

'You need to be more careful where you put things,' Burnsy joked. 'Righto, what's her name and I'll have a look in the system?'

'Thanks, Burnsy... Tatum, Ruth Tatum.' Nate waited as Burnsy checked the files. He could hear the sounds of him typing as he opened and closed screens.

'Sorry, Nate, not a thing. No one by that name anywhere on the system. She hasn't even got a driver's licence that I can find.'

'That so? Is there a Ruth Sabel in the system? Maybe she hasn't changed her licence name.' Again, he waited. He was sorely tempted to casually mention the cricket bat delivered to Adam, and the name of Allan Sheffield, but he had agreed – rightly or wrongly – to let Tom look into it, given it was connected to the Murphy family.

'Nope, nothing, like she never existed,' Burnsy said returning on the line and interrupting Nate's thoughts. 'For that Tatum name, there is a minor police record for a Ron Tatum – a misdemeanour, disorderly conduct dating back a few decades. I don't know if it's the husband or a relative, but do you want the address?'

'Yeah, thanks, that'd be great.' Nate took it down. 'Appreciate it. Talk later.' Nate hung up and sat back, perplexed. Did Mrs Tatum drive to his office that day without a licence? Was she married to Ron Tatum? Could someone have targeted mother and son?

He thought back on Burnsy's words... *like she never existed*, and opening his search engine did a quick search for her missing son, Aden Sabel, to see if he had any social media footprint. A few faces came up, but none of them matched the photo Mrs Tatum had given him of her son. He put in Ruth Tatum's name, and again photos of different Ruth Tatums of all ages came on the screen. But like Burnsy said, none that were Mrs Tatum who sat in his office, and she had a face he wouldn't forget. He tried Ron Tatum and got a selection of heads that meant nothing to him.

Nate sat back, resigned to not being able to find Mrs Tatum and having to wait until she contacted him. He had taken her deposit and had no intention of refunding it, especially if she didn't make herself known to him again. He waded through some emails and saw one from Adam. It had the link to the news story about Allan Sheffield – Uncle Allan's release. He clicked on it and read the story. He searched for an update, found a more comprehensive story with earlier photos of Allan as a young man and photos of the kidnapped boy, Dean Beals.

'Weird,' he muttered, seeing the man he remembered as Uncle Allan being arrested all those years ago. Now he and Adam were the same age as Allan Sheffield was then.

Nate scrolled down further to photos of Sheffield walking from prison. He stopped. For a moment he thought he had confused the images in his mind with what he just saw on screen; the photo of Allan now was so different to the younger man they knew. It was familiar, shockingly familiar. He stood, walked to the front of his desk, and exhaled.

Nate rubbed his hands over his face.

'Fuck, holy fuck,' he said and walked back to his laptop. Nope, it was there, it was correct.

Nate strode to his office door, swung it open so quickly that he startled Jessica at her reception desk and glanced towards Adam's door.

'Is he alone?' he asked.

'He is, for about two hours… he's doing reports.'

Nate raised his voice and yelled. 'Adam, I need you.'

Jessica winced again. 'You couldn't walk that distance?'

He disappeared back into his office.

*****

Adam's office door opened and he surfaced, looked around for Nate, then glanced Jessica's way.

'What's he on about?'

'Nate wants you to come out and play,' she said, and Adam grinned.

He shook his head. 'Nothing changes.' He headed to Nate's office and found him standing behind his desk, his hands on his hips.

'You're not going to believe this... I don't believe it... holy fuck...'

'What?' Adam asked, a feeling of alarm rising in him.

'The email link you sent me, the story on Allan Sheffield being released from prison last week,' Nate said and pointed to the screen. 'For two days I've been waiting for Mrs Tatum to contact me again and all the time this has been out there.'

'Slow down, you've lost me.' Adam went to the desk and lowered himself into Nate's chair; seeing the story on the screen he frowned. The headline read: *Child kidnapper's time up*. 'Yeah, so we know what Allan did and that he's been released...' he said, a little confused and scanning the article.

Jessica came in to join them.

'Need anything?' she asked.

'Yes,' Nate said, 'check out this article, quickly.'

She hurried behind Adam and he moved aside to let her read the headline and first few pars. Nate loosened his tie and continued to pace as Adam read.

Adam read. 'Allan Sheffield, the convicted kidnapper and murderer of Brisbane schoolboy, Dean Beals, was released on Friday morning after serving a life sentence with no parole. The young boy disappeared on his way to school in 1989 and was never found. Sheffield's car was spotted in the area of Dean Beals's abduction, and police found evidence of blood and hair in the back seat. Early police investigations revealed Sheffield was grooming two young boys and claiming to be their uncle to build trust. Bloodied items of the boy's clothing found in the boot convinced the jury of Dean's death. The family paid the ransom for the boys' safe return, but his body was never found. Dean Beals's death shocked and frightened the nation and made every parent vigilant.'

'That's enough,' Nate interrupted, 'scroll down to the photo of Allan Sheffield.'

Adam did as he was directed.

'Okay,' Adam studied the image. 'That's how we remember him, isn't it?' He glanced at Nate and then back at the screen. 'Weird seeing him again.'

Nate nodded. 'I know.'

'Wow, so this is the guy who gave you both a lift home and used to hang around you?' Jessica said, studying the photo of Sheffield in his thirties.

'That's the creep,' Nate confirmed. 'Now click on the link… *Sheffield released* and go to the *now* picture.' Again, Adam did as instructed, and his eyes widened. Jessica looked closer and gasped.

'It's her, isn't it? Mrs Tatum. Allan Sheffield is Mrs Tatum,' Nate said, leaning over Adam and studying the photo again. He moved away and exhaled, puffing his cheeks out in shock.

'What sort of game is this?' Adam asked, rising. 'He was here, in this office.'

Nate nodded, hands on hips. 'He didn't see you or ask to see you, but he knew you were working as a psychologist with me, I remember.'

'He saw me. We locked eyes on his way out, but he looked away quickly.' Adam stood behind Nate's desk, looking at the image on the screen. 'I thought he looked familiar, but never in my wildest dreams…'

'Mine either.'

'So, she or he came here asking you to find a boy – not the boy he kidnapped and murdered 20 years ago because we know his name was Dean. So who's this guy?' Adam pointed to the photograph Mrs Tatum left behind.

'I don't know, and I don't know who to call first.'

'You could sound out Burnsy, but no crime's been committed, yet,' Adam said. 'What about the missing son? Is there any mention of Allan having a son in anything you've read? If the drug story is a lie, has he hired you to find the son he was separated from? Is his wife still around?'

'I don't know any of that,' Nate said. 'If Allan's wife was pregnant, I doubt she would have given the kid Sheffield's name. I wonder if Sabel was her maiden name.'

'So, Aden Sabel could be his real son that he never knew while he was in prison, or the photo could be a prop and the so-called missing son he has you searching for doesn't really exist,' Adam said.

'I'll check marriage and birth records online, hold on,' Jessica said, sitting at Nate's keyboard and calling up the state's *Birth, Deaths and Marriages* index.

They both paused and breathed out, looking at each other and not sure what to do next. Jessica tapped away.

'I've got a Sheffield, Allan Edgar, marrying a Millicent Ann Chamberlain around the timeline of when you were boys,' Jessica said.

'That's them,' Adam said, 'he called her Millie.'

'No birth records for that couple and…' she tapped away on the keyboard, 'no children to Millicent under her married name or maiden name. I can look up if she remarried and had kids but they wouldn't be Allan Sheffield's kids then.'

'Thanks, Jess,' Adam said. 'If Millie did have a kid, she could have legally changed her surname. Or if she went ahead with the IVF – which the newspaper report said was the reason he needed the money – then there was no biological connection to Uncle Allan anyway.'

Jessica sat back and stared at Nate's whiteboard with his list of clients written down one column including Mrs Tatum and Aden Sabel, the son.

Nate sighed. 'For all we know, Aden Sabel was just a made-up kid so Allan Sheffield – dressed as Mrs Tatum – had a reason to hire me and see you, Adam. Or Millie had a kid by that name and Allan Sheffield's found about it.'

'Don't you see it?' Jessica asked. Their blank faces answered the question. 'Aden Sabel does exist, or he existed, but it's not really his or her son.'

'What do you mean?' Nate asked, still freaked out.

'I'm good at puzzles,' Jessica said. 'Aden Sabel is an anagram.'

'What's an anagram again?' Nate frowned.

She grabbed the green whiteboard marker and wrote on Nate's whiteboard the name Aden Sabel and using all the same letters, she wrote Dean Beals above it, marking off each letter as she used them.

'Aden Sabel is an anagram for Dean Beals. Mrs Tatum or Allan Sheffield is not looking for a lost son, he's playing you. He's got you looking for the boy he murdered.'

'Holy crap,' Nate said.

'Clever Uncle Allan,' Adam said, the words hissed between clenched teeth. 'He's screwed us again. He was right here, in our midst, and must have been enjoying the ride.'

'He's had twenty years behind bars to prepare for it,' Nate said.

'But why is he looking for Dean? Is he trying to prove his innocence or that Dean is still alive?' Jessica asked.

'Or is he trying to find the body and can't remember where he put it?' Nate asked.

'Maybe he's unbalanced and seriously thinks Dean is his son,' Adam said with a shrug.

'I need to find him, her, Mrs Tatum, to see for myself she is him,' Nate said. 'Burnsy had nothing but gave me an address for a Ron Tatum. Could be a relative, could be no relation.' He returned to his desk and grabbed his car keys, phone, and wallet.

'I think you should stand down on this,' Adam said, seating himself on the window ledge and crossing his arms as if expecting an argument. 'I'll give it to Tom. He can make himself useful and come with me to check it out.'

Nate scoffed. 'Do you think the pair of you would get to the address before you killed each other? I'm checking it out,' he said decisively.

Adam stood his ground, a rare thing where Nate was concerned. 'I think we've already proven that hanging around with me is dangerous. You've got a daughter now, it ends here.' He stood as if the conversation was over.

'I'll just go and check on... something,' Jessica said, leaving the two men staring at each other.

Nate cleared his throat and turned to his friend. 'I was in the police service for close to a decade where I put myself on the line every day for people who I didn't even know, or didn't deserve it in a lot of cases. So if you think I'm letting this lie, you're dreaming.'

Adam went to speak, and Nate shut him down. 'Seriously, I'm not.'

'Just let me win this one,' Adam said.

'It's not happening.'

'Fine. I'm coming with you,' Adam said.

Nate smiled at him. 'Of course you are. Wouldn't be the same if you weren't leading me into trouble.'

Adam rolled his eyes and followed Nate out of the office.

'Don't forget you've got the angry guy at four-thirty,' Jessica called after Adam. He grimaced at her nickname, and she shrugged. 'I have to differentiate them and maintain their privacy.'

Business as usual.

Chapter 23

Now...

He waited until his mate went to work before he came out of his room in drag. His mate didn't care, but Allan wanted his privacy – something he never got in prison. He'd looked after his mate with cars in his pre-prison days and now the favour was being returned – lodgings and use of a car until he got on his feet. Allan Sheffield readjusted the wig on his head, pushing the tufts of his greying hair under the edges, and looked at himself in the mirror to make sure it sat right. God, he was ugly; he laughed at the thought. Still, he'd fooled Nate Delaney, even if Nate looked at him suspiciously a few times. He wasn't sure he'd fooled Adam Murphy, though. They locked eyes for just a moment, but he saw Adam's frown, his eyes narrowed in concentration. He had to admit it was good to see the boys all grown up now and successful, doing their own thing. A credit to them, especially Adam, who had so little fatherly guidance.

Allan Sheffield dabbed some make-up on his face. He didn't have to be perfect today, he wasn't intending on seeing anyone, but he was doing a drive-by and he didn't want to raise any suspicion. He didn't want to be Allan Sheffield driving around the areas where he once worked, lived and haunted. Where he took the kid. Where he once lived with his wife and planned a future.

Enough, he coached himself. Focus on the plan. Nate will be looking for me now to tell me he couldn't find my son. The son that doesn't exist. If he's any good at his job, he will have found out who that boy in the photo is and then the game will be on. He will have worked out who Aden Sabel is and realised he's not dealing with just any ordinary Johnny here. He'll need to be on his game.

He applied the lipstick, blotted on a tissue and reapplied like he had seen his wife do many a time, and with a final glance, Allan Sheffield decided he was ready to go out. He stood, straightened the dress and practised his more feminine walk as he headed out of his room, down the hall and with a glance to make sure there was no one around, Mrs Ruth Tatum headed to the garage and the borrowed car.

*****

'I don't go this far on holidays,' Nate grumbled impatiently as Adam indicated to enter the freeway to Logan, about thirty minutes' drive from their Stones Corner office.

Adam laughed. 'Well, you need to get out more. I went to Uni with a girl who lived in Logan. I came down here a few times for her study group.'

'I bet you did,' Nate said, giving him a sly look.

'Nuh, it was not like that, well maybe it was for a short while,' he said, thinking back. 'We were better suited than me and Stephanie.'

'I still can't work out how you ever got with Steph,' Nate said. 'Don't get me wrong, I like her, even if you don't anymore, but you are complete opposites. Blind Freddy could see she'd drive you nuts in time.'

Adam shrugged and paused as Navman instructed him how far to go and which coming exit to take.

'She was sexy and... yeah, that was pretty much it. I was young, she was hot, and Mum loved her,' he said and sighed. 'My days of trying to impress Mum are over.'

'So, you're more suited to Kesley? You're very first love,' Nate stirred his best friend and saw him visibly relax and smile. 'Say no more.'

'Remember your first girlfriend?' Adam asked.

'Which one?'

'Charlotte Duffy, my security detail,' Adam said, 'the terminator.'

Nate laughed. 'Ah, Charlie. God, I was mad for her, even if she was nearly thirty and I was ten. I spent an entire week's pocket money on that Valentine card and chocolates for her!'

'Can't believe she didn't wait for you to come of age,' Adam joked.

'Do you ever hear from you?'

'Yeah, she always calls on my birthday and we talk, and she sends a Christmas card every year. I send a late one. She's still in London, it usually arrives three weeks after Christmas,' Adam said. 'Still, it's a good thing she rejected you, she's fifty this year. Can't see you two lasting.'

Nate scoffed and refrained from replying as Navman told the two men to turn right and then immediately left. Ten minutes later, it informed them they had reached their destination. They eyed the neat street of timber two-story homes, circa 1970s, and pulled up in front of number six, Ron Tatum's house. There was a small fence, and the gate was wide open.

'No dog, that's a good thing,' Nate said. 'Leave your jacket in the car, I don't want to look like the heavies.'

The front door opened as they walked up the path and a small, white-haired old man appeared, studying them. Nate introduced himself and Adam, and asked could they talk about a family connection.

'You'd better come in then,' he said and they followed Ron Tatum inside.

Nate glanced back at Adam, who followed. They were not sure what to expect, but Ron Tatum was too old to be Mrs Tatum's husband – if Mrs Tatum existed – he was more the age of a father or an uncle.

The house was tidy and fussy. An old-fashioned fabric couch with a crochet blanket draped over it took up one wall, and a sideboard took up the rest of the small room. There were several framed photos along it, and lace doilies were in vogue.

'The Mrs is gone now,' he said, 'died three years back, but I try to keep it presentable.' He waved them to a seat. 'I get a bit of cleaning help and *Meals on Wheels* drop in. I'll make some tea.'

'I'll help,' Nate offered and left Adam to loiter in the lounge room and study the photos. Nate was still not sure if Ron Tatum could help them, but apparently, Ron didn't care who they were; he was keen for the company.

Once returned and seated with tea and biscuits, Ron asked, 'So what brings you lads to the neighbourhood? One of my relatives, you say?'

'We were wondering if you knew a Ruth Tatum,' Adam

said and accepted the offer of a biscuit – a shortbread with jam in it – which he polished off like it was breakfast.

Ron frowned. 'Well, that's a few of us Tatums around,' he said, 'but Ruth, hey?'

'She has a son, Aden,' Nate said, feeding him crumbs of information.

Ron shook his head. 'Sorry lads, I'm sure I would remember Ruth and her son, but she's not in my immediate family circle. Can I ask why you ask? Is she a relative of yours too or is she in trouble?'

'No, not a relative,' Adam answered a little too quickly. 'She's connected to a man I knew in my childhood. A man called Allan Sheffield.'

'Allan Sheffield! The man who was jailed for taking that little boy?' Ron said and put his cup down.

'That's him,' Nate said, watching the old guy.

'Now Allan Sheffield I can tell you about.'

Chapter 24

Now…

Danielle emerged from the boardroom and joined Jessica at the reception desk. Together, they watched Tom Hartigan as he finished his security audit.

'Nice butt,' Danielle said under her breath as he leaned over in the doorway of Adam's office in his well-fitted jeans. Jessica grinned.

'So inappropriate,' Jessica said.

'Aren't I?' Dan agreed.

Tom emerged from Adam's office oblivious to their admiration.

'Okay, done,' he said, addressing the two ladies. 'I've checked the car park, and Adam, Nate and Rob's offices.' He looked at his pad with a list of what security he needed to arrange for the offices of *Delaney and Murphy*. 'Glad you've got the video entry, at least,' he said to Jessica. 'You know not to let anyone upstairs without an appointment even if they say they spoke with one of the guys directly?'

'Okay,' she said, 'but you're freaking me out a little.'

'It's just good security, that's all. Lots of businesses have it,' he assured her, trying to play the situation down. 'However, I'm going to give you all a distress code.'

'What's that?' Dan asked.

'If you are frightened or threatened at the door when you punch in your entry code, you put in this one instead. It will still let you in, but it will signal me straight away that you are under threat... someone is around, behind you or forcing you to enter.'

'Creepy,' Jessica said and shuddered.

He sat on the armchair edge of the reception couch and explained: 'The assailant won't know that you have signalled for help, it will be a four-digit number like you put in every day and will open the door as usual, but I'll be on the way with back up. You need to ensure that Nate, Rob, and Adam remember it too. Quiz them on it at your regular team meetings.'

'I can do that,' Jessica said.

'So, are you and Adam okay? No love lost between you two, huh?' Dan asked.

'No, he can hold a grudge,' Tom said.

'Sounds like you deserve it,' Dan said, not holding back. 'I missed the first part of the meeting, but I heard you bonked his mum while she was still married to his dad, and when you should have been on kid-watch. If you did that to my family, I'd bring you down.'

'That so?' Tom said and grinned. 'I like a fiery woman.'

Danielle gave a less than glamorous snort of derision.

'Adam was always a quiet, cold sort of kid, not like Nate,' Tom said and Danielle cut him off.

'Adam's anything but cold. He's really sweet and caring,' she shot back.

Tom gave her a smirk. 'Sounds like you're keen for him.'

'It's called loyalty, you should try it sometime, Captain,' she said, crossing her arms across her chest and raising an eyebrow in his direction.

He smiled and looked at her, impressed. 'It's an excellent trait in a soldier, the type of person I'd like on my team. Anyway, it's not Adam's fault, it was a weird household and being raised by that odd old girl wouldn't have helped.'

'I met Audrey, she's fabulous, and yeah, a bit eccentric,' Jessica conceded. 'She clearly dotes on him, and Nate.'

'Yeah, she's alright, the old girl. Just a bit out there. She raised his father after all,' Tom said. 'She'd make sure Adam listened to the news and talkback radio every day with her on the way to school and she'd ask him questions. If I had a dollar for every time I heard her say "a well-rounded person can talk on any subject and if not, ask questions," I'd be retired and surfing all day.'

Jessica pushed for more information. 'What was so weird about Adam's household? They had money and his mum was famous, but he's not the only kid to grow up with that.'

'True, but Winsome never got him. She wanted him to be like her… a model, a star. She wanted to parade him around, kind of like the yummy mummy thing that happens now… she was before her time. His dad was happy for him to be a kid star too. Everyone was keen on the marketing and dollars that could come from it, everyone except Adam. If he was born ugly, he wouldn't have had the problem, but he was a really good-looking kid,' Tom said. 'Add to that the rumours about him being the ex-prime minister's son and everyone wanted a piece of him.'

Jessica nodded her agreement. 'I saw those pics of Winsome with him when he was a baby and toddler.'

'Yeah, he was the face of a few brands before he could walk,' Tom said.

Danielle shrugged. 'Kids are busting their asses to be stars these days...'

'Yeah, but Adam wasn't one of them. He was an introvert who didn't want to stand out at school for being different or pushed around for being a pretty boy. If Nate was Winsome and James's son, it would have been an entirely different situation.'

'The big ham would love it,' Jessica said and laughed.

'It infuriated Winsome,' Tom said, thinking back on those years. 'She'd complain to me about it no end. And she lost interest in Adam because he wasn't into the one thing that fuelled her. James was too busy running around managing Winsome and his media investments to take much notice of Adam, so Adam spent half of his life at Nate's house, in their family home. Nate's parents loved him, Nate was an only child, so they were like brothers, and they were oblivious that security detail was in Nate's street the whole time.'

'Wow, really?' Jessica said. 'Do they know now, does Nate?'

Tom shrugged. 'I don't know.'

'I saw Winsome's *Vogue Living* shots when Adam was a kid... they had an enormous house on the river, wouldn't the boys want to hang there?' Jessica asked, storing the information like a fangirl.

'They'd come to Adam's place to swim or play cricket on the tennis court, but the kid was home alone with Audrey most of the time. Whereas Nate's mum worked during school hours, so she was there when they were. She'd cook, spoil them. Nate's father worked regular hours and would take them places like the football.'

Danielle glanced at the door. 'I don't want to be caught talking about him.'

'I'd see them on the security screen coming up the stairs,' Jessica assured her.

'Oh yeah,' Danielle brightened. 'So when did Adam's modelling career stop?'

'What am I, the president of the Murphy fan club?' Tom asked, grimacing at them both.

'Get out of here, you're as bad as Nate, you love the attention and knowing something we don't,' Danielle ribbed him and Tom laughed.

'So, how long did he model for?' Dan pushed him again and Tom sighed, then thought for a moment.

'He just turned nine when it all wound up. This is strictly between us?'

Danielle and Jessica both nodded.

'In the vault,' Danielle said and Jessica made a cross over her heart and held up a boy scout salute and added: 'Cross my heart, promise.'

'Okay. Well, there was a shit-fight… I had to take him to a shoot for his ninth birthday. A magazine spread with him and his mum. When we got there, Adam wouldn't get out of the car,' Tom said and shook his head. 'Fucking drama. I dragged him in literally kicking and screaming.'

'Yeah, no wonder he didn't feel a bond with you,' Dan said and Tom gave her a wry look.

'Poor Adam. Did the shoot get done?' Jessica asked.

'Yeah, his father sedated him.'

Both of their eyes were wide.

'You've got to be joking!' Danielle exclaimed.

Tom shook his head. 'He said the boy was distraught, and it was for the best. The shoot was done. Adam smiled when he was told to, stood where he was supposed to stand, I took him home straight after, he slept all the way home in the car.

They went too far, and they knew it. I carried him in, and on seeing him, Audrey was outraged. That was it, she put a stop to it.'

'Yeah, I got the impression she wasn't a fan of Winsome,' Jessica said.

'True. And if there's one person who had more influence over James than Winsome, that was Audrey. He did what he was told.'

'I'm surprised Adam managed to keep a low profile for the rest of his teen years,' Danielle said, and Tom shrugged.

'It's like all things, eventually, Winsome's star began to wane and new models and stars stepped in. When James died, Winsome and Adam were back in the spotlight again for a brief while – shots of the funeral, stories about her career, that sort of thing. And Adam had a girlfriend at Uni that sold photos of the two of them to a magazine for a tidy fee.'

'What a cow!' Danielle exclaimed.

'His ex-wife did the same, Stephanie,' Tom said. 'She sold her story to a magazine – an insider exposé on what it was like being a celebrity wife or some bullshit. The magazine gave her hardly any column space and wrote the whole thing about the *"Reclusive son of Australia's sweetheart"*. I heard that went down a treat.'

Jessica shook her head. 'No wonder he is slow to get close to people. Not saying he's cold, just careful,' she added.

'Yeah,' Tom concluded. 'He's about as fucked in the head as his patients.' He grabbed his notepad. 'Well, it's been lovely chatting, ladies. Tell the boys I'll be back with a tradie to fit some extra security in the next few days. Keep up your fitness, Private Dan.'

She gave him a smile and a nod.

'He's pretty hot, for a guy in his fifties,' Jessica said after Tom had left the building.

'Yeah, don't worry, he knows it,' Danielle told her. 'He has a reputation amongst the Army Reserve girls for sleeping around. Fucked in the head or not, I'd take Adam's integrity over Tom any day. He is sexy, though.'

Jessica laughed. 'Yeah, if you like an older man.' She sobered. 'Still makes me worry about Adam a bit.'

'Has Nate asked you to the wedding yet?' Danielle asked.

'Nope. You?'

'Nah, I'm not expecting to be invited but I want to go.' She brightened. 'I might just get myself on the security team now. It's all who you know,' Danielle said with a wink and a smile before departing.

Chapter 25

Now…

It had been twenty years, but Allan Sheffield was on automatic pilot – driving the route like he had been there yesterday. Except it wasn't yesterday.

'Holy crap,' he muttered, eyeing the progress and increased traffic in the suburbs he used to drive daily for work. The area seemed so congested, uglier than he remembered.

His first port of call was his old home. He knew his wife, ex-wife, was long gone, but he wanted to see the house. He indicated, turning into the street and felt a rush of nerves, even fear.

'I've done my time,' he said aloud, like a mantra, 'I've got a right to drive anywhere I want.' Then he remembered he was dressed as Mrs Tatum and relaxed a little. He slowed as he came towards the house but didn't stop. He didn't need some *Neighbourhood Watch* old biddy writing down his car rego and reporting him for looking suspicious.

His breath caught when he saw the house. It looked so different – smaller, shabby, but the garden had taken flight, the plants were fully established. A young man was mowing the lawn down the side of the yard. Mrs Tatum drove by.

When he got to the corner, he breathed in sharply and fought back tears.

'Move on, stick to the plan,' he said and straightened up, then wiped his face on his sleeve along with a stain of powder make-up.

He drove on further to the wealthier parts of the suburb on the river, back where the Murphys lived. He didn't know if they still owned the place or if Adam still lived there. It was a big place; he might do so. He knew Adam's father had died, he saw the funeral footage on television and saw Adam, then 15 or 16 years old, with his mum on his arm. Still a good-looking kid.

And there it was. That had changed, too.

'Christ,' he muttered. It was bigger than he remembered, more austere.

He shook his head and drove by, noting the CCTV security around the edges of the property. He was glad he'd dressed as Mrs Tatum.

'Right, it's time,' he said aloud, to make it official. The last time, he got the wrong kid, it had all backfired. This time he wouldn't make that mistake. He'd get it right, get Adam. Then his wife would be pleased and take him back. Everything would be back on track.

For a moment he forgot it was 20 years ago, he was doing that a lot lately. He automatically started driving back to his old street, his old house. Remembering, he turned sharply and returned to his mate's house. He needed to get changed before anyone saw him. But he intended to dress up again soon, maybe even tonight. He had a visit to make.

*****

Nate poured the old guy a second cup of tea. He would have happily accepted something stronger but topped up his own cup and Adam's as well.

'Thanks, Mum,' Adam said and earned a smirk from Nate. Ron Tatum chuckled.

'My neighbour makes these biscuits – shortbread jam drops,' Ron said, offering the boys another and taking one himself.

'Best thing I've had today,' Nate told him, not wanting to rush the old guy.

'So, Allan Sheffield,' Ron said, and shook his head. 'Broke my Hazel's heart, he did.'

'Tell us how you know him,' Adam said, encouraging him like he was one of his counselling patients.

'The couple next door, long gone now – Julie and Scott Sheffield – were battlers. Most people were doing it tough in this area back then, but Julie and Scott, well, they worked hard, kept the place tidy, had three boys and kept them in line. Then Scott cleared out. He had an affair, and he left poor old Julie with three kids and a part-time job to pay the mortgage, feed and dress the boys, and survive on.'

'No parents to help?' Nate asked.

Ron shook his head. 'Not locally. Scott's parents were never much involved in his life and Julie's parents lived out west. She thought about moving, but we stepped in – we were old enough to be Julie's parents and we had no grandchildren of our own, so it was a good thing for all of us. We babysat, I looked after the maintenance of the house, Hazel cooked and did after school care for the boys while Julie found herself full-time work. We loved that family and they loved us.'

'Perfect arrangement,' Adam said.

Ron agreed and sipped his tea while the men waited patiently.

'We'd lost our boy, you see,' Ron said. 'Our only child. He got his P-plates, and off he went in the car we'd bought him. Died a week after he got his licence... him and his best friend speeding and straight into a tree.'

'Ron, that's terrible, a lot to bear,' Nate said. He recalled when he and Adam first got their licences and thought they were invincible.

Adam shook his head. 'Happens all too often.'

'Well, we threw ourselves into looking after these three boys – Allan and his two brothers. He was a good kid, Allan. Polite, ambitious... when he was arrested, I never thought Hazel would recover. She loved him so much. We even visited him in prison a few times before she died.'

'Did you see it coming? Any inkling that he could be violent?' Adam asked.

'No, the brothers fought like normal brothers, but if I was going to put it on one of the three, it wouldn't have been Allan,' Ron said. 'Before you ask, the two brothers both live in Victoria now and Julie moved there after the court sentenced Allan to twenty years. She was so mortified.'

Adam and Nate took it all in.

'Did you ever meet Allan's wife?' Adam asked.

'Of course – Millie – a lovely girl. Can't tell you what happened to her, though. She took off and Allan was asking us to help find her every time we visited him in prison. We didn't search, of course, but we didn't tell him that. We just told him we'd had no luck and she mustn't have wanted to be found,' Ron said.

'Did they have any kids? Because we read in the paper the ransom Allan Sheffield requested was to pay for IVF,' Nate said.

'Not while Allan was a free man. But I guess clinically she could have been impregnated and we didn't know. Maybe she thanked her lucky stars they didn't have a kid together,' Ron said. He rose and asked the men to wait a moment while he went to the sideboard and opened several drawers.

Nate gathered up their empty plates and took them to the kitchen.

'When did you become so domestic?' Adam asked, surprised.

'I've always been the perfect houseguest,' Nate said, feigning shock. 'How do you not know this?'

Adam smiled and shook his head. Ron returned and sat down again near the men. He showed them a few photos.

'This is Allan and his brothers when they were boys.'

'I can see the boy in the man,' Adam said, studying the photo. 'Have you seen him since he was recently released?'

'It's been years since I saw him,' Ron said. 'Last time was when Hazel and I visited him in prison. Now, this photo...' he passed it to Adam, 'this is at Allan's wedding, to his lovely young wife, Millie. We were so proud of him that day. That's Hazel and me there in the front row at the church.'

The men admired the photo and acknowledged Hazel.

'And this one,' Ron said, handing over a photo of an unattractive young man around eighteen, with a big grin, bad skin and a bad haircut, standing in front of his car. 'This was my lad.'

Nate's breath hitched and Adam covered for him, offering their sympathies again.

They knew the boy. This was the photo Mrs Tatum – Allan Sheffield – gave Nate. The boy she said she was trying to find – Aden Sabel. Allan Sheffield was playing them again at the expense of the man who loved him like a grandfather.

'I miss the lad every day,' Ron said, looking at the photo as Nate handed it back to him.

When Ron rose to return the album to the sideboard drawer, Adam muttered for Nate's ears only: 'Allan Sheffield has absolutely no moral compass.'

Chapter 26

Now...

His house was Adam's place of escape. He loved it, like he loved all of his minimal possessions. He earned them; somehow, that made them worthwhile. It was a white timber one-level home on a pleasant street – a cul-de-sac – in a good neighbourhood. It didn't stand out on the street but was a character home like the other homes nearby. The yard was a little larger than average. Maybe one day kids would play in it, and ride their bikes up and down the street, maybe not. A verandah wrapped around the front of the house, the interior ceilings were high, the walls were timber VJ boards, all white, cool and calm with timber polished floors. The garden was thriving on neglect; he hadn't touched it since buying the house a few years back, except to mow and water it occasionally, but Kelsey eyed it with interest every time she came to stay; her thumb was green.

Tonight, however, Kelsey was at her conference. It was nearing 9pm when Adam pushed aside his patient's notes, rose from the couch, turned off the sports channel and took his cereal bowl that had earlier boasted Nutri-Grain for dinner, to the kitchen. As he reached the sink, the house fell into darkness.

Total black.

Adam froze.

A slideshow of faces went through his mind… people he had worked with, dangerous patients, and opportunists. Allan Sheffield.

He listened, his breathing tightened and hitched while he strained to hear a noise, any noise, like the sound of footsteps or glass breaking.

Not a sound.

He glanced to the lounge room where his phone sat on the coffee table, in reach if he moved quickly. As his eyes adjusted to the light, he gingerly made his way to the lounge room window, opened the blind and looked to the street. Everyone else had power on, just not him.

Great, he groaned softly, the sound of his rapid heartbeat thumping loud enough to hear. Adam grabbed his phone and found the torch app, pressing it on. It was a narrow light but enough to get him to the cupboard in the hallway where he kept a brighter torch with a long-range throw of light. He silently opened the cupboard, and pulled it out, flicking it on.

Probably nothing, just a fuse, he told himself, but his mind kept going to Allan Sheffield. He was out of prison and knew where Adam lived. Sheffield had visited to drop off the cricket bat only days before. Adam took a quick gasp of air as if he'd forgotten to breathe until now.

Silently going through the motions of what had to be done – he moved to the front door, checked it was locked, and then moved to the windows nearest the power box.

Glancing out and around, no one was in sight. He relaxed a little now, and made his way to the backdoor, let himself out and stood on the back deck surveying his yard. There was no one there, no motion he could see. But his senses were on alert. Using the torch to see his way around to the power box at the side of the house, he paused in front of it – a glance around – no one was nearby. Adam opened the door of the power box. Someone had turned the main switch off. With a flick, the house lit up.

It could have been a surge in power that flicked the switch…
Or was it turned off on purpose?

Adam's skin crawled as he walked back to the deck, his senses heightened, listening, waiting for Allan Sheffield to step into the open on this dark night.

Someone was watching him; he could feel it. He made it back inside without running, but he wanted to.

Back door locked.
Check.
I'll have to tell Tom. Great.

He exhaled and turning off the torch, entered the lit lounge room. Adam stopped dead. In the middle of the coffee table was an exercise pad. In two strides he was beside it but didn't touch it. On the front cover, it read: *Adam Murphy, Science, Year 5, St Joseph's School.*

Another returned gift from Uncle Allan.

He glanced around. Was Sheffield still in the house?

Adam grabbed his phone, thought for a moment and then called Sergeant Matt Burns. He move to the edge of the room so his back was against the wall, and he could see any movement ahead and in his peripheral vision. The sergeant answered on the second ring.

'Murph? You alright?'

'Burnsy, I've just had a visit from Allan Sheffield,' Adam said and looked around the room as he spoke.

'What the hell? Sheffield the kid murderer?'

'Yes.'

'Why?'

'Long story, but he cut the power and left a reminder of our time together.'

'Time together? Tell me later. Are you alright? Give me the abridged version?' Burnsy snapped commands at him.

'Unfinished business with my family,' Adam told him. 'He wants to catch up.'

'For the love of God. So, he could still be in the house?' Burnsy asked voice raised.

Adam frowned. 'Probably not.'

'For Christ's sake. I'm on my way with a squad car.'

'No! Mate, no! The neighbours here don't know me and don't care who I am. I don't need the attention. No cops, no cop cars. But if you could come...'

'Fine, but listen to me. Go and visit a neighbour, ask if they lost their power, whatever you have to say to justify a visit, or go lock yourself in your car now and wait for me. Just get out of the house. Do you understand?'

'Yes. Thanks.'

Burnsy hung up and Adam pocketed his phone. He took a breath and calmed himself. Silently he moved to stand nearer to the door so he could make a quick exit if needed and not be trapped inside.

He cleared his throat and called out: 'Uncle Allan, want to talk?'

Nothing happened. There was no sound in the house.

'Uncle Allan?'

He's gone.

Fifteen minutes later, Burnsy pulled into the driveway in his sedate black sedan, exited and ran to the house. Adam let him in.

'I don't see you waiting outside for me,' he snapped.

'He's not here.'

'Let's make sure.'

They split up and canvassed the house, meeting back in the living room afterwards.

'The second bedroom window was open,' Burnsy said.

'Christ,' Adam muttered. 'He could have been waiting in there for hours.' The thought creeped him out.

Burnsy studied the school exercise pad that Allan Sheffield had left on the coffee table.

'Have you touched it?'

'No,' Adam said. 'I share an office with an ex-cop. I know the drill.'

Burnsy nodded. 'I'll bag it and take it. You've got to get out of this place for a while.'

Adam sighed. 'This could go on for a long time... what am I supposed to do, live in fear?'

'Hell yeah, I would,' Burnsy said. 'This guy is a nutter and a killer. He's killed once before.'

'Yeah. He's delusional but even if his prints are all over the second room window, a break and enter charge will have him back on the street in no time. It's a game and I have to play it.'

'Not alone you don't.'

'Sorry to bring you out this late.'

Burnsy shrugged. 'I was just watching TV.'

'Beer?'

'Thought you'd never ask.'

Adam got them both a drink and they sat on the couch.

'What do you think this is about?' Burnsy asked. 'Why would he contact you again?'

Adam thought for a moment. 'He's righting a wrong, I'd say. If I'm right, he won't stop until he feels vindicated.'

'What's that even mean?' Burnsy asked taking a swig of his beer.

Adam didn't want to go into detail, not yet, and not with Burnsy. Audrey had hired Tom to protect the family and he should have called him but, it was Tom.

He cleared his throat. 'In Sheffield's mind, my family owe him something. I suspect that grudge has got bigger with every year he was in jail.'

'Christ,' Burnsy said again. 'You need some form of security.'

'Don't worry, my grandmother has hired some. I would have called him instead of you but he's a dick.'

Burnsy laughed and then sobered. 'There are some screwed up people out there.'

'Tell me about it,' Adam said, and they looked at each other.

'Not us though,' Burnsy joked.

'Definitely not us,' Adam agreed and smiled.

Then...

Charlie Duffy looked at both of the boys and gave them a nod of approval. She moved Nate slightly to rebalance him and adjusted the height of Adam's hands.

'It's all about your centre of gravity, boys,' Charlie said, as she took a stance next to them showing them what she meant – feet apart, shoulders straight, back and stomach tight. The muscles in her lean arms were at best advantage, and her fighting fit body looked ready for action in her fitted black pants and singlet.

'Centre of gravity,' Adam repeated, committing the phrase to memory.

'When you go to defend yourself,' Charlie said, choosing her words carefully and not saying *fight*, 'your centre of gravity helps you keep your balance and swing powerfully.'

'So, we don't land on our arse before getting one good hit in,' Nate added, and Charlie grinned, shaking her head at him.

'I'm hoping they run away from you before it comes to that,' she said. 'Now look at me, right in the eye,' she said, and both boys did. 'You need to show me your serious face, and that you are not backing down.'

Both boys gave Charlie their most intense look, and she did her best not to smile at the young lads. Instead, she returned the favour with her stare-down face, narrowing her eyes.

'Excellent. If you are not sure if the person with you is safe or if they are trying to harm you, you can just call out really loudly "Stranger!" or "Go away" and it will attract attention,' she said. The boys nodded. 'It might also stop that person in their tracks which leads me to the most important lesson of all.'

The boys exchanged smiles looking forward to some bad-ass moves.

'And the most important lesson of all,' she said solemnly, noticing their complete attention, 'is to run!'

Charlie took off across the lawn of Adam's family's vast estate and could hear the boys laughing and chasing her. 'Did I mention I'm a sprint champion?' she called back.

Chapter 27

Now...

Tom Hartigan had requested a thirty-minute meeting with Adam and Nate at their office. The two men sat opposite him, around Nate's office table.

'I want to find out just what sort of threat this Allan Sheffield is going to be,' Tom started. 'He knows where you live, Adam, he knows where you used to live – Audrey's still there.'

'Right,' Adam agreed.

'Should we put on extra security for her?' Nate asked, and Adam laughed.

'Good luck with that. Maybe release a German Shepherd on the grounds at night, that'd be her speed,' Adam said.

Tom raised an eyebrow in Adam's direction. 'She actually suggested that when I broached the subject with her.'

'So you've spoken with Audrey, kitted out the office, why are we here then?' Adam cut to the chase.

'Yeah, sorry to waste your time and worry about your security,' Tom continued and Nate rolled his eyes.

'Do you think you two could learn to play nice together? Or at least pretend?' Nate asked like he was talking to his five-year-old daughter.

'We'll have a shot at pretending,' Adam said with a smirk in Nate's direction.

'Just a few quick questions,' Tom continued, 'then I'll let you get back to your all-important work of reading heads.'

Nate sighed and adopted a look of resignation.

'I've got security for your office underway. But what security have you both got at your homes?' Tom asked.

Nate answered first: 'Deadlock windows and doors, CCTV at the front of the house that runs on a loop, and plenty of child restraint locks.'

Tom looked impressed.

Nate shrugged. 'I'm an ex-cop and believe it or not, some crims might have a grudge against me. Plus, I don't need a husband I've outed for cheating making a revenge house call.'

'Good thinking,' Tom said. He looked at Adam for his response.

'Just your standard locks on the doors and windows... no actual security, I guess,' he answered.

'Really?' Tom said, frustrated. 'You're the son of—' he saw Adam's expression and dropped it. But not before issuing a few swear words as he moved on to the next question. 'Have either of you felt anyone following you or watching you?' he continued and started with Nate.

'Nope, that's usually my job, so I'd notice,' Nate answered.

'Adam?' Tom asked, and Nate laughed.

Adam exhaled, trying to take the question seriously. 'Pretty much every day for thirty years,' he said.

'Great,' Tom said.

'Allan Sheffield's been around again, so some security is probably not a bad idea,' Adam conceded.

'When?' Tom snapped, bolting upright in his seat.

'Last night.'

'For the love of God, why didn't you call me?' Tom demanded.

'Or me, more importantly?' Nate asked. Tom gave him a less-than-impressed look.

'Thanks, but I'm sure you've both got lives. Burnsy came over,' Adam said. 'We cased the place inside and out. Sheffield just dropped off another item from my school bag and departed. A science exercise pad.'

'Where did he leave it?' Tom asked, not letting up.

Adam hesitated and exhaled before answering. 'He cut the power and when I went out to the power box to flick it on, he must have entered and left it on the coffee table.'

Nate groaned and Tom snapped. 'You have to be fucking kidding me?'

'Christ,' Nate said. 'Why didn't you come over and crash at my place.'

'Yeah, I didn't sleep well after that, but once the drop was done and the house locked up, I figured his show-and-tell was over for the night,' Adam said.

Tom shook his head and looked away in frustration.

'That it?' Nate asked, surprised.

'For now, I guess so,' Adam said.

Tom rose. 'I need to complete a full security detail for both of your homes, starting with yours, Adam. Can you leave an entry key and address with Jessica for me? I'll be in touch.'

He departed, frustrated as hell and oddly interested in seeing how both men lived.

*****

Allan Sheffield went over and over last night's events in his head in minute detail, a smile of satisfaction on his face. It was an amazing night. He took a walk around his neighbourhood and in the park, his hands clasped behind his back, a straw hat perched on his head and looking like any senior man taking his daily exercise. He nodded and greeted those he passed, like good citizens and community members do. Today he was a happy man.

His plan had gone to perfection; he still couldn't believe it. He had parked his car some distance from Adam's house in a street with a lot of units, where cars parked up and down the road was common, and he had walked the short distance to Adam's house. As soon as it was dark, and he could not be seen, he entered the property. Adam would not be home until after 7pm at least, he knew, he had studied his movements. The girlfriend appeared to be away at the moment too, it was all coming together beautifully.

He cased the house back and sides. Breaking in was easy, he'd learnt a few tricks over the years but the second bedroom window made it easier. It was also in the perfect location, if he leaned out and used something long and solid, he could flick the power off without having to be outside. Sheffield looked around and saw a rake leaning against the fence. Perfect. The old casement window slipped up, and in the dark, he pushed open the old fly screen enough to get in. He left them both open and placed the rake within reach. With the screen closed, it was hard to tell the window was open. Another victory. But he needed to have ease of access for now, so he left the screen and the power box door open. He slipped into the room and practised reaching the power box switch with the rake, but didn't flip it, yet. It worked, everything was going to plan, better than plan!

In his jacket pocket he had Adam's exercise pad he intended to leave as a gift, he knew Adam would appreciate it. Now there was just the wait. He carefully wandered around inside the house, avoiding the windows where the curtains were open. The house was in darkness, but best not to draw attention to himself if passing headlights should catch his silhouette. As the hour approached, he returned to the second bedroom and stood behind the curtains. He could see the loungeroom through the open door and was confident Adam wouldn't be entering the second room, the light had not come on in this room all week. He took his preparation very seriously.

Around quarter past the hour, car headlights shone into the house.

He's home. Sheffield's adrenaline spiked. The game was on. He waited, motionless and heard Adam enter the house, saw the lights flicker on. Adam dumped his keys and phone, shucked off his jacket and disappeared up the hallway to change in his own room. The shower came on and Sheffield waited. He felt a little melancholy – this was the boy who loved him once, loved his Uncle Allan, and that feeling was euphoric, he might have been just like Allan's son if all had gone to plan. But there was no son, and he had missed years of Adam's life.

The shower went off and soon after, Adam walked down the hallway in a T-shirt and shorts. He heard the kitchen cupboard and fridge opening and then through the doorway, saw Adam sit on the couch, flick on the television to the sports channel and eat from a bowl. Cereal, he was eating cereal for dinner. Allan's heart saddened, the boy needed a wife, like Millie. He watched him for a long while, while Adam did his paperwork, changed channels, spoke with his girlfriend on the phone – all the time, Adam was oblivious to his observation.

It was time.

Sheffield leant out the window through the open screen and quietly and carefully flipped the switch. The house fell into darkness. He pulled himself back in and quietly closed the screen to hide the open window, and then he waited. When his eyes adjusted, he could see Adam's hesitation and his trepidation. What are you thinking, lad? Sheffield wondered. He stayed well behind the curtains when the torch came out and heard Adam exit the house.

Now!

He quietly left the security of the curtains, hurrying to the lounge room, and placed Adam's primary school exercise pad on the coffee table. Sheffield wanted to stay, to talk, to share a drink but he couldn't, not yet. He ran back to the window but didn't get behind the curtains until he heard Adam flick the power back on and his footsteps retreating to the house. Adam didn't notice the window was open behind the screen. Sheffield couldn't believe his luck tonight. With Adam gone, he slipped back behind the curtain but he didn't leave just yet, he wanted to see Adam's reaction.

It was worth it. He looked at the pad with wonder and fear.

Then Sheffield silently lifted the screen, lowered himself out and closed it. He heard Adam call out to him. He hesitated, but no, now was not the time. Stick to the plan. It was time to go; he had done all he intended to do tonight.

He smiled again thinking about his success. Sheffield knew he had to strike while the iron was hot, so the next visit would be sooner rather than later. Very, very soon.

Chapter 28

Now...

Adam saw his last patient, Lily – 'hungry girl' – to the door. Her skeletal frame still shocked him. Anorexia was an insidious disease and hard to understand, but he knew all her fears and triggers. He wished Lily was hungry enough to eat, to not fear her food, and to get back out there and have a normal life with her friends. Worse still, he wasn't sure if they were making progress. It always felt like one step forward and two steps back with her.

He thought about his security guard, Charlie... when she was young and had a super-fit body. It was weird to think she was his age then, 30, when she took over from Tom. Her friendship and kindness, not to mention protection of him and Nate, never made them feel like they were dumb kids wasting her time. He could never think of Charlie without missing her or smiling at the memories of the eight years she was by his side, like a big sister, like a surrogate mother. When he turned 18, the family terminated her contract.

If only he could get his anorexic patient to develop a

body like Charlie – that balance of food, health and fitness. He knew of a new program that was being developed and he wanted Lily to undertake it with his referral.

'I'll definitely think about it,' she said, turning at the door on her way out. 'It's just that I've got a lot going on at the moment, in my head. And at work, I'm snowed under... I'm tired,' she gave him all her excuses.

Adam nodded his understanding. He knew them all, and had used them himself occasionally. 'It's okay to take a rest day, you know?'

'Yes.'

'Really. It's okay to do that, Lily. Some people sit and read a book. Some watch television, others will stay in bed and do both. That's okay, you've earned it.'

Her eyes welled with tears and she swallowed. 'I don't think I could. I'd feel so guilty.'

Adam continued. 'I had this manager once, when I first started work. He worked late every day and seven days a week. He was so loyal to the company.'

'What happened to him?' she asked.

'He had a breakdown. They replaced him at work and the next guy did normal hours. The company is still going.' Adam hoped he'd made his point.

'And the manager, what became of him?'

'He's still doing the same thing over and over. Burn out, break down... life goes on with or without him,' Adam said, bringing home his point. 'Have a rest. Take some annual leave or sick leave and try this new program. You and the other attendees can enjoy being managed for a little while instead of you doing all the managing. Some time out of your own head.'

'I'll think about it, I really will,' she said again. 'Thank you, Adam. I'll see you next week.'

'Sure.' He watched her walk down the stairs, so brindle she could snap and break. Adam knew if she turned down the program, this helpline, there was not much more he could do for her. With a sigh, he turned and re-entered the office, locking the door behind him and closing the blind. It was the equivalent of putting out the closed sign on the door.

Normally Jessica worked back late on the nights he did, but tonight she had a family dinner and Adam was secretly pleased. He liked to have some time alone each day to get things done... first thing in the morning before everyone arrived at the office, or last thing at night after they had left. He wasn't in a hurry to go home to an empty house, especially given his last house guest was a stalker. Thinking of his stalker made him think of Tom. Adam wondered what he had been telling Jessica about their history; she had been looking at him weirdly all afternoon... more than usual.

He made a coffee and returned to his desk to write up some notes on Lily, and fire away some emails, including a request to the program organisers to continue to hold a place for her. When he next looked up, an hour had passed. It was nearing seven; he decided to call it a day.

The office buzzer went off, startling him and breaking the silence. It was dark outside, and gloomy in the section of the hallway of the *Delaney and Murphy* office. Adam rose and went to Jessica's desk where the remote security video was located. There was no one in the video frame at the buzzer downstairs. Probably someone who had pressed the wrong button and moved on, or locked themselves out and was trying all the buttons in the hope someone let them in.

He barely got back to his office before it buzzed again.

Now his body was on alert. He returned to the desk and pressed the speaker.

'Hello, can I help you?' he asked and then a face appeared on the video screen.

A smiling face, a woman.

'Hello, Adam.'

Adam froze.

'It's Mrs Tatum here, I'm looking for Nate,' she said and smiled. 'I hear he's been looking for me.'

'Mrs Tatum… Allan,' Adam said, watching the video screen like it was a horror movie.

Then she reached up and pulled the wig off and said: 'Clever you. It's your long-lost Uncle Allan. Come on down, Adam,' he said and laughed.

Adam broke out of his frozen state and ran for the door.

No thought of what he was going to do.

No thought of the danger he might be in.

He ran down the two flights of stairs and to the front door buzzer. Allan was gone.

He burst through the door and looked around. The footpath was empty.

No one was there. Not a man or woman in sight.

Adam raced out further onto the street, looking left and right, but he found himself completely alone.

*****

'Slow down, calm down,' Nate said as he closed his front door behind Adam. 'What happened?'

'At work, she came, he came, but I lost him!' Adam said, 'fuck!'

'Okay, okay, stop. Is there an emergency?'

'No. Yes… no.' Adam exhaled.

'Right, I'll get us a drink. Sit down, we'll talk, we'll decide what to do next,' Nate ordered him. Years of dealing with emergencies and panicked people in his police service gave Nate the upper hand on this occasion.

'We should call Tom.'

Nate stopped and turned back to look at Adam. 'Really? This is an emergency if you want to call Tom.' He waited, but Adam didn't withdraw the request. 'Right then,' Nate said and grabbing his mobile, hit on Tom's number. He watched Adam slip off his jacket and throw it along with his keys and phone on an empty chair.

Tom answered.

'Yeah, hi, are you around? No, my place.' Nate checked Tom had the address and hung up. 'Give me a minute. Sit down,' he said again to the pacing Adam before disappearing into the kitchen. He returned with two beers and sat opposite Adam, turning down the football re-run on TV. 'Drink, then talk.'

Adam did as ordered. He leaned forward after swallowing a mouthful. 'It was him, her, Mrs Tatum, and then Uncle Allan, on the buzzer at work. I couldn't believe it,' Adam said, his mind racing. 'I ran down but couldn't find him, he was gone.'

'You ran down?'

Adam stopped to think about his actions and gave a small shrug.

'What time was this?' Nate asked.

'Just now…' Adam glanced at Nate's clock, 'thirty minutes ago. He asked for you first when he was dressed as Mrs Tatum but he would have known you weren't there. He was lucid, in the now.'

Nate recognised Adam was reading Sheffield's head space.

'He wasn't confused and looking for me, he was there to play a game, involving us both,' Adam continued.

'Tell me from the start,' Nate said. 'Don't miss a detail.'

Fifteen minutes later, Tom arrived.

'Nice place,' he said. 'Didn't picture you for a house with a white picket fence and verandah.'

'The wife, ex-wife, liked it... more than me, but not enough to stay,' Nate added drily and Tom smiled.

'Yeah, I can see you're a bachelor now.' Tom studied the tasteful colouring of the pale blue walls against a mixed match of furniture.

'Get out of here,' Nate said. 'This is called modernism, isn't it? Beer?'

'Depends. Do I need to hunt anyone down tonight?' he looked from Nate to Adam and back.

'Nope, that bird has flown the coop,' Nate said with a glance to Adam.

Nate went to grab the beer, hoping the two men might strike up a conversation; he heard the resounding silence coming from his living room. Adam was used to silence, he listened for a living; Tom was used to discipline, he could probably go months without saying a word if ordered to do so. They were both as bad as each other. Returning, he found Tom distracted by a row of framed photographs that Nate had displayed along a wall rail – one in particular of the two men as teenagers, tanned and grinning. Nate held up a fishing rod with a twig on the end of it and Adam was laughing. Tom took the beer and took a seat on a cream leather couch next to Nate, opposite Adam, like they were interviewing him.

'What's happened?' Tom asked, and Adam ran through the story again.

'And you ran down there?' Tom said, throwing up his hands in frustration.

'I've already covered that,' Nate added.

A calmer Adam nodded. 'Yeah, probably wasn't the smartest thing I've done this week, but I wasn't going to stay in the office and be stalked.'

'No, you call me,' Tom said like he was talking to a child. 'I'm your security.'

'Yeah, that's always worked so well in the past,' Adam snapped back, and Nate sighed. 'Besides, he is smart enough to be long gone by the time you got there.'

'You two are going to have to move on from this,' Nate said. 'Can't you pretend as if you've never met?'

Tom continued. 'Doesn't matter if you think he's bolted or not. You call me. I arrive, sweep the area and give you the all-clear to leave your office or house. That's how it is done. So, he's now visited you at work and home several times, and he's clearly playing a game.'

'I'll give Burnsy a heads-up,' Nate said and turned to Tom. 'Sheffield hasn't committed a crime yet, but he's on his way there.'

'What's he want?' Adam asked, rising and pacing again. He turned to face Tom. 'They never found the body of Dean Beals, did they?'

'Oh, no you don't,' Tom said, shaking his head. 'You two will not play that game. If Sheffield is unbalanced enough to abduct you and kidnap another kid twenty years ago, you're not playing his game to find a body. You'll get yourselves knocked off.'

'Adam's right though, why the game?' Nate said and put his feet, clad in runners, on the coffee table. 'Is he angry that he didn't get away with it and blames us for his being caught?'

'Every chance,' Adam agreed. 'For twenty years he's sat in prison stewing and thinking about what went wrong. If Tom hadn't intercepted him that day, it might have all gone to plan.'

'Yeah, remember that day I saved your life?' Tom said to Adam and the two men smirked at each other. 'You've still got the family home on the river...' Tom was thinking out loud.

Adam nodded. 'Yeah, as you know, Audrey still lives there in the separate cottage.'

Nate smiled. 'Which is bigger than my house now... just saying.'

'Who's in the main house?' Tom continued.

'No one. Audrey's offered to move out or she'd be happy if Mum subdivided the block and sold off the main house, but Mum likes to keep it for the half a dozen times she visits every year. She and Jack will stay there before the wedding.'

'I want you to move there. Take your girlfriend, take Nate since he's part of Sheffield's game. There's a high fence, it's got CCTV in place and I can ramp that up, and hire an outdoor patrol.'

Adam grimaced.

'He doesn't know where I live,' Nate said, 'and he's not interested in me. No point me moving there.'

'It wouldn't be hard to find out where you live and he once had you both in that car... he might want a re-enactment,' Tom said with a glance at Adam.

Adam nodded. 'Yeah, who knows what is going on in Sheffield's head.'

'How often do you have visitation rights?' Tom asked Nate.

Nate glanced at the photo of his five-year-old daughter, Matilda.

'Every second weekend, but she's interstate at the grandparents' place for school holidays.'

Tom nodded. 'Good. Something going right tonight then.'

'You should both stay at the house then when Matilda visits,' Adam said.

'I agree.' Tom said and he and Adam looked warily at each other. It wasn't often they agreed on anything, if ever.

'A holiday!' Nate said. 'At least the house is big enough, we might not see each other.'

'You'd miss me,' Adam said automatically, going back into their banter.

'Yeah, you're right. Let's share a room.'

'What about Danielle? She's moved into your place, hasn't she?' Adam asked.

'She's about to,' Nate said.

'She'll be safe there. I'd say he's got no interest in anyone but you two,' Tom said.

'I'll put it to her. She might have a friend who'll stay there with her,' Nate said, thinking aloud.

Tom interrupted him. 'How soon can you both move?'

Adam exhaled as he thought about it. 'I've got to talk with Kelsey, and check Audrey's alright with that.'

'Audrey will be fine with it. I'll see to her,' Tom said, taking charge. 'Plan on moving tomorrow. I'm going back to your office now. He'll be on the CCTV footage and I want to see it for myself.'

Nate saw him out and returned to Adam.

'Want to crash here the night?' he asked.

'Nah, but thanks. I'm hoping Uncle Allan drops by home. We've got some catching up to do.'

Nate looked worried. He debated whether to let his best friend walk out or tackle him to the ground and knock some sense into him. 'Got a cricket bat you can put beside your bed if you need it?' he asked, half-joking.

'I have now. Don't worry,' Adam said and smiled. 'I've got my centre of gravity right where it should be.'

'Lord help us,' Nate said and smiled at the memory of their self-defence classes with Charlie.

'He won't come near my place tonight,' Adam assured Nate as he grabbed his coat, phone and keys to go.

'How do you know that?' Nate asked, following him to the front door. 'You've worked him out and you're in his head?'

'Maybe. He wants the game to last. He's made his appearance for the day… he knows he will have freaked me out, and that you and I would talk about it tonight. He'll be at his home – wherever his cave is – planning his next appearance,' Adam said, and shrugged. 'That's what I'd be doing if I were him.'

'I hope you've analysed this one right,' Nate said, and watched with a rising sense of dread as moments later, his best friend drove off into the night.

Chapter 29

Now...

Sergeant Matt Burns saw plenty of Nate and Adam after hours, but he was happy to have an excuse to come to the office and catch up with Jessica. He remembered her when she worked in administration for the Police Service, and he knew she was single. She was standing near the printer when he entered after being buzzed in; he appreciated how good she looked in a fitted red dress and tanned high heels. He suspected Nate did as well.

'The new security is an excellent idea,' he told her, a file tucked under his arm, and his uniform straightened in the stairwell before entering.

'Yeah, we're full of bright ideas here,' she said with a smile, returning to her desk. 'Nate will be five minutes at most,' she said with a glance to Nate's closed office door.

'Can't believe he's busy,' Burnsy said and Jessica laughed.

'He gets a steady stream of missing people, missing items, cheating couples and business partners. Not all of it exciting but now and then he gets his teeth into a case that keeps him motivated.'

'Like finding out what happened to the guy from the

asylum,' Burnsy said. 'And to think he left his fortune to Nate and Adam. He was insane.'

'There's a lesson in that for all of us,' Jessica said and laughed. 'Got any insane relatives you could get chummy with?'

'Most of them, and it's not like I haven't tried,' Burnsy confessed with a grin. There was a moment of lull as Burnsy desperately thought of something to say to keep the conversation going.

'Want a tea or coffee?' Jessica asked filling in the silence.

He was just about to accept when Nate's office door swung open and an older man in a grey suit exited, with Nate on his heels. The older man gave a wave of thanks to Jessica.

'Thank you, Mr Larson,' she called after him.

'Be right with you, Burnsy,' Nate said and saw the client to the door, shook his hand and closed the door after him.

'Let me guess,' Burnsy said once the client had left and the door was closed, 'the wife's cheating on the poor old bloke?'

'Embezzlement, allegedly,' Nate said. 'A business partner who has suddenly started living the high life and hasn't won the lotto.'

Burnsy shook his head. 'People suck.'

'Thank God, or we'd all be out of work,' Nate agreed. 'Are you here for me? Of course you are!'

'Sadly yes,' Burnsy joked and accepting the offer of coffee from Jessica, he headed into Nate's office with a final glance back at Jessica which didn't go unnoticed by Nate.

They moved to the small table by the window in Nate's office.

Burnsy glanced downstairs to the street. 'Just checking on the car,' he said.

'So, are you going to make your move?' Nate asked.

Burnsy looked confused and then realised Nate was talking about Jessica. He sat down and lowered his voice. 'Depends on where you stand.'

Nate shrugged. 'Why would that matter?'

Burnsy studied him for a few moments and then changed the subject. 'Where's your partner? Reading heads somewhere else?'

'Yeah, he has a group session at the prison every Tuesday.'

'Christ, that'd be a hoot, wouldn't it?'

'He has his favourites,' Nate joked. 'Bruiser, Lefty, and I'm sure some of the boys love him – tall, dark and handsome that he is.' Nate shuddered at his own joke and then with a glance to the file on the table asked: 'What have you got for me?'

Jessica came in with a coffee for the men and they thanked her. Both of them did their best not to watch her leave. Burnsy opened the file he had been carrying and gave the top sheets to Nate.

'I can't leave the file with you, but that's a copy you can keep. It's Allan Sheffield's testimony when he was arrested.'

'Fantastic, thanks, really appreciate this,' Nate said, leaning forward and looking over the document.

'Why do you want it? Have you discovered something? Has something happened since Sheffield visited Adam the other night?'

'No, nothing to report. But if anything changes, you'll be the first to know.'

'Sheffield has been out for about two weeks and he's already causing problems,' Burnsy said, his voice laced with frustration as if time in prison should straighten out every crook by the time they were released.

Nate looked up. 'Yeah… they never found the body of

that kid he killed, did they? Adam and I dodged a bullet there.'

Burnsy gave him a raised eyebrow. 'What's that kid got to do with you and Adam? I thought Sheffield had a history with the Murphys, he was the driver...'

'Nothing, you're right. Mr Murphy used him occasionally, I believe,' Nate hurriedly assured him. Too hurriedly. 'I was just saying it was bad business with the kid.' Nate saw the look Burnsy gave him and rolled his eyes. 'You're a tough interrogator,' he joked. 'Fine then. We knew him when we were kids, Adam and I.'

'For Christ's sake... what is it with you two?' Burnsy asked. 'Hanging around the insane asylum and bloody murderers. Where were your parents?'

'We were raised by monkeys,' Nate joked.

'Explains a lot.'

'Trust me, my parents didn't know about Allan Sheffield,' Nate said. 'Well not that I know about.' He frowned wondering if perhaps they did. 'Then again, they knew about our friend, Joe from the asylum, but never told me.'

They heard the buzzer going and Jessica chatting to a male voice. Moments later, Tom Hartigan appeared in the doorway of Nate's office. Burnsy rose to shake hands as Nate did the introductions.

'The team's growing,' Burnsy said.

'No, I'm a security contractor, just here to improve the building security,' Tom said with a glance to Nate.

Burnsy knew the uniform had that effect on people, they clammed up. He smelled a rat and his eyes narrowed. 'Okay, you want to spill what's going on? First, you want info on Allan Sheffield, now security is being upgraded. Are you expecting a drama?'

Tom spoke up. 'No, I'm hired by Adam's family… because of Winsome's wedding.'

'Ah, gotcha,' Burnsy said and nodded his understanding. 'Yeah, Adam mentioned Audrey had hired additional security. But there's more going on here.'

The outside office door opened again, no buzzer this time and again a male voice could be heard talking with Jessica.

Burnsy looked to Nate who explained: 'We're very busy and important.'

Burnsy scoffed.

'Fine then, it's Adam,' Nate conceded and soon Adam appeared in the doorway of Nate's office. He glanced from Burnsy to Nate to Tom.

'Ah, all my favourites,' he said drily, and the men chuckled.

'How were the prison boys?' Nate asked.

'Good, they send their love, and Reg said thanks for the nude photo,' Adam shot back with a smile. 'What's going on?'

'I just dropped in Allan Sheffield's testimony that Nate requested,' Burnsy said, rising.

'Did you?' Adam asked and looked to Nate.

Burnsy winced. 'Sorry,' he said to Nate. 'I thought you told each other everything.'

'We do, and I'm devastated,' Adam joked. 'Is there someone else?'

Burnsy saw a look between the two men. 'I saw that,' he said.

'Don't look at me,' Tom said holding up his hands, as the police sergeant took in all three men.

'Something is going on. Maybe you better tell me in advance… or I'll have to find something to arrest you on… both of you,' Burnsy suggested.

Nate frowned at Adam. 'Boardroom,' he said rising as there wasn't room for four people in his office. He led the way, arguing with Adam all the way.

'You've got no poker face. You should have played along.'

'I didn't know that I wasn't supposed to know,' Adam defended himself. 'What are we talking about anyway?'

'Exactly, just like that, play dumb.'

Chapter 30

Now...

Danielle pulled into the carpark at the Correctional Centre in the outer suburb of Wacol and turned her vehicle into a park beside a post. She liked to reduce the number of idiots that could park next to her and risk scratching or denting the paintwork on her relatively new red Mazda hatch. It made sense, she thought, that the Correctional Centre was so far out in the burbs – no-one wanted jailbirds for neighbours despite the inconvenience of the drive. After Tom's tirade about Adam's unconventional childhood, Danielle was undertaking some of her own research and had called in a favour.

Locking the car, she entered the centre and went through the procedures to get in, then waited. A huge man in uniform appeared and grinned on seeing her.

'Danielle Walters, as I live and breathe,' he said. 'You're looking good, darlin." He checked her out.

'Stevie Faulkner the first!' she said, he laughed.

'Yeah, the one and only, and you're the only person

who calls me Stevie and lives.' He gave her a bear hug and released her. 'Come on, I'm on my break, I'll shout you a prison-issued coffee.'

'Who could resist that?' she asked, following him into an empty staff room and leaning on the counter, as he prepared two coffees from the machine. 'So this is what you've done with your security qualifications... moved in to mind the bad asses.'

'Yeah, I'm big enough and ugly enough. You know the moment you walk through here you'll be every man's fantasy tonight,' he teased, 'including mine.'

She laughed. 'Nice to give something back,' she grinned.

'So, tell me why you wanted my help,' he said.

'I like a man who gets straight down to business,' Dan said. 'I'm working for an ex-cop who runs a P.I. agency. This visit is related to a case,' she said, accepting the coffee with thanks. They moved to a table near the barred windows and she caught him checking out her butt in the tight jeans she was wearing.

'Alright?' she asked.

'Fantastic,' he growled.

'You're lucky I don't work here. You'd have to rein in all those sexist comments.'

'Don't worry, I'm safe here. There's no one I'd risk get a rap over the knuckles for in this joint,' he sighed, disappointed.

'So, you got me the interview? He was happy to see me?' Dan asked getting back on track.

'Yeah, happy for the company and a break from the routine. You've got a 40-minute visitation.' He glanced to the clock, cutting to the chase.

'I love you,' Dan said and Stevie laughed.

'Of course you do. Want to tell me why? I'll keep it to myself.'

'Why I love you? What's not to love?' she segued.

He grinned and shook his head. 'Righto, I'll read between the lines. Shut up and mind my own business. Did you bring the cigs for him?'

'You bet.' She patted the tote bag beside her that security had checked and let her bring in.

They talked small talk for the rest of the time, swapping notes about their class colleagues and where they ended up, and then Danielle followed Stevie through the prison to visit the man who for the last seven years had shared a cell with Allan Sheffield – Uncle Allan.

*****

'I'm glad to be rid of him,' Doug Gill said upfront.

Danielle studied the small and wiry man opposite her. He smelled of cigarettes and his skin was dark and leathery; years of sun exposure had done its damage.

'You got a man?' he asked.

'Several,' she said and made him laugh.

'Good for you, love, good for you. You're a looker.'

'I'd be lying if I returned the compliment,' she said, and Doug put his head back and laughed.

'Yeah, you're sassy too. Okay, so you want to talk about that boring prick.'

'Maybe next time we can talk about you,' she teased, and he winked.

'I'll take you up on that. Before I tell you about Sheffield, tell me why you want to know? You don't look related.'

'No, thank God,' she said. 'I'm doing some undercover work, some security stuff, and he's linked to my client,' she said without going into detail.

'Sounds boring,' he said. 'Is you Dad black or your Mum, or both?'

Dan smiled at him; she liked a direct person and that would bode well for her questions.

'Both. Saltwater people.'

'Geez, I'd bloody love to swim in saltwater again. I can't tell you the last time I felt the ocean on my skin,' he said, a wistful look on his face. 'I worked for over a decade in Darwin, love the heat.'

'That's where I'm from,' she said, and then changed the subject. She was homesick and talking about it would bring her no comfort. 'What are you in for?' she asked, not worrying about diplomacy given Doug didn't seem to know much about the concept.

'Not murder, so relax,' he said and chuckled. 'Break and enter, theft, a few other charges for good measure.'

'And you got to share a room with a kid murderer?'

Doug shook his head. 'It's a bloody miracle he survived, and trust me, I didn't have his back. He was one of those guys who thought the world owed him. Always complaining that he drew the short straw... got sacked, couldn't get the wife pregnant, got caught by the cops, always the victim.'

Danielle nodded her understanding. She opened the bag she was allowed to bring in and pulled a long narrow box wrapped in brown paper from it.

'This is not a bribe, just a *thanks-for-seeing-me* gift,' she said pushing a week's supply of cigarettes to him and the brand he smoked.

He looked inside and smiled. 'Ah, you're a treasure,' he said, eyes lighting up at the sight of them. 'Thank you, Luv.'

'You're welcome. It's the kid I want to talk about,' Dan said. 'The kid Allan Sheffield stole and killed wasn't the first kid he tried it with.'

'I know, I heard all about it,' Doug said and rolled his eyes.

Dan sat forward, now he had her attention. 'Can you tell me everything he said about the first and last kid?' She asked and then tried it on and gave him a wink, 'including where he buried the boy?'

Doug laughed. 'Yeah, you've got spunk.' He sat back. 'Allan Sheffield,' he said almost under his breath, and then he began his tale.

Chapter 31

Now...

Kelsey was no stranger to Adam's family home – she had visited the grounds quite a few times in the months they had been going out, each time to lunch with Audrey on Sundays in the grounds of her cottage. But she had never been in the main house – the white elephant – and Adam had never offered her a tour.

He put her two suitcases in the boot of the Mercedes and they entered the car and departed from Kelsey's unit.

'You look great,' he said, reaching for her hand across the console. The other he kept on the steering wheel. 'I love it when you wear your hair out.'

'Thanks, and yes, I know,' she said, 'you might have mentioned it a few dozen times.' Kelsey smiled and ran a hand through her long red waves.

Adam cleared his throat. 'I know we haven't spoken about moving in together and this is just a temporary thing, but you can have your own room if you prefer.'

She snapped to look at him, surprised. 'No! Do you want your own room?'

'No, hell no, I just thought you might want some time out.'

She squeezed his hand. 'No. I want time in.' She gave him a sexy smile.

Adam grinned and returned his attention to the road.

'But there is something I would like...' she started.

'What's that?' he asked, a little concerned.

'My own bathroom. Can we have separate bathrooms?'

He relaxed and smiled. 'Absolutely. In our wing, there's three to choose from, take your pick.'

She shook her head in disbelief. They drove for a while talking about the house and what else Kelsey might expect to find there. Then they returned to the subject of Allan Sheffield.

'Did Tom say how long he'd like us to stay there?'

'No. We really don't know what Allan Sheffield's doing or why he's doing it.' He hesitated, then added: 'He came to the office... twice.'

'Uncle Allan? No!' she exclaimed, eyes wide. 'When?'

'Once pretending to be a woman and hiring Nate to find a lost child...'

Kelsey shuddered. 'That's just creepy, especially knowing he killed that little boy.'

Adam nodded and turned down a street leading to his family's home. The river glistened beside them. He continued: 'Then he came to see me when I was working late. I saw him, dressed as a woman, on the screen. By the time I got downstairs, he was gone.'

She turned to face him. 'Why would you leave the office? Adam, he could have killed you.'

'So I've been told,' he assured her. 'Sorry. I don't mean to spook you but you should be forewarned.'

'Thank you,' she said. 'I've been through worse; I like to know what's coming.'

'I know you do,' Adam said, turning into the street where his family home was located and driving into the property.

He hit the button on his key ring and the large black gates on the exterior of the property opened. He drove them into the grounds of the house he had grown up in, nothing like the suburban timber home he now owned. The gates closed behind them.

'Do you play tennis?' Kelsey asked as they passed the court.

'Like Nadal,' Adam joked and she laughed.

She noted the cameras on the gates as she took in the grounds. 'You've got a bit of security around at least.'

'Yeah,' he agreed. 'But we're not here just because of Sheffield… with the wedding coming, it might be trickier getting in and out of our places if some media want cheap filler stories.'

'You and I are so cheap,' she agreed and laughed. 'You're assuming they'll be interested in me,' Kelsey said, doubt in her voice.

'Trust me, if they are still interested in me, they'll be very interested in you,' Adam said with a sigh. 'I don't get it.'

Kelsey shrugged. 'There's a lot of online content that has to be generated all the time, and it is all so disposable. It's just feeding the machine.'

Adam scoffed. 'Doesn't it work on clicks, though? If no one is interested, then we'll be dropped quickly.'

'They're interested, especially in celebrity gossip. You know, if you and I were the type, we could be influencers living the life here and posting every day of our amazing lifestyle and how much we are in love.'

He parked in one of the four carpark spots in the garage, cut the ignition and looked at her, his expression was hard to read. Kelsey laughed.

'Stop freaking out. I'm not interested in doing that,' she said and leaned over to kiss him.

Adam exhaled with relief. 'Thank God, I thought you might have had a change of heart.' People had tricked him before.

They exited and Adam grabbed their suitcases from the car before putting them down again at the front door as he grabbed for the house key.

'Want me to carry you across the threshold?' he asked, and she smiled and gave it serious consideration.

'No, I think I'll wait for the official carry, but thanks,' she said and smiled at the thought. 'I am excited about having a pool though, fantastic!' Her pale grey-blue eyes lit up at the sight of it behind Adam, taking up an enormous footprint of the garden. 'What happens if we are still here when Winsome comes home for the wedding?'

'She likes the rooms away from the river, oddly… she's scared of water.'

Kelsey interrupted him as Adam unlocked the front door and handed her a set of keys.

'Your mum bought a house on the river and has an Olympic-sized swimming pool but is scared of water?'

'Yeah, Dad liked it,' Adam said as if that explained everything. They walked in and Adam headed to the bedroom with a bag in each hand. 'So, Mum and Jack will take the garden wing, we'll stay in the river wing, and Nate can have the main wing, unless he gets lonely,' he said and Kelsey laughed.

'He can stay with us,' Kelsey said, and then she laughed again. 'The garden and river wings… it's all too weird.'

He shrugged; Adam knew no different, but it felt different already with Kelsey beside him.

It felt like how a home should feel.

Chapter 32

Now...

Doug Gill's expression looked like he'd eaten something that disagreed with him.

'He used to talk about those two boys like they were his property,' he started telling Danielle. 'The first one, the name was Adam...'

Danielle nodded. 'That's him, he's my point of interest,' she said, being upfront with Doug. She liked him, he was a down-to-earth type, and she wasn't the type to judge someone who committed a crime like a robbery. Who knows what motivates anyone to do anything – a lesson she'd learnt first-hand, but she drew the line at child killers and wife bashers.

'Yeah, Adam,' Doug continued. 'He spoke about that kid like he really was his uncle, like he loved him. He told me Adam was good at cricket, was a really good-looking kid, slow to smile, but when he did, it was worth it. What the hell? This is a kid he was going to kidnap!'

'Given that, do you think if he'd managed to kidnap Adam that he would have killed him?' Danielle asked.

'Yeah, I do,' Doug said. 'Because he talked about the second kid, Dean, the same way. He said he was a good little swimmer, a really nice kid, as if he was proud of him.'

Danielle nodded and Doug continued: 'I think Sheffield got a lit bit loopy with time,' he said, circling his finger around his temple. 'From what he told me, he was desperate to pull that plan off and once he got the money, he didn't care what happened to the kid.'

Danielle exhaled. 'Did he tell you what happened with Dean?'

Doug nodded. 'Not just me. He talked to anyone who'd listen. He thought he was the victim and it was unfair he didn't get to have a kid with his wife.'

'Did she ever visit?'

'Can't say, but he didn't get a lot of visitors. I think his grandparents dropped in a few times.'

Danielle brought him back to the topic of the boys. 'So, Dean?'

'Yeah, Dean. He told me he took the kid's father to the airport and knew that Dean was expecting his father at his swimming final, so he went along instead. He said the kid was so pleased to see him that the parents didn't deserve the kid.'

'That's interesting,' Danielle said.

'Is it? Why's that?' Doug asked.

Dan ignored the question and asked: 'If he drove Dean's dad around, I wonder if that's how he met Adam's parents?'

'Was Adam's father a manager, media manager or something like that?' Doug asked.

'Yeah, something like that,' Dan said without mentioning James Murphy's media business interests, Winsome and Adam's history.

'Then yeah, I think Sheffield might have driven Adam's dad around, too. Couldn't say for sure though, but it's somewhere in my memory banks,' Doug said and tapped his head.

'What else did he say about the first boy, Adam?'

'Lots. He'd rave on about how it was criminal to neglect that kid. Ironic, isn't it? It's alright for him to kill the kid but not neglect him.' Doug shook his head. 'Sheffield said both of the boys' parents didn't deserve them, they didn't deserve to be parents when he and his wife were desperately trying to have kids.'

'Wow,' Dan said.

'Yeah, I told you he had a victim mentality.'

But that wasn't what Danielle was thinking. She was amazed at Sheffield's grooming of the boys – that he found Adam and Dean, both young boys neglected by successful parents – easy pickings for a driver who built relationships with his clients and became trusted like family.

'I don't know how he killed the boy, but I can tell you something.'

'Great, anything. What?' Dan asked, and Doug grinned.

'There was a redevelopment about to happen some years back... they were going to reclaim some of an old cemetery where no one had been buried since forever and develop it into commercial land. Every time a story about the St Nicholas Cemetery came on the news or TV, he would freeze. Like he expected them to say they found something there and then he'd relax and breathe again when the story was over.'

'St Nicholas Cemetery... haven't heard of it.'

'Well, not saying that's where he buried the lad but could be worth a look. It's been 20 years, I'm not sure anything there will look recently dug,' he said and chuckled.

'Doug, you're worth your weight in smokes,' Dan said and Doug laughed.

'Come again, hey? It's nice to have a visitor.'

'I might just do that,' she said and left him with a smile on his face.

Chapter 33

Then...

Charlie Duffy – dressed in her standard-issue black pants, black boots, and black T-shirt, with her hair tied back in a pony tail, looked ready for action. It was her work gear and since she had come on board as Adam's security detail, she had monitored where the boys went for sports days, who their friends were, access points around their homes and had made herself known to Adam's teachers and sports coaches.

She had also checked out where they went on their bikes and, by the time she finished her surveillance, knew the area around the river and rear of the asylum like the back of her hand. Charlie was satisfied she had taught them enough moves and responses to get out of a hairy situation and, more importantly, she had taught them how not to get into one in the first place – running and shouting were good strategies. She didn't like James Murphy telling his son to trust no one... Adam had told her about it. She appreciated where he was going with it, but it made her job more difficult.

Charlie glanced over at Adam as she drove him to school. It was Audrey's bridge day and Nate was in the backseat, getting a ride and staring at her with love-eyes. At least that's what Adam called them and made her laugh.

They were playing 'Ice Breaker.' It was a game Charlie made up so she could snoop on the boys without drilling them on what they were up to and who they were speaking with – a mistake the former security guard made She had heard that Tom threatened and coerced Adam, which just made the young boy clam up. With *Ice Breaker*, you got to find out more about a person by asking anything you like. Nothing was off-limits, or so she told them.

'Okay, my turn,' Charlie said. 'Have you ever met anyone hiding out in the woods where you ride your bikes?' She asked as if it was a great mystery, dangerous and fun.

Adam turned to glance back at Nate and let him answer.

'We met a guy once who got away from the asylum, he was wearing all white. But we were on bikes so we left really quick, he couldn't catch us,' Nate said.

'We were super-fast,' Adam agreed. 'And some older kids were smoking, but they didn't stay for long, so we just kind of avoided them.'

Charlie nodded, satisfied. 'Very clever you two. All good soldiers know how to read a scene and when to get out.' She saw their pleased reaction.

'My turn,' Adam said. 'Have you ever killed anyone, Charlie?'

'No,' Charlie said 'but I would if I had to.'

'Wow, like Tom was going to kill Uncle Allan, I reckon,' Adam said.

Charlie gave a little shrug and tried to keep it casual. 'If I had to save you or Nate from someone and the only way to do that was to kill them, I'd do it like that,' she said snapping her fingers. She saw the boys glance at each other and look impressed. She wanted to be their first port of call if they were frightened.

'Your turn, Nate,' Charlie said.

'Have you got a boyfriend?' he asked.

Charlie smiled. 'No, but there is a guy I like,' she said and saw his face drop. 'Two guys actually, but I'll have to wait until they grow up.'

Adam laughed. Nate grinned and looked away, pleased with the answer.

They did another round of questions and Adam asked: 'If you killed someone, Charlie, where would you bury them?'

'Hmm, good question,' she said. 'I have to think like a criminal now. But there's only one logical place…'

'Where?' Nate asked, leaning forward.

'The cemetery, of course!'

*****

Now…

Nate drove for a change. His silver Holden SUV was not as comfortable as Adam's Mercedes, but it did the job.

'You're brilliant, Dan,' Adam said, after hearing for the second time the discussion between Danielle and Allan Sheffield's prison roommate, Doug Gill.

'I am, thank you,' she agreed and Nate glanced in the rear-view mirror to give her a smirk. 'Doug liked to talk, so he sang like a choir.'

'Or a canary,' Nate corrected her.

'That old cliché,' Danielle sighed. 'One thing I took away

from it though, was that your Uncle Allan has a massive chip on his shoulder and might be out for revenge, giving he thinks he was wronged.'

'You know he's not related, right?' Adam asked, with a glance back to her.

'Yeah, but are you sure he knows that?' Danielle asked.

'No. I'm not sure he knew it then or now,' Adam said.

Nate elaborated: 'All this started because Allan Sheffield wanted to get cashed up for the IVF program. It was planned, calculated and kids groomed, let's keep that in sight.'

Adam turned to Dan again. 'I appreciate you pulling favours and getting the info.'

'You've earned your stripes this week, Dan,' Nate agreed. He nudged Adam. 'Update the directions, Navigator.'

Adam glanced at his phone. 'St Nicholas Cemetery, turn into the third street coming on your left,' he said.

'I have Navman,' Nate said, 'just because it's not built-in like it is in some cars.'

'The phone is easy,' Adam said.

'Why aren't we in the Merc?' Danielle grumbled from the back, which she shared with Matilda's car booster seat. 'No point having a good car if you don't show it off.'

'Because if Allan Sheffield is monitoring this place, he doesn't know my car, but he probably knows Adams from the online shots of the model here, avoiding the paparazzi,' Nate said, nodding towards Adam with a grin.

'At least it's a career fallback option,' Adam joked.

'You'd starve,' Nate told him.

'Thanks! Tell me again why we have to go here at night?' Adam said.

'It's scarier,' Nate answered and Danielle laughed. Nate sighed like he was talking to a child: 'For the same reason we're using my car – to keep a low profile. If Doug Gill reckons Sheffield reacted every time the cemetery name or area was mentioned in media, then he's probably been visiting here as well to make sure his work stays hidden,' Nate said.

'Yeah, but he'd probably visit at night, like we are,' Adam said.

'Not if he is being careful and smart, and we know Allan is no idiot,' Nate said. 'If I were him, thinking with my criminal mind...' he looked to Adam for his comeback but got a nod to continue, 'I'd come dressed as Mrs Tatum and carrying flowers during the day. No-one is going to look twice at a poor older woman mourning someone.'

'Yeah, that's good,' Adam said. 'You'd make a great criminal.'

'Thank you,' Nate said and followed Adam's directions to take the turn.

Danielle stuck her head between the two front seats as far as she could while strapped in with the seatbelt. 'So the lowdown on the cemetery... it's tiny, thank God, about one hundred graves. The first grave was in the 1850s, lots of infant burials but that's pretty normal for the times, and you'll be interested in this... one mass grave of over 200 bodies moved from the Asylum Cemetery and re-interred here.'

'Our asylum?' Nate asked as if the inhospitable place looming in their childhood playground was theirs to claim.

'The very one,' Dan said.

'Glad we didn't know that when we were looking for Joe,' Adam said, 'we might have spent a lot of time looking in the wrong place. When was the last burial or is it still current?'

'Lucky for us it was around the late 1960s and early seventies, which means any recent graves will be obvious,' Dan said.

'Not that obvious. We're talking 20 years ago that Uncle Allan would have buried Dean Beals and he wouldn't have put a headstone on Dean's grave if this was where he buried him. But there might a marker,' Adam said and pointed to another turn. 'It's at the end of this road.'

Nate drove to the end and turned into the small and dark grounds of the St Nicholas' Cemetery.

'Saint Nicholas – the patron saint of children,' Adam said, and they both looked at him. 'Catholic school,' he added.

'Very apt though,' Nate muttered under his breath, as they exited the car and he locked it.

'So we're looking for a marker that might be recent or relevant, fresh flowers, or any recent tread marks?' Danielle asked.

'That's about it. And avoid using the torches if you can,' Nate directed, taking the lead and walking through the small timber archway, Adam and Danielle right behind him.

Chapter 34

Now…

The three friends divided the cemetery amongst them – Danielle took the middle section, which included rows of tiny headstones with nothing but a number inscribed on them – the asylum dead. Nate claimed the older area, including the children's burial ground filled with small statues of angels, and Adam sectioned himself in the newest burial area – covering the 1930s to 1970s and included all ages of 'residents.' There was enough moonlight to get the job done once their eyes had adjusted away from the streetlights.

Large trees and monuments felt like guardians watching them as they moved between the shadows. The chill of the night settled in, the grass was long and cool, and the crunch of twigs and dried leaves beneath their feet was the only sound other than their breathing.

Adam had to admit, despite its openness and the widely spread out tombstones, the place was creepy. He thought about the last time he was somewhere creepy at night. It just happened to be with Nate, again, who had dragged him into an abandoned and derelict asylum. He glanced up at his best friend, sighed, and then returned to the job.

The headstones were worn and hard to read; there was no recent activity in the first few wide rows he weaved himself between. Occasional small graves sat alone, out of order, and away from the other sleepers – shunned. Rusty, small iron fences hemmed several plots. Adam read one headstone – Evelyn, died 2 October 1932, aged three. '*Our angel, never forgotten.*' Adam took comfort in the fact that Evelyn's parents would now be gone too and free from that pain.

He saw his surname on a grave and stopped to read it. '*Lawrence Murphy, March 1942, accidentally killed. Aged 39. Loved husband and father.*' What's your story, Lawrence, he wondered. Now and then, Adam looked up to check on the other two – he noticed Nate was constantly on alert… his cop training kicking in. Danielle was concentrating with great intensity – if Dean was to be found here, she wanted to be the one to find him. She was competitive; Nate would have the same mission.

He turned and gave a start, stepping back in fright.

'Christ,' he muttered, exhaling as the tree he had rounded hid a headless angel monument easily his height. He glanced at the base and the wording '*My beloved Theresa, 1927*'.

He heard a short, sharp scream and snapped to look for Danielle and Nate.

Danielle held her hands up in apology. 'Sorry, rabbit. Scared the shit out of me,' she said panting.

Nate and Adam grinned.

'Did you think it was a hand out of the grave to grab your ankle and drag you below?' Nate called out theatrically, his voice quavering.

'Something like that,' she said and patted her heart.

'Don't worry. I just met the walking dead,' Adam said, indicating the statue behind him. 'I nearly took it on.'

Nate and Danielle laughed, and they all resumed their combing of the grounds. As Adam neared the last row of his section, he stopped on finding a grave with a cross on the ground made of white pebbles. He squatted to have a look. It was hard to tell how recent it was and there was no name or other markings. No fresh flowers.

'Adam!'

Adam shot to full height on hearing Nate yell out his name. 'What?' he asked, alarmed.

Nate shook his head, throwing his arms up into the air. 'For Christ's sake, I thought you'd been abducted or fallen into a grave.'

'It'd save time and money,' Adam conceded as he strode towards Nate. 'There's a grave in the back row worth checking out.'

'Tell me where and I'll mark it up,' Danielle said. 'I've got the cemetery map.' She fished a pen and a folded map from her pocket.

'So organised,' Adam said.

'I don't come cheap, but I'm good,' she said with a smile in Nate's direction. 'I'll contact the St Nicholas' Friends of the Cemetery group and see if they can identify the grave and who's lying there. They'll know the history and have the church records,' she said. 'If they don't know, then it's a possibility it could be Dean.'

'The cemetery has friends?' Nate asked. 'Why didn't I know this?'

Danielle shuddered. 'Who wants to hang out here at the best of times?'

'Yeah,' Adam agreed, 'I used to be scared of cemeteries too, when I was alive,' he said and slowly turned his gaze to Danielle, his eyes fixed.

'Don't!' she scolded him, 'that's not funny.'

Adam laughed and then looked at her. 'Seriously? That freaks you out? I thought you were invincible.'

She lowered her voice: 'It's the resting place of the dead,' she said as if that explained everything.

'They can't hear you,' Nate said.

Danielle rolled her eyes.

'I wish they could. It'd make our job a lot easier,' Adam said, and cupping his hands around his mouth, called out, 'Are you here, Dean? Anyone seen Dean?'

They waited for a second, as if expecting a response. Nate put his hand to his ear, concentrating on listening.

'Dead silence,' he said and sighed.

'You two are idiots,' Dan scolded them. 'Take me to the grave you want checked out and I'll mark it up on my map,' she ordered Adam.

He led the way to the grave with the white stone cross, sorely tempted to spook her some more. He knew Nate would, but he couldn't bring himself to do it.

'Over here when you're done,' Nate called. Minutes later they joined him at a grave with a homemade wooden cross for a headstone. It had a small tin trophy leaning against it. No name, no sport.

'Swimming trophy?' Nate asked.

'Could be, but I suspect any fingerprints would be long gone,' Adam said.

'I'll note this one too then,' Danielle said and snapped a photo with her phone and marked it on her map.

'Are we done here?' Adam asked, feeling the night getting cooler.

'Done. Let's go have a drink somewhere, it's only nine o'clock,' Danielle said.

Adam thought of Kelsey waiting for him at their new temporary home. Nate was moving in tomorrow.

'Mum's place is nearby and Kelsey's there, I can text her and see if she's up for an invasion?'

'Perfect,' Nate said.

Adam noted Danielle's eyes widened with interest but she played cool and gave a quick nod.

'Jessica will be so jealous I've been to Winsome's house,' she said.

'Really?' Adam asked frowning. 'Why?'

Danielle shrugged. 'You don't get it because it's all you know. When are you moving?' she asked Nate.

'Tomorrow. The sooner the better apparently... Tom's orders. Now you can run wild at my place while I'm away.'

'I'll do my best,' she joked.

'We should have a BBQ soon and invite Jess around, let her see Winsome's bedroom. We'll all fit in. What do you think?' Nate asked Adam who shrugged.

'Sure, why not.' He sent a quick message to Kelsey who sent back a thumbs-up.

They walked towards the car and Nate continued, adopting a plummy voice: 'Or instead of a barbeque, we could enjoy hors d'oeuvres in the gazebo and have a hit of tennis.'

'How terribly civilised,' Adam agreed.

Nate continued. 'Then have cocktails by the pool, supper, and port and cigars in the library after.'

'There's a library?' Danielle asked.

'No, there's no library!' Adam smirked at Nate as they returned to his car. 'You're hilarious.'

'That I am,' he said, hitting Adam on the back. 'Even in a cemetery, I can lift your spirits.'

Adam groaned and studied the cemetery as they departed. It could be him buried in there somewhere, unclaimed, separated from his family and friends. Despite being with Nate and Dan, and safely ensconced in the car, the thought chilled him to the bone.

Chapter 35

Now...

Tom Hartigan supervised the two tradesmen he brought with him to install panic buttons and security alarms to the desks, doors, and windows of the *Delaney and Murphy* office. Tom looked less like a security operator and more like an office manager in black suit pants, a crisp white shirt, no tie, and black boots – a compromise between office wear and clothes that would let him chase someone if he needed to do so. As the 'tradies' finished work on the front door and Jessica's desk at reception, Tom wrote the panic code for the alarm on a card and gave it to her.

'Make sure the whole team, Rob included, learn that number,' Tom said.

She looked at the number. 'You don't think this is a bit over the top?' Jessica asked as she watched from her chair in the reception area.

'Nope. Over the top would be a security guard at the door all day and one in the carpark,' he said with a smile in her direction. 'Where's Nate this morning?'

'Out with Dan, working on his embezzlement case. He's about to wrap it up, I believe.'

'I'll do his office next while he's not here.' He looked at Adam's closed door. 'Is he in there?'

'Yep, with a client,' Jessica said and glanced at the clock. 'He'll be finished in fifteen minutes, then he's got forty-five minutes before his next one.'

'Wow, lots of screwed people around, hey? What about Rob?'

'He's in there,' she said with a nod to the closed office door behind her. 'He's not seeing clients so you can probably interrupt him anytime.'

'Finished here,' one of the tradies said and Tom thanked him and said to Jessica. 'I'll get the guys started in Nate's office and come back and show you how to use what they've installed.'

He returned moments later and sat beside her behind the reception desk, noting she moved as far as way from him as she could. *What's that about,* he wondered, it's not like he'd tried to come onto her. He ran her through the alarm usage, disarming it, using the panic code, and filing the CCTV footage daily.

'Call me if you forget any of it, I can quickly step you through it via phone.'

'Thanks, I will.'

He rose and checked on the boys in Nate's office. Finding them finished, he left them momentarily on hearing Adam's office door open. An athletic guy in jeans and a long-sleeve black T-shirt, with a buzz cut and a tattoo on his neck, exited. He looked Jessica's way and thanked her, and figuring out the new system – pressed the green button to depart – headed out the door and out of sight.

'Good, well that worked,' Tom said, watching the client depart.

Adam appeared in the doorway and, on seeing Tom, went back into his office.

Tom strode across reception and followed him in. 'Adam, I need fifteen minutes in your office to install the security alarm.'

'Now's good,' Adam said and walked out again.

'You don't have to evacuate,' Tom said and, finding himself alone, rolled his eyes. It was one step forward and two steps back with Adam. He stuck his head out the door. 'In here, lads,' he called across the room to them. He returned to Jessica. 'I'll do Rob's office next.'

'Adam's in there now, so let me know when you're ready and I'll interrupt them.'

Tom nodded and lingered on a fact-finding mission. 'What's the story with Rob?' he asked, lowering his voice.

'He works here three days a week,' Jessica said, telling him what she knew.

'Doing what?' Tom asked with the authority of one who needed to know for security reasons.

'He focuses on class actions. He and Adam are finishing up one now with former asylum patients, and there's a PTSD class action case too, just kicking off.' She nodded to the door to indicate the man who just departed.

'What's Rob to Adam?' Tom asked, cutting to the chase.

'They go way back. Rob was Adam's advisor when Adam was doing his PhD. Now he's Adam's supervisor.'

Tom looked surprised. 'I thought Adam was the boss. He's working for himself, isn't he?'

'He is,' Jessica said, 'but all psychologists need to complete personal development and training each year to maintain their registration, apparently. I think it's about thirty hours or something like that.'

'Really?' Tom asked. 'I didn't know that.'

'Me either, until I came to work here. But I guess it's like cops in the police service having bosses up the line and resources at their disposal, same as you in the military,' she said with a questioning look.

'Yeah, I guess so,' Tom said. 'In my time, they weren't so much into checking on you... as long as you did the job, all was well. Now they've got all the touchy-feely stuff, probably a good thing,' he mused, thinking about his state of mind after being discharged with injuries. It was straight after that he was assigned the job of guarding Adam and stuffed that up. He cleared his throat and got back on track. 'So Rob supervises Adam to make sure he's of sound mind, so to speak?'

'He does. Not for the whole thirty hours, but some of that has to be consulting or supervision.'

Tom narrowed his eyes. 'Can Rob prevent him from practising?'

'I guess so,' Jessica said with a shrug. 'But I think Adam would have to be doing something unethical for him to do that... you know, like taking drugs or being drunk on the job. But Rob can suggest he takes a break or counsel him if he thinks he is stressed or going off the rails.'

'Hmm. Makes sense. I wondered why Rob was with him when we had that first meeting and I saw him give Adam a look and a nudge once or twice.'

The tradies came out of Adam's office and interrupted his thought process. He turned back to Jessica.

'Can you see if we can evacuate the two of them?' he said with a nod to Rob's door.

'I'm on it,' she said and rising, tapped on the door.

Tom glanced out of the office front window as he thought. 'Good to know,' he mumbled. He suspected there was worse to come and Uncle Allan Sheffield was just warming up.

Chapter 36

Now...

Allan Sheffield enjoyed being Mrs Tatum. He'd never admit that out loud, or to anyone, but he felt great anonymity dressed as her. He enjoyed the sympathy – first Nate when Mrs Tatum called on him, looking for the son that never existed, and recently as the bereaved mother in the cemetery when the elderly couple passing offered him condolences.

He laid out all the remnants he owned on his bed. Little things that reminded him of the two boys he was once so close to. He didn't like parting with Adam's cricket bat, but he knew Adam would be excited to get it back. He looked at Dean's bathers and towel from his swimming bag. He touched the swimming goggles. Beside it was Adam's cricket cap and glove, two more school exercise pads with his name on them, and his math and English exercises inside.

Tomorrow he would visit Dean. He knew Dean would know him even if he was wearing a dress. He'd explain everything. How he wasn't meant to die, how he would have been a much better father to him and Adam than their fathers, who didn't have the time of day for them. Dean and

Adam would be so happy to see him. Soon they'd all live together like it was meant to be. Like he deserved.

*****

Adam heard the office numbers being punched into the pad, followed by a thump against the door that didn't open.

Nate, he thought. He'd been waiting for him to arrive. Rising he came to his office door to greet him and watched the charade of Nate trying to enter as he tried again. Jessica paused with the watering can and pressed the button under her desk to let him in. He barged in, swearing under his breath.

'Stupid door.'

'Morning, happy,' she said.

'Some idiot is parked in my parking spot. I bloody hate that,' he said, then calmed down. 'Morning Jess, Adam.'

He saw the small smile on her face. 'What's so funny? That would piss you off too.'

'Sure would,' she agreed, 'especially when there are two visitor parks there for visitors.'

'Exactly!' Nate continued his rant: 'You'd think an in-your-face sign with *RESERVED* written on it and my car rego would deter someone, but no! If they're not legally blind, I'm having them towed.'

'I hate to point out the obvious,' Jessica said, continuing to water the office plants, 'but if they're legally blind, they wouldn't be driving.'

Adam nodded sympathetically. 'I hate that too,' he said and glanced at Jessica.

Nate looked at both of them. 'What's wrong with you two, shared some happy pills?' he asked and stormed into his office. Adam and Jessica exchanged a smile and waited. Moments later he reappeared in the doorway dangling some keys in his hand.

'Either of you lose your keys? They were on my desk.'

'I think they fit the car some *idiot* parked in your spot,' Adam said with a sly smile.

Nate stared at him for a moment before realisation hit. He looked at the keyring and the Audi symbol and frowned.

'No?' he said, looking from Adam to Jessica. 'No way.'

'Yeah. Happy birthday from Mum. Paid-up rego and insurance papers are in the glove box. She couldn't get it in pink.'

Nate laughed and shook his head in astonishment. 'Nah, I can't accept this.'

'Of course you can,' Adam said. 'All the years you kept me out of her hair, I'm surprised she didn't pay your pocket money during that time. But I can have it towed,' Adam suggested.

'No way. C'mon,' he said and bolted out the door.

Adam grinned and looked at Jessica.

'You've got two hours free,' she said, and he raced into his office, grabbed his phone and followed his best friend to the carpark.

Arriving, he slid into the passenger seat of the navy-blue Audi, closed the door and inhaled the new car smell of the cream leather and pristine interior. Beside him, Nate sat looking at the dash as the car was idling. Nate pressed a few buttons and adjusted his seat.

'It's amazing,' Nate said. He turned to look into the back seat and touched the leather interior of his new Audi sedan. He inhaled the crisp smell and returned to the front, running his hand over the steering wheel. 'Amazing.'

'Can we drive?' Adam asked, and Nate gave him a smirk. He reversed, snapped it into drive, and smiled at its purr. They pulled out of the car park.

'Where do you want to go?' Nate asked, getting a feel for it.

'Let's go past St Nicholas's Cemetery. No one will recognise your car and you can give it a go on the back road,' Adam suggested.

'Brilliant!'

Adam laughed at Nate's expression – Nate couldn't wipe the smile off his face. They drove in silence while Nate adjusted to his new ride. 'I can't accept it.'

'You're accepting it. It's just money.'

'Nah, it's crazy. You didn't tell Winsome that I wanted the new Audi from her, did you?' he glanced at his best friend, concern etched on his face.

'No, of course not,' Adam said, truthfully. 'She asked would you like a Mercedes too for your thirtieth after she gave me mine. So I said, sure, you'd love one. But I suggested the Audi.'

Nate shook his head again. 'Unbelievable. I've never had a new car. Brand new. It's too much.'

'It's all good. Let me put it into perspective for you,' Adam said. 'The contract Mum just signed for the new *Winsome* perfume was $2.8 million. That doesn't include a percentage of future sales. Then there's the book contract advance on the thirtieth anniversary of the affair, the wedding rights sold to some magazine, her investments that Dad set up, she's the face of some beauty product that she earns a living from, yaddah, yaddah, yaddah. Thirty is a significant birthday and you've earned it.'

Nate exhaled and grinned. 'I guess I have put up with you for a long time.'

Adam smiled and shook his head.

'I'll ring and thank her later. Can't believe it.' He laughed at the thought. He glanced in the back seat again. 'I'll have to get Matilda's booster seat put in. Sell the SUV.'

'Yeah, you're all grown up,' Adam ribbed him.

They turned off to the street that ran alongside the St Nicholas' Cemetery.

'Ready?' Nate asked, preparing to put his foot down and test her speed.

'Pull over, quick, behind those trees,' Adam ordered, and sat bolt upright in his seat, his hand grabbing the dashboard in front of him.

'What?' Nate asked, alarmed. He looked around and pulled the car behind three enormous gum trees.

'Christ,' Adam said. His eyes were wide and his breath hissed through his teeth.

There was an older couple in the cemetery's corner, gardening.

'Probably friends of the cemetery,' Nate said, 'what's the big deal?'

'No, there!' Adam pointed to a figure moving out of the shadow of the angel statue with no wings.

Walking through the graves was Mrs Tatum holding a bunch of flowers. She walked with the ungainly gait of a man dressed as a woman. She had a tanned handbag over her arm and wore red lipstick, her wig of shoulder-length brown hair was brushed neatly in place. They watched as the older couple greeted her.

Adam ran a hand over his mouth, his breathing increased.

'It's okay, stay in the now,' Nate said, reading his reaction. 'You're not a kid anymore.' Nate continued in a low calm voice. 'We're going to watch where he goes. There are other people around, so today we're just going to watch where he puts the flowers.'

Adam exhaled and breathed in sharply again.

'Are you okay?'

Adam nodded, his breathing coming fast. He wasn't afraid of Allan Sheffield; only days before he had run after him at work. It was knowing Dean was his age, that Dean wouldn't be in the hole covered with dirt if Tom hadn't stopped them that day. It would be him that Allan Sheffield was visiting. He could feel the dirt on his chest, in his mouth and nose.

Adam had to get out. He pushed open the car door, stumbling out, and leaned over, panting. He heard Nate swear and follow him out, trying not to attract attention their way. Nate's hand rested on his shoulder.

'We'll call Burnsy, get him here.'

'Sheffield hasn't committed a crime,' Adam said between pants.

'He's going to the grave of Dean Beals,' Nate said.

'He's done his time for that.'

They watched as Mrs Tatum lay the flowers on the earth.

'Can you get back in the car, in case we have to get out of here fast?' Nate asked, studying him. Adam straightened, took a huge breath, and got back in. He closed the door quietly; Nate got back in the driver's seat and did the same. All three people in the cemetery were far enough away on the other side not to hear Nate and Adam's car doors closing.

The pair sat watching. Adam could feel Nate studying him.

'I'm okay, don't worry.'

'Uh-huh. You look grey.'

'I think he's at the grave with the little trophy,' Adam said getting his bearings from seeing it last night.

'Yeah, I think you're right. And, I'd say we've just found where Dean Beals was buried.'

'We can give him back to his family,' Adam agreed.

'We can do more than that,' Nate added. 'We can either follow Sheffield home and find out which hole he's living in these days. Then, we're on the front foot—'

'Or?' Adam asked.

'Call Burnsy, wait here and have them find him at Dean Beal's grave.'

'What if it's not Dean's grave?' Adam asked. 'What if it's some friend or family member he's visiting?'

'So, what are you suggesting we do?' Nate asked, impatient for action.

'We tell Burnsy about the grave later, when Sheffield's not here in case we're wrong. And we leave now.'

'Why?' Nate snapped to look at Adam. 'We should follow him.'

Adam frowned and turned to Nate. 'If there's any chance Sheffield sees us or even suspects we're onto him, he could have that body removed and buried somewhere else before we know it.'

Nate grunted an unhappy agreement.

'We've got nothing to gain from following him home,' Adam continued. 'He's done nothing wrong, yet.'

'Except stalk you. He's dropped off your cricket bat, entered your house to leave the school book and dropped into work. But, yeah,' Nate agreed, 'it'd be a rap over the knuckles.'

'He freaks me out. He's lucid enough to want to play this cat-and-mouse game with us, but yet from what Dan told us, he's also delusional and takes a strange pride in us.'

Nate grabbed his phone and tapped out a message, sending it.

'Who are you messaging?' Adam asked.

'Just giving Tom a heads-up.'

Adam knew better. He was pretty sure Nate had just asked Danielle to get here now and follow Sheffield home.

With a frustrated glance back at the 'woman' kneeling at the grave, Nate started the car and backed away out of the sight line of the cemetery before turning and departing.

'Ring Burnsy and tell him,' Nate said and listened in as Adam made the call.

They left the body behind, for now.

Chapter 37

Then...

'That's a very impressive trophy,' Uncle Allan said, with a glance towards Dean in the passenger seat of his limousine.

'I couldn't believe it,' Dean gushed, gripping the trophy between his legs as if it might disappear. He beamed over at Uncle Allan. 'I thought I was doing okay, but I wasn't in the lead, not until the turn.'

'You were right on the lead's tale, though at the end of that first lap,' Uncle Allan said, showing he had been watching attentively. 'Your turn was better than his.'

'Was it? I've been working on my turns.'

'You deserve success when you are so dedicated to it, Dean,' Uncle Allan said. 'It's a shame your dad missed it.'

'Yeah.' Dean held up the trophy and looked at it again, his smile fading as he thought of his father. He pushed his hand through his blonde hair. Allan carefully studied the boy between glances while driving. He looked so much like his father. He hoped his son would take after him.

'Thanks for coming, Uncle Allan,' Dean said sincerely.

'I wouldn't have missed it for the world, Son. I would have fought wild beast and dragons to get here.'

Dean laughed. He felt important. 'I'm going to keep this trophy forever.'

'You should. You're the champion,' Uncle Allan said.

Uncle Allan kept the trophy for over twenty years.

*****

Now...

The security guard at the Correctional Centre unscrewed the seal on the top of the large four-litre container of water and sniffed.

'I promise, it's just salt water,' Danielle said. She stood tall in her high-heeled boots, fitted black jeans and black tank top, daring him to find it otherwise.

He gave her a look that said he was not convinced, put his fingers into the water, wet them, and sniffed before licking.

'Salt water,' he said, and frowned.

Danielle smirked. 'Yep. Salt water.'

'Why?' he asked, screwing the lid back on.

'One of the prisoners, Doug Gill, really helped me out with a case I'm researching,' she said with a casual shrug. 'He said he missed going to the beach and swimming in salt water. So, I brought him some. Unless he's allowed a day pass?'

The guard laughed.

'Yeah, didn't think so. It's not enough to swim in, but he can pour it over himself in the shower or fill a sink and splash it on.'

The security guard smiled. 'Yep, I've seen it all now.'

Danielle laughed. 'Is Steve Faulkner in?' she asked after her friend.

'You just missed him. He was on the early shift,' the guard said. 'So do you want to give this to Doug Gill yourself?'

'No, thanks,' she said and grabbing a black marker from her handbag, wrote on the side: "*Saltwater. Thanks, Danielle x*"

'I'll see he gets it,' the guard said.

'Thank you,' Danielle said and gave him her most appreciative smile. She turned and strode out with her best walk on-show. It doesn't hurt to keep everyone happy, she reasoned.

Chapter 38

Now...

Jessica was so shocked she nearly didn't respond to the office door buzzer. Jack Bernham – singing star, legend, and Adam's godfather – buzzed again, which jolted her into action. She cleared her throat.

'*Delaney and Murphy,* may I help you?' she said, watching him in the intercom the whole time.

'Hi there, I was looking for Adam if he's in please, or Nate? It's Jack Bernham.'

'Please come up to the second floor,' she said and buzzed him in.

Oh my God, Jack Bernham! She grabbed her handbag beside her and the make-up kit within and then gave up. She wouldn't have time to touch up before he arrived at the office door.

Jessica straightened her dress, sucked everything in and pushed out what should be pushed out, and went to the door just as he arrived.

'Hello, I'm Jessica Johnson, office manager. Come in please,' she said, managing to speak without stumbling.

Jack entered and offered his hand. 'Jack Bernham, good to meet you.'

'Oh, I know who you are,' she assured him. 'Mum and I went to your last two concerts,' Jessica gushed.

'Did you? Well, thank you for that,' he smiled.

'You were so great.'

Jack laughed. Even in his fifties, he was gorgeous, she thought, even more so than some of the earlier and younger photos of him in the bad fashion of the time with the bad haircuts. Now he was suave, slim, and his voice was low and sexy. He wore a dark suit, crisp white shirt and no tie, and looked like the poster guy for mature men.

She remembered herself. 'Adam and Nate will be back any minute. Can you wait? Can I make you a cup of tea?'

'Yes, to both, thank you, but any chance of a coffee instead?' Jack answered. He was no stranger to gushing women.

'Absolutely. Take a seat if you like,' she said, but was pleased he didn't. Jack leaned over her desk and talked with her as she made coffee in the kitchen behind the reception area.

'Well, Jessica Johnson, office manager, you've got your work cut out for you managing those two,' he said, taking in the intimate office surrounds.

'Tell me about it,' she said, thrilled Jack remembered her name and title. 'Adam's easy enough, although he takes on too much and cuts it fine for his appointment times. Nate, well he's all over the shop.'

Jack grinned. 'You sound like you know them well.'

'I've known Nate for years, we used to work together when he was in the police service, I was in police admin. I'm new to Adam and his ways,' she said.

'How is he?' Jack asked, with genuine sincerity.

Jessica gave a small smile. 'I'd say he was happy in love, happy here at work with Nate, but looks like he could sleep a little more and have a good meal.'

Jack nodded, taking in her words. She placed the coffee on the reception table and he thanked her.

'So Adam wasn't expecting you? Does he know you are in town?' Jessica asked.

'No, I thought I'd surprise him. I've got a couple of meetings with management and the concert venue people... I'm going to do a few concerts before the wedding since we're in town anyway,' he said casually.

'Oh wow, how fantastic.'

'Don't buy a ticket if you're inclined. I'll organise you some,' he offered.

'Yes please, that would be great, thank you. Did Winsome come with you?'

'No, I'm only here for two nights. It would take her two days to pack,' he said and gave Jessica a wink before taking a sip of his coffee.

Jessica laughed. 'They're here now,' she said, seeing Nate and Adam drive into the garage on the CCTV camera.

'Ah, I'll surprise him if he hasn't got any skeletons or clients hiding in his office?' Jack asked.

'No, all safe,' she assured him.

The phone rang and Jessica indicated which one was Adam's office and Jack thanked her, took his coffee and entered, closing the door. A few minutes later, the men barged in. She was still on the phone, but heard Nate say he'd wait for Burnsy. Something must have happened.

'Two o'clock tomorrow will be fine,' she said before she had a chance to talk with either of them and with a wave to her, Adam opened his office door and disappeared behind it.

*****

He wasn't expecting to find anyone in there, but regardless, Adam was on alert. He opened the door, narrowed his eyes from the glare of the windows, and entered, closing the door.

'Adam!'

He wheeled around in alarm as a male figure stepped out from behind the door.

'Jack! Christ,' he said and stumbled back with his hand over his heart. 'You're the last person I expected to see,' Adam exhaled and smiled.

Jack held up his hands in a placating manner. 'Just me, sorry. Are you alright?'

Adam straightened, hands on hips, still breathing faster than usual. 'Of course,' he moved to his godfather and embraced him.

After a few moments, Jack pulled away and, gripping Adam by the shoulders, studied him.

'You've looked better. What's going on?'

'Nothing. I'm good, I'm better than good,' he said and pulled away. 'Is Mum here?'

'Just me, a business trip for two nights.'

'Great,' Adam said and moved further away, slipping off his jacket and placing it over a chair. 'Are you staying at home?'

'If that's okay? I hear that you, Kelsey and Nate are living there.'

Adam looked surprised and Jack added: 'Tom told me. He's coordinating security for the wedding and so on.'

'Right. Yeah, we're just there temporarily, but there's plenty of room,' he teased his godfather.

Jack laughed. He was no stranger to the house. Over the years, he and Winsome had returned there as a couple many a time when in Brisbane on business. Then he sobered. 'Tom told me about Allan Sheffield being released.'

Adam nodded.

'Is that why you look like you haven't slept for a month?' Jack asked, concerned.

'No, I always look like this,' Adam said and smiled for his godfather's benefit. He glanced at the clock.

'I'm keeping you,' Jack said.

'No, never. But I've got a client in fifteen minutes. I just need to read over our last meeting notes. How about dinner tonight, at the house?'

'Great,' Jack brightened. 'Invite your group. I look forward to meeting Kelsey at last – the girl who has stolen my godson's heart,' he teased, 'and catching up with Nate again. Is Nate seeing anyone?'

'Not yet, but I'm hoping,' Adam said with a nod to Jessica outside the door.

'Good, invite Jessica too if you like, the more the merrier.' He moved closer to Adam again. 'It's good to see you, Son.' Jack had always called him that, being his godfather and his closest male relative once James passed away.

'Thanks, Jack. It's good to see you too.'

'Soon you'll officially be my stepson. I'll be able to send you to your room.'

Adam laughed. 'Yeah, give that a try. I might even enjoy it.'

He pulled Adam in for a hug again, finishing up with a slap on the back. 'Tomorrow night though, if you're free, just you and me, a drink or dinner before I go home. Yeah?'

Adam nodded. 'For sure. Need a car?'

Jack pulled some keys out of his pocket. 'Hired one. See you tonight.'

Chapter 39

Now…

The office was busy, which happened when Adam, Rob and Nate were all in attendance. Adam had a client in the office – hungry girl – and Danielle had dropped in with a report for Nate, and was in his office. Add to that, the phone was going off. Tom Hartigan arrived, punched the code in, entered and with a wave to Jessica, who was on another call, entered Nate's office. Moments later, she buzzed in Burnsy – Sergeant Matt Burns – who also went straight into Nate's office. The three men and Danielle appeared moments later as Jessica hung up.

'I'll be gone for a few hours,' Nate said. He moved closer to Jessica's desk and lowered his voice: 'Try not to mention to Adam that we were all here,' he asked of her with a glance at Adam's door.

'Sure,' she said confused and gave them a wave, noting Burnsy's gaze lingered on her longer than normal as he was the last to leave. *What the hell was going on?*

Adam's door opened at the same time and he walked his

patient out. She apologised for something and he told her he understood, it was her choice. But Jessica could tell he didn't understand. He'd about had a gutful by the look of his body language, and she was getting better at reading Adam these past few months of working together.

He turned to her after the patient had left. 'Was that Burnsy?'

Jessica hesitated, so much for not telling. 'Yes.'

'Was he with Tom and Nate?'

'And Dan,' Jessica added.

'Right,' Adam said, his jaw locking.

Rob's office door opened and he stepped out. 'Central station here this afternoon,' he said.

'It's crazy,' Jessica said. 'What's going on… with Nate, Burnsy and Tom? Why are they here?' She looked from Adam to Rob and back to Adam.

Adam cleared his throat. 'We think we found Dean Beals's body.'

Jessica gasped. 'So, why aren't you—'

Adam cut her off, knowing what she was asking. 'Because Nate, for some reason, thinks I'll freak out when they dig the body up.'

'Oh,' Jessica said and glanced at Rob.

'Right, I've got notes to write up,' Adam said and went back to his office, closing the door.

'Is he freaking out?' she asked Rob.

'No. But it's pretty close to home for him,' Rob said. He turned to look in the direction of Adam's office, and then followed, knocking and entering straight away.

The phone rang and Jessica sighed. 'Crazy all-round,' she muttered.

*****

Rob closed the door behind him. Adam sat, feet on the corner of his desk, staring at the window.

'Just thought you might want to talk if you're not in the middle of writing notes,' he said with a smile, and sat down in front of Adam's desk. 'How are you?'

Adam turned to him. His eyes were dark from lack of sleep. He looked thinner than usual.

'Good. How are you?'

Rob gave him a frustrated expression. 'You know what I'm asking. This is opening a lot of old wounds for you.'

'No, it's ancient history, dealt with, gone,' Adam said with a wave of his hand, dismissing his supervisor's comments.

Rob waited, saying nothing. They were both masters of silence and comfortable in it, so neither of them spoke for some time.

Then Adam dropped his feet off the table and swung around in his chair to face Rob. 'It's not that, it's not about Uncle Allan or Dean Beals or Mrs Tatum,' he said. 'She turned down the course – her anorexia struggle has got to the point of no return. I can't help her; she will die and I can't even talk her into taking this course. I told her I would have to refer her elsewhere, maybe a female psychologist can help her get there. I can't help her anymore.'

Adam exhaled, his thin cheeks puffing out a long breath, and he sat back in his seat, staring at the window.

'You did your best, that's all we can do. Guide and hope for the best,' Rob said. 'But you've had challenges like this before, Adam.'

Adam conceded with a small nod.

'You know what I think?' Rob asked.

'What?' Adam knew he might as well ask; he was going to hear it anyway.

'Your client can't admit she needs to do this course, and you can't admit the ghosts of the past are affecting you. You're both in denial.'

Adam narrowed his eyes. 'Did Nate tell you about... the cemetery?' He refrained from mentioning the panic attack in case Nate had not told Rob about it.

'He might have said, only because he was worried about you, that you were... a bit unhinged.'

Adam stood, angry, and paced to the window. 'Unhinged? For fuck's sake.'

'You're not?' Rob asked.

Adam folded his arms across his chest and ran a tongue over his lower lip as he thought. A few minutes later, he returned to his seat and turned his attention to Rob.

'I'm just not sure that what I do has value anymore. Have you ever felt like that?'

'Hell yeah,' Rob said.

'It's bullshit,' Adam continued. 'All this help crap... who is it helping? I don't know... I want to throw it in.'

'Right, and do what?' Rob asked calmy, knowing better than to react.

'I'll go model,' Adam said and laughed at the thought.

'You're not okay...'

Adam rubbed a hand across his mouth.

'You need to step away for a moment until we sort all this out.'

'Sort what out?' Adam asked. 'Living at Mum's place because there's a stalker out there who has legally done nothing wrong yet and could taunt me for years? Dealing with the kid whose body is about to be dug up that should be mine? Putting up with Tom running around organising security crap for a wedding that's going to be a circus, not to mention the patient who won't get out of her way to help herself?'

Rob continued as if he hadn't been interrupted. 'Have a week or two off… go away with Kelsey or…'

'I've got appointments.'

'If they can't be rescheduled, I'll take over your clients. Part-time retirement can go on hold for a few weeks.'

Adam shook his head. 'No.' He placed his hands on the desk in front of him. 'No. You've just caught me frustrated after the last session. I'm in control.'

Rob studied him. 'Okay. But we're going to talk every day for a while.'

Adam grimaced.

'Every day. Not negotiable.'

Adam gave a curt nod and rose.

'So where are you going now?' Rob asked.

'St Nicholas's cemetery to catch up with Nate.'

Chapter 40

Now...

Audrey heard it on the news before her grandson, Adam, or security detail, Tom, had the chance to tell her. It was all over the media. The police had exhumed the body of a young boy at St Nicholas's Cemetery, believed to be that of kidnapped victim, 10-year-old Dean Beals. The man charged with his murder had been seen in disguise, visiting the site. On his arrival home in the late afternoon, Audrey was at Adam's side before he had even exited the car, Jack – who had arrived earlier – alongside her.

'Darling, they haven't associated the boy's remains with you, have they?' she asked, shocked.

Adam shook his head. 'No. I was there, but as soon as we saw it was the remains of a young boy, I got out of there. Nate did the interviews with the media... told them about Mrs Tatum, the ex-prisoner Allan Sheffield, looking for her son and the game she played.'

'They'll make the connection for sure,' Jack said, leaning up against Adam's car.

'I don't know that they will,' Adam said. 'Dad kept it out

206

of the media all those years ago. No one ever knew that Sheffield had picked me up before Dean.'

'That's true,' Audrey confirmed. 'James told the police, but in the strictest of confidence. A miracle it didn't make the papers.'

'You can say that again. What happens now?' Jack asked.

'We've got friends coming for a BBQ around the pool,' Adam said, and smiled. 'Audrey, you have to join us.'

She clapped her hands. 'Delightful. I'd love to. See Jack, your visit is good for us all.'

'I do my best, Audrey,' he said with a laugh, placing an arm around her.

The three walked to the house together.

'What a shame Winsome isn't here,' Jack said, looking at his godson and Audrey, happy in their company.

'Yeah,' Adam said, Audrey did not respond.

'But back to my former question, what does happen now, Son?' Jack asked before they entered, knowing Kelsey was in the house and not knowing how much, if anything, she knew.

'Nothing happens. Sheffield's done the time for the crime,' Adam said. 'It's just fortunate that Dean's body has been found so now his family can reclaim him.'

'But the visit to your office, the cricket bat... is that just supposed to be his idea of fun or is he dangerous? You're a psychologist, what do you think?' Jack asked.

'We're keeping Tom on,' Audrey said before Adam could respond. 'Not just for the wedding but after if needed. Until we know what this man is playing at.'

'I agree,' Jack said.

Adam nodded. 'I don't know yet what Allan Sheffield intends to do or why he is doing this. He might just be attention-seeking, or he might be angry because he got caught all those years ago, and this is revenge. It'll play out.'

'That's what I'm worried about,' Audrey said.

*****

Adam raced up the stairs and Kelsey smiled as he entered the kitchen. She wore an apron, her hair was tied up in a high ponytail, and several salads sat on the counter, sealed and ready to serve. Beside her was a bowl of whipped cream and cut up strawberries.

'Domestic bliss.' She grinned and leaned up to kiss him.

'This looks great, thanks for doing the prep,' Adam said winding an arm around her. He wanted to say more – how glad he was to come home to her, how she made his day – but it didn't come easy, so instead he kissed her and held her close enjoying her excitement at tonight's gathering with people they were comfortable with.

'Jack did the desserts. There's a lemon meringue tart in the fridge and he's dressing the pavlova,' she said with a nod to the strawberries. Jack entered as she spoke.

'Get out of here,' Adam said, and grinned. 'I wouldn't have picked you for a dessert chef.'

'Son, there is no end to my talents, I'm surprised *Masterchef* hasn't called me to be a judge,' he joked. 'You should see what I can do with a steak on the BBQ.'

'Ooh, you'll need to fight Nate for the BBQ tongs. He thinks he's the BBQ king,' Kelsey said. 'Although, technically, this is your domain.'

Jack held up his hands. 'No, I'm a guest tonight and happy to be so.'

Adam was still holding Kelsey tight and she looked at

him, studying him. When Jack went to change, she turned to face him.

'Don't ask,' he said, putting his chin on the top of her head and hugging her.

'I understand,' she said and held him tighter. Kelsey was no stranger to running from the past. 'We're a fine pair.'

He chuckled. 'A perfect fit.'

They heard running up the stairs and Nate appeared.

'Let the BBQ begin!' he exclaimed with a smile. 'As soon as I get changed,' he said heading to the rooms that had been assigned to him and he disappeared down the hallway.

Chapter 41

Now...

Jack took the phone call away from the group on the pretence he couldn't hear over the noisy guests. He moved towards the tennis court, watching as the group mingled, enjoying the mixture of young and mature, the self-deprecating humour between old friends. He loved seeing his godson with a network around him. Casual in jeans, white runners and a white T-shirt, he thought Adam almost looked relaxed, except for the air of vigilance about him.

Jack glanced at the name on the screen and answered.

'My love, how are you?' he asked, his voice softening. For as long as he could remember, he had been in love with Winsome Keeley. He would have married her in a heartbeat but she accepted James's hand instead, and so he remained a friend of both of them – so close the pair had made him godson to their only child, Adam. But he had bided his time; now they were a couple, soon to be wed.

They spoke of their day and then Winsome asked: 'What's Kelsey like?'

'Lovely. She's attractive, clever, gentle, and good for him. They look good together… a fit,' Jack said with a glance to Kelsey. 'Quite the opposite to Stephanie in personality.'

'I'll never know what went wrong with those two,' Winsome sighed, her voice soft and girlish. It made him miss her more. 'Do you think I should involve Kesley in the wedding party somehow, for Adam's sake?'

'No! I definitely wouldn't. I don't think she would be comfortable with that at all. She's quite reserved, like him. Best you leave them to arrive and sit together.'

'And how is Adam?' she asked.

'He's fine. His new office with Nate is great, and he has a good network of friends around him. One of them here tonight is a cop. I'd be lying if I didn't tell you he looks a little stressed out with the whole Allan Sheffield thing.'

'Will he look okay for photos?'

Jack resisted a chuckle. Winsome was always thinking of the front page. He assured her: 'Adam's just a little gaunt, otherwise, still a striking looking young man. To be honest, when he walked into his office, he looked so much like James that it floored me for a moment. I thought it was him.'

'That what Audrey says too. She also says it's the wedding and all the hoo-ha that is stressing him out,' Winsome said. 'She can't seriously think that we'll all never move on from darling James.'

'Don't stress about that, Darling.' Jack told her what she wanted to hear. He watched James do it for years and knew how to meet her needs. 'Adam hasn't mentioned the wedding, so I doubt he is too worried about it.'

'Good. One photo the magazine wants is a family shot; I'll need to talk him around,' she said. 'Hopefully, the gift to Nate has softened him.'

'Nate loves that car,' Jack said and chuckled. 'You've never seen a car so clean and polished.'

'Boys and their toys,' Winsome teased. She changed the subject. 'I spoke with Tom earlier. He said the security plan is all in place, but he's getting a frosty atmosphere from Adam.'

'Tom and Adam will never be best friends, but that's not a bad thing. A bit of professional distance might serve them better.'

He talked for a minute more about the concerts before hanging up and returning to the group.

'Your mum sends her best,' he told Adam.

'Did she ask if I would do any photoshoots for the wedding?' Adam asked, his eyes narrowing with suspicion.

Jack laughed. 'Only once and only one shoot.'

'How exciting,' Jessica said and then, seeing Adam's expression, changed her mind. 'Or not, of course.'

The irony was not lost on the group that Adam's entire childhood had been chronicled and staged managed, always ensuring his mother's best angle in the photos. It continued now in his thirtieth year.

Jack noticed Kelsey looked at Adam, and he gave her a subtle shake of his head in the negative. Jack wondered what she had to fear from all the publicity. Then Danielle said what Jack was thinking.

She turned to Nate. 'Are you sure you two weren't swapped at birth? Nate would happily do that shoot for Winsome, I'm sure of it, he's such a ham,' Danielle teased.

'I wouldn't just do any shoot,' Nate said, correcting her. 'Maybe Mr January in the *Private Eye Calendar*.'

Adam laughed. 'Only January? You're selling yourself short.'

'I'd buy that calendar,' Jessica said. 'I need a laugh during the workday.'

Nate gave her a well-earned smirk. 'I can't do it though,' he sighed dramatically. 'I need to have some anonymity for my work, so being a star just won't work if I'm mobbed everywhere. Jack understands.'

Jack chuckled. 'So true. It can be tricky just wandering down to grab a latte. Even worse if they think you are someone else!'

'Speaking of being mobbed,' Jessica said, still in awe of Jack, 'can I have a photo with you please, Jack?'

'Absolutely.' He rose and Jessica gave her phone to Nate to snap the shot.

'Want one with me too?' Nate asked her.

'Could be handy for the *Most Wanted* list,' she deadpanned.

'The real question we are avoiding is if Winsome wants Adam to do a photoshoot, is he model material?' Nate ribbed his friend. 'Do chicks like the dark, brooding type?'

Kelsey laughed as Adam gave his best friend a disbelieving look. She grabbed his chin and kissed him.

'Of course they do,' Adam said as if that were proof. 'This face could launch a thousand ships.'

'The *Titanic* has already sunk,' Burnsy reminded him. 'I think they like the rugged, thinning hair types,' he said running a hand over his hair and making the group laugh.

Jessica ignored them as she looked at the photo of herself and Jack.

'Some like the mature type too,' Jack added with a grin seeing her studying it, she laughed and showed it to Kelsey.

Adam looked over her shoulder. He abruptly grabbed the phone from Jessica's hand and hit the photo to full screen. Stretching the image, he stood and looked to the side gate.

'He's here.'

'Who?' Nate asked, not catching on.

'Sheffield.' Adam issued orders. 'Dan, stay with the girls. Jack, call Tom and get him here now.' He took off running toward the boundary.

'What the hell?' Nate rose and ran after him. Burnsy followed.

Jack called Tom and beckoned for Jessica's phone. She showed him the photo. In the background on her side of the photo was a lady. The shot was clear enough to see the dark wig and the dark dress, but definitely a woman. Mrs Tatum was looking through the fence.

*****

'This has got to stop,' Tom said, an hour after sweeping the grounds. Kelsey and Audrey had called it a night once they were sure they were safe on the premises. Burnsy had walked Jessica to her car, checked inside it and saw her off. Danielle remained.

'He's long gone,' Adam said with a shrug. 'He's made his point, again, he's still got some control.'

Burnsy shook his head. 'You need to apply for a restraining order to keep him away from yourself, your girlfriend, Audrey and Nate too. Come down to the station tomorrow and I'll see to it.'

Adam thanked him and accepted another beer from Nate as the remaining group sat around the outdoor table.

Jack turned to Tom. 'What do you suggest we do, Tom? Other than taking out a restraining order, how do we protect everyone here?'

Tom's eyes narrowed with frustration. 'Our hands are tied. If he breaks the restraining order, we can have him arrested, but again that's a short-term solution.'

'We need to understand why he's doing this,' Adam said getting back to the matter of Allan Sheffield's mind.

'I agree,' Nate said. 'Is it a game or is he just crazy?'

'I don't think he's going away anytime soon,' Danielle said and gulped her diet coke.

'What makes you say that?' Tom asked.

'When I was talking to Sheffield's prison flatmate, Doug Gill, he said that Sheffield spoke about Dean and Adam like he was their uncle, like he loved him. Doug said Sheffield was proud of the boys.'

Nate frowned. 'So, you think Uncle Allan wants to resume his relationship with Adam... that's he's lost the plot and seriously thinks he's family?'

Danielle nodded. 'Doug called him loopy. He told me that Sheffield said the kids should have been his, and their parents didn't deserve them.'

Adam's jaw locked, not keen on having his relationship with his parents scrutinised by the group.

'What else?' Nate moved the conversation along.

'He said he should have done it right the first time,' Danielle said.

Everyone talked at once with their analysis of Sheffield's words, and then Adam interrupted. 'Back up everyone, Dan's just told us what we need to hear.'

They all looked at him.

Adam continued. 'He thinks he should have done it right the first time... he is still visiting me and Dean. He's stuck somewhere between there and now. We need to re-enact the scene, push him over the edge and get him into a specialist mental health unit before he chooses some more nephews.'

'No way,' Tom said. 'If you think you're getting back in the car with him, you're the crazy one.'

Adam smiled at him. 'You saved me once before, Tom. You can do it again, can't you?'

Red rag to a bull.

Chapter 42

Now…

Tom Hartigan was not happy. He sat in the boardroom at *Delaney and Murphy* with the private eye and security team of Nate and Danielle, and the two psychologists – Adam and Rob, to discuss Uncle Allan, Mrs Tatum and Allan Sheffield – one and the same. The door remained open and outside at her desk, Jessica worked and listened in.

'The idea's crazy,' Tom said again, and sat back with a shake of his head, crossing his arms, which were notably muscle-defined in his black polo shirt.

'Hold up,' Nate said. 'Let's try to work out why Sheffield is doing this and then we can work out if Adam catching up with Uncle Allan is the best way forward.' Nate's police negotiation techniques were coming to the fore.

'So, profile him for us,' Danielle said, sipping her coffee and keen to hear more about Uncle Allan.

Adam looked at Rob to explain.

'Bear in mind we haven't clinically met with Sheffield, so we're "typecasting" for want of a better word… it's just a profile,' Rob said.

'Good enough,' Tom said.

Rob continued. 'Well, different things motivate different kidnappers. For example, some have a sexual need and fantasy script that makes them behave in a certain way. But that's not the case here because Allan Sheffield never touched Dean and Adam. Sheffield's motives were financially and emotionally driven.'

Adam added: 'But we know from what Doug Gill told Dan about his jail flatmate, Sheffield feels unjustly done by. He has a victim mentality. He believes it should have been him who fathered Dean and me. It would be safe to say that Uncle Allan was, and most likely still is, totally focussed on his needs to the extent that kidnapping and killing Dean to get ahead himself is perfectly acceptable. There's no remorse, no consideration for the pain he has put the family through – everything in the world revolves around him and his needs and meeting those needs.'

Tom nodded his understanding. 'Add to that he planned and groomed you boys. He built those relations as if he were your uncle.'

'It sounds like he also started to believe his lies,' Danielle said. 'He was the uncle, the rescuer. According to Doug, his cellmate, he still does believe it.'

'And that's a personality disorder,' Rob said. 'He may not feel or understand the emotions of others, like Adam, Dean, or the parents, nor his own for that matter.'

'But he's feeling love for Adam and Dean,' Danielle said. 'He's proud of them. Doug said he used to boast about them.'

'That's the delusional part of his personality,' Rob said.

'Gee, he's got it all going on,' Nate huffed. 'He must have had some assessment or treatment in prison though, surely. Adam has a prison group. Did you ever see him in there?'

Adam shook his head. 'His name was on my list when I started taking the group, but I had to refer him to another psych. I'm not allowed to counsel him and I didn't want to.'

'I didn't know that,' Rob said, surprised.

'You're in trouble now,' Danielle said with a grin to Adam, who smiled at her before offering an apologetic look to Rob.

'It was a while back,' he said by way of excuse. 'But yeah, obviously Sheffield's psychologist thought he was sane enough to return to the community, I guess.'

'Got that wrong,' Tom said.

'Well, he probably presents as very sane,' Rob said. 'And has no problem justifying all his actions.'

'It's more sinister than just greed though. He didn't need to kill Dean Beals,' Tom said. 'Once he got the ransom, he could have let the kid go.'

'We don't know how Dean died yet,' Nate reminded him. 'Sheffield might not have meant to kill him. It will be interesting to see if they can turn up anything from the bones after twenty years.'

'Sheffield must have expected there would be a point at which Dean or Adam realised they were in trouble and fought back. That he'd have to use violence to subdue them or Dean in this case. Surely, he planned for that?' Danielle asked.

Adam shrugged. 'Maybe not. Research has shown that kidnappers or abductors, do what Sheffield did – invent a relationship with their victim, convince them they are family, even believe that their victims want to be there – which Dean and I did initially when we didn't sense any danger. These types often make their victims believe they are being held for their own safety or it is for the best.'

'That's when the Stockholm syndrome kicks in?' Nate asked.

'Sometimes,' Rob agreed. 'When the victims feel empathy or develop a relationship, a complicated one, with their abductor.'

Tom sat forward. 'So, what is Allan Sheffield thinking and doing now based on what's going on up here?' he said and tapped his head.

Adam thought for a moment. 'Twenty years ago he had a plan. He selected two victims, and it failed. From what Dan found out from Doug Gill, and given Sheffield's current actions, I think he's delusional and believes he has to complete it.'

Adam looked to Rob who concurred. 'Once he's fixed it, he believes all will be well in his world again. But it's not fixable, so it has to come to a head.'

Tom took in a deep breath and shook his head. 'You plan to meet up with Uncle Allan and do what? Let him try to kill you so he can be jailed again? Or just prove he's crazy and have him committed?'

'Yeah, the latter preferably,' Adam said with a smirk, and Tom huffed again.

'I have a specialist mental health unit in mind,' Rob said, 'they'll accept him as an involuntary inpatient.'

'Can they hold him permanently?' Tom asked.

Rob grimaced. 'That's not so easy to manage, but he'll be assessed regularly.'

'He apparently "assesses well" given he's out on the street now,' Nate said, unimpressed.

Adam leaned over and called out to Jessica, asking if she was free. She entered.

'Can you do something for me, something creative?' Adam asked.

'Of course, what?' she asked.

'One minute,' Adam said, rose and departed to his office.

'See, there it is again,' Nate frowned. 'You never say "of course" when I ask you for help.'

She rolled her eyes. 'Because you need a personal assistant around the clock. You can't even get in the front door yet.'

The group laughed, relieved for a break in the tension that existed when Adam and Tom were in the same room.

Adam returned with a school writing pad. The front had his name on it written in his childhood handwriting – *Adam Murphy, English, Year 5, St Joseph's School.*

'How cute,' Nate said, giving him a smirk. 'You've kept this all these years, very sentimental.'

'My best work yet,' Adam joked with Nate. 'But no, I haven't kept last week's notes, let alone this.' Then he saw Tom's expression.

'Don't tell me this is another one?' Tom's jaw locked. 'When the fuck did you get this?'

Adam exhaled. 'Sheffield left it at home in the letterbox, after the cricket bat and the other exercise pad appeared.'

Tom shook his head. 'For the love of God. And you didn't think to mention it?'

'You were moving me out to Mum's place anyway. What difference would it make?'

'Could you just work with me?' he demanded angrily, and the room stilled, waiting for Adam's reaction.

'Sure,' he said, looking intensely at Tom, and everyone breathed again.

Rob leaned over slightly to get Adam's attention. 'In light of Sheffield being on your prison counselling list, if you could work with me too, that would be appreciated,' he said with a half-smile.

'Right,' Adam said, and turned to Nate. 'Nothing from you?'

Nate shook his head. 'Pretty sure we're already working together, given the sign on the door,' he said and gave his best friend a supportive smile.

Adam gave him a small chin-up movement of thanks. He turned to Jessica. 'Using my kid-like handwriting style, can you write a letter for me?'

'Sure. As long as it is short, you haven't got the whole alphabet here.'

Adam turned to Rob. 'What do you think? Something like "Dear Uncle Allan, see you at cricket on Friday?" or whatever day works for Tom,' he said with a wry look in Tom's direction.

'That would do the trick,' Rob said. 'How will you deliver it?'

'We'll put it in his letterbox. Nate knows where he's staying,' Adam said with a glance at his best friend.

Nate snapped to look at Adam, his eyes widened in surprise.

Adam continued. 'I know you had Sheffield followed from the cemetery when I suggested not to.' Adam looked at Danielle, and she looked sheepish. 'You were right,' Adam said, 'we should have followed him.'

Nate nodded. 'Sorry, I just wanted to keep you as removed as possible. It was a lot for you to take in.'

'I get it,' Adam said.

'I'll create the letter now,' Jessica said, and took Adam's exercise pad with her back to her desk.

'That it?' Adam said, rising to depart.

'I'm coming with you to meet him,' Nate told Adam. 'He'll remember me.'

'No, you can have a hit of cricket with me, but you're not coming on the ride,' Adam shut him down, the group packed up to leave, the meeting for now, over.

'He'll expect me too,' Nate protested, 'like the first time he took us home in the back of the limo.'

'And he'll know that didn't work, so he'll wait for the second time when I'm alone. Let's cut to the chase.' Adam turned to his mentor for agreement. 'Don't you think?'

'As much as I'd like you there, Nate, I think on this occasion that Adam is right.'

Adam shrugged. 'It's no big deal. I'm not a kid he can overpower. Let's just do this, I'll tell you when and where.'

'Crazy,' Tom mumbled, getting to his feet and heading straight out the door, less than impressed.

Chapter 43

Then...

Uncle Allan looked over at Adam in the passenger seat of his car. They were alone, at last. The boy looked small in the corner.

'This is not the way to my place,' Adam said, with a glance around.

'No, I took a shortcut, I know a lot of them from my line of work. I could take you on shortcuts all around town,' Uncle Allan boasted, with a glance and smile in Adam's direction. 'I was thinking... would you like to come and stay with me for a while?'

Adam's eyes widened. 'Sure, that'd be great. Like on a holiday, you mean?'

'Yeah, we could go fishing, take the boat out on the water.'

'Cool. Could Nate come?'

'If he's allowed,' Uncle Allan said. 'I know your dad hasn't got time to do that sort of stuff, but I'll always have time. There's a good air show on too.'

'Wow, I'd love to see the planes,' Adam said, smiling at his uncle. 'Do you think they'd let us sit in one, in the cockpit?'

'I think so if you know the right people,' Uncle Allan said and tapped his nose. Adam laughed.

They talked about planes for a short time; Allan impatiently kept to the speed limit.

'This is a long shortcut,' Adam said, with another glance around him. 'Hey someone left some clothes in your back seat, women's clothes,' he said innocently.

'Ah, they belong to my wife, your Aunty Millie. She leaves her stuff everywhere, you should see the bedroom,' he said and forced a laugh.

Adam grinned. 'Nate's room is a disaster. His mum says it looks like a spaceship landed in it and everything got twirled around before it took off.'

They both laughed at the image.

'And your room, is it clean?' Allan asked knowing it would be. The kid had an orderly mind and his cricket gear was well kept.

Adam nodded. 'Audrey won't give me my pocket money unless my room is clean and my shoes are shiny.'

'It means you show pride in your things,' Allan said. 'Look at my shoes.' He lifted one foot momentarily off the floor – the foot that wasn't on the pedal – and showed Adam.

'That's like a soldier's shiny shoe,' Adam said. 'Tom's are like that.'

Allan looked into the rear-view mirror; a car was advancing on him, fast.

'Do you like having that security man with you all the time?' Uncle Allan asked, as his eyes kept flicking to the mirror and the advancing car.

'Tom's okay, but I wish he didn't have to watch me get in the school gate. I'm not a little kid anymore.'

'That's right, you're not.'

Adam glanced around to see what Uncle Allan was watching in the rear-view mirror. He was too small in the seat to see the advancing car.

Allan was in no doubt now that the driver of the car was coming for him, coming to rescue Adam.

'Adam, I want you to listen very carefully now.'

The boy snapped to look at him.

'What's wrong?' he asked wide-eyed, not used to his uncle talking like his father.

'Not a thing. But listen now… no matter what Tom tells you, no matter what they say to you about me, I want you to know that I am your uncle, I am very proud of you and…'

'Wow!' Adam yelled as a car shot past them at an incredible speed. 'That's Tom's Commodore.'

Allan swerved to the edge of the road, hitting the brakes, as the car passed within a hair's breadth and stopped further up in front of them, swerving to block the road.

Adam yelled in fright as they came to within inches of hitting it. They jerked forward. Adam snapped back in his seat with the force of the seatbelt.

'Uncle Allan, it's Tom. What's he doing?' Adam asked, panicked.

'Don't be frightened,' Allan yelled as he scrambled to lock the door, his fingers fumbling as Tom was running towards them.

The door burst open with enough force to pull it from its hinges. Allan felt the strong security man's hands around his throat as Tom Hartigan pulled him out of the driver's seat and shoved him against the car. The first blow hit him.

Behind him, Allan could hear Adam screaming for Tom to stop. The blood was flowing from his nose now, his eyes were watering and he doubled in pain before being straightened and punched again.

Allan didn't know how long it went on for… it was slow and fast, over in minutes. Adam saved him when the kid took off.

The security guard called out ordering the boy to stop. Adam ignored him. Swearing, the security guard shoved Allan to the ground and took off after Adam.

Allan pulled himself off the ground and hurriedly slumped into the driver's seat of his car. He leaned over, wincing, and grabbing Adam's ajar door, slammed it shut, locked the doors, spun the car around, and left.

Adam's cricket bat and school bag were on the floor.

'Thank you, little mate,' he said to Adam in the mirror as the scene faded from sight. 'Thank you for saving your Uncle Allan.'

Chapter 44

Now...

It was just after 7.30pm when Nate joined Danielle for surveillance in a hole-in-the-wall jazz club in the West End. It was a small den, not smoky as expected since smoking was banned, but the jazz quartet in the corner had created a welcome atmosphere and the intimate crowd ranged from Bohemian to suits. Nate had spotted Danielle on entry; she wasn't hard to miss. Sexy, confident, in her customary black gear, but this time it was a dress with killer heels, her hair loose and long. He joined her and they talked about everything and nothing. They had almost finished their drinks, but as yet, their client's job was not completed.

'Since you're here, you could have just done the shift and saved yourself money not having to pay me,' Danielle said, indicating it was his shout.

'But then I'm taking money off you,' Nate said, 'and besides I might not stick around, I just had to get out of the house for a while.'

Danielle laughed. 'You're living in a mansion on the river... feeling closed in, were you?'

'Nuh, just wanted to give Adam and Kelsey some time alone. Being around couples that still like each other is exhausting. Same again?'

'Please,' she said, keeping her attention on the man in the corner who was cheating, according to his wife, and the wife wanted proof.

'I hate cheating surveillance,' she muttered as a woman walked in, saw the subject and went straight to his table. They kissed and then she sat opposite, extending her hand and the subject held it. Danielle sighed, subtly snapped a few pics on her phone while pretending to be messaging, including the one where he leaned over and kissed her. She checked the photos worked, and satisfied, put the phone away.

Nate returned with a beer and coke, pushing the coke to Danielle.

'Job done. Want something stronger now?' he said with a glance at the pair in the corner.

'Maybe when I finish this one, thanks,' she said, and they clinked glasses in a toast, took a mouthful and relaxed to enjoy the music.

After a while, Danielle cut to the chase. 'So, are you feeling sadly single?'

'Not really. Sometimes you just want to chill and have a drink somewhere different. I haven't been here for years.'

Danielle shook her head, unconvinced. 'Just ask Jessica out or I'm telling you, she'll accept Burnsy's invitation if you don't.'

Nate's eyes widened. 'He's done it? Asked Jess out?'

'Only a couple of times, but she keeps coming up with excuses. She likes him. Burnsy's a nice guy and he's got a good bod.'

Nate smirked. 'That's all you need then.'

'She likes you more, that's why she's stalling. You like her a lot. What's the problem?'

'If it doesn't work, we're supposed to keep on working together?'

'Nuh, she can work anywhere. Office management is hardly a career. Besides, you might be able to stay frenemies and keep working together.'

Nate made an unconvinced snorting sound.

'Can I be blunt?' Danielle asked.

'When are you ever not?' He chuckled.

'Your ex-wife is not sitting around moping for you.'

Nate's countenance changed. She had hit an open wound. He looked away, glaring in the band's direction.

Danielle continued. 'She's not, Nate. Whether you like it or not, she's moved on and soon there will be someone else in her life and Matilda's.'

He recoiled at the idea. 'I'll be running a police check on him before he puts a foot in my daughter's life.'

'And you should,' Danielle agreed. 'But you and Jessica have got something going on. Ask her to go to the wedding with you, then you can stall going on a normal date.'

'The wedding's two months away, you think she'll wait around until then with no action?' Nate said.

'Yeah, I do. By the time she plans her dress, talks about it non-stop with friends and organises you, the time will fly and if it goes well, then that's your first date. If not, you'll both know it and can carry on like you are. It's a brilliant plan,' she said, congratulating herself.

Nate chuckled. 'Yeah, brilliant.'

'But ask her soon, now, to secure her.'

Nate contemplated her words. 'So, you seriously think if I ask her to come with me, she'll turn down Burnsy for the next two months?'

'Yep. Trust me, it's the beginning, and she knows it.'

He pursed his lips while he thought. 'I'll give it some serious thought.'

'Just do it.'

'What about you?' Nate asked. 'You've given up on Adam, I'm guessing?'

Danielle sighed. 'I've lost him, but I like Kelsey, so I can live with that, I guess. You were right,' she said with a shrug.

'Yeah?' he said, surprised.

'They're good together, better than Adam and me.'

Nate nodded. 'Dan, you're a sexy, sassy chic. Trust me, half a dozen guys are checking you out as we sit here. Take the advice you've given me and move on.'

'I'm planning on it,' she said with a mysterious smile.

'Yeah? That's a relief. Got someone in mind then?' he asked a little louder as the jazz band started a new number.

'As a matter of fact, I do,' she said, crossing her legs and showing off her shapely figure. She took a sip of her glass of Coke, not giving him the satisfaction of knowing who she had in mind.

'Not the prison bird?' Nate asked, alarmed.

'Don't be ridiculous,' Danielle laughed. 'No, someone we both know.'

'Yeah? From work or play? Are you waiting to go for Burnsy if Jess isn't interested?'

She shook her head and put him out of his misery.

'I've no interest in Burnsy, but I've always liked an older guy, a salt-and-pepper man. Someone fit, confident and together.'

'Tom? Seriously?'

'Maybe,' she said with a shrug. 'We'll see. I'm on his security team for the wedding.'

'Are you?' Nate laughed, surprised.

'Of course. Who better to watch over your table… you and Jess, Adam and Kelsey? I'm the perfect woman for the job.'

'Dan, you never stop surprising me,' he said and smiled.

'And I've just wrapped up another case. I'll send you the photos and my bill.'

'Send them to Jess,' he said. 'You'll have more chance of being paid that way.'

'Here's to you and Jess,' Danielle said, raising her glass. 'Hear that song?'

'Yeah, if I didn't know better, I'd assume you and the band were in cohorts,' he said and smiled, enjoying the band's rendition of *I'm in the Mood for Love.*

Chapter 45

Now...

'*Delaney and Murphy*,' Jessica answered the phone again. 'No, I'm sorry. Dr Murphy is booked out for several weeks. Do you have a referral?'

Jessica looked up and rolled her eyes as Nate, outside the office, pinned in the wrong number to the security door pad again, while attempting to do up as his tie at the same time. She buzzed him in.

'That's confirmed and please arrive ten minutes early just to fill in the paperwork we require for new patients. We'll see you then, thank you,' she said and hung up.

'The nutters are calling early this morning,' Nate said.

'Indeed, and on your side of the business, I've checked the bank account – your embezzlement client has paid his account.'

'I'm sure he has,' Nate said, 'I got all his money back.'

'I thought you and Adam would commute together,' Jessica said as she rose to fill the paper tray in the photocopier.

'No, I wanted to swim laps before work, which I can do while staying at the Murphy Mansion,' he joked, as he headed to his office.

Five minutes later, he called out to Jessica: 'Got a minute?'

'On my way,' she said, and swanned into his office in her sassy short skirt and fitted jacket. 'What's up?'

Jessica found him standing behind his desk.

Nate cleared his throat. 'I was wondering if you, um, would like to come to Winsome's wedding with me as my plus one?'

'Oh, thanks, Nate,' she said and smiled, noticing how uncomfortable he was. If he had been rehearsing asking her, he had wasted his time. 'But no, thanks.'

Nate's face fell. She could tell he hadn't expected that, not for a moment.

'I thought you wanted to go?' he said.

'I did, I do. But you took too long. You knew I was keen, but you weren't interested in asking me earlier. So, did someone else fall through?' she asked, crossing her arms over her chest.

'No! I haven't asked anyone else, and I didn't want to take anyone else. I was just not ready.'

Jessica raised an eyebrow. 'And you thought if you asked me, I'd be so flattered and would assume that you were keen to have a relationship with me. That I'd fall in love with you and I would trap you?' She dragged out the word "love" as if she were a teenager on a first date.

Nate shrugged. 'Crossed my mind.'

'I'm surprised we can both fit in here with your colossal head,' she snapped.

Nate exhaled, frustrated. 'I didn't want to lead you on if I wasn't ready to date,' he said, cutting to the chase.

'And now you are?'

'Yes. No, I don't know,' he said, putting his hands up in the air. 'Forget it. I just thought you might like to come and thought I'd ask you. Whatever.'

'Thanks anyway,' she said and left, hearing him swear behind her.

Adam came out of his office and headed to Nate's office, as Jessica returned to her desk at reception.

'Don't go in there. He's cranky,' Jessica warned.

'I'm used to that,' Adam said and wandered in.

The phone rang, and Jessica frowned. She was hoping to overhear their conversation. *Bummer.*

*****

'What's up?' Adam asked as he studied a fuming Nate sitting behind his desk.

'Close the door,' Nate said.

He did so and moved to the chair opposite Nate's desk, standing and leaning on the back of it. 'What's happened?'

'I asked Jessica to come to Winsome and Jack's wedding with me, and she turned me down because I took too long to ask her,' he said and scoffed.

Adam thought about it. 'Yeah, fair enough.'

'Seriously?' Nate asked, rising and striding across the floor to his window that looked down on Stones Corner.

Adam gave a small shrug. 'She probably feels like an afterthought. Besides, Jack invited her to come along and bring a friend. He took a real liking to her.'

Nate threw up his hands for the second time. 'Oh great. So now she'll take a date of her own and what am I supposed to do?'

'You don't have to take a plus one,' Adam said. 'I don't get why everyone wants to go anyway.'

'Well, you're probably the only one in the city who doesn't get it. It's a society wedding allegedly or some crap like that,' Nate said and frowned as he focussed his gaze on the streets below. The morning traffic was dwindling as workers arrived at their destinations. Adam stood upright and went to the door. He opened it and given Jessica was off the phone asked: 'Jess, got a minute?'

'Of course,' she said, and ignoring Nate's panicked look, Adam opened the door wider for Jessica to enter.

'Again with the "of course",' Nate said, frowning at Jessica. 'You don't say that to me when I ask.'

'From now on I will, Sir,' she said and rolled her eyes.

Adam ignored them both and, putting his hands in his suit pant pockets, he rocked on his heels and cleared his throat to get their attention.

'Jessica, I believe you have an invitation to the wedding and can bring a guest.'

She nodded. 'I do indeed,' she said smugly. 'I'm very much looking forward to seeing Jack marry his love, Winsome.'

Adam smiled, amused at her enthusiasm. He continued. 'Nate is hoping you might invite him to be your plus one to Mum and Jack's wedding. He'd very much like to attend with you.'

Nate rolled his eyes and looked out to the street, expecting her to put him in his place.

'I'd be delighted to invite Nate. Would you care to accompany me as my guest, Nathaniel?' she asked sweetly.

He turned to look at her, frowned, and then, seeing her smug expression, smiled.

'It would be my pleasure, Jessica, thank you for asking me,' he said and returned her smile.

'My work is done here,' Adam said and turned, leaving them looking at each other with satisfaction, trying to work out which one of them won that round.

While passing, Adam opened the front office door for Rob as he arrived.

'Morning,' Rob said. 'Got you working the door now, have they?'

Adam laughed. 'Yeah, the tips are good.'

'When's your first appointment?' Rob asked, heading to his office.

'Thirty minutes,' Adam said with a glance to the clock.

'Great, let's catch up, just for ten minutes,' Rob said and headed into his office.

Adam suppressed a groan, wishing he had said five minutes.

'Adam?' Rob called out.

'Coming.' He inhaled and headed into Rob's office closing the door. He took a seat, as Rob logged into his laptop. Rob looked neat and pressed in his pale grey suit, white shirt and flowered-patterned tie.

'Nice tie,' Adam said.

Rob ran his hand down it. 'Birthday present from my son... some time ago,' he said.

'How is he?'

'Doing his time. At least the prison officials are letting him study. He'll have his masters done by the time he gets out.' Rob sighed. 'But to you.'

Adam straightened and could see Rob had opened a supervision form on his monitor.

'How are you feeling about your patient not accepting the course now that you've had some separation from it?' he asked and gave his full attention to Adam.

'The same. I'm going to refer her elsewhere; I don't feel like I can do anything more for her.'

Rob nodded. 'Tell me what you are feeling about her decision.'

Adam shrugged. 'Anger, frustration, annoyance, impatience...' he raced through the answers flippantly with a wave of his hand.

Rob cut him off. 'Tell me the predominant feeling, the one feeling that you can't move past because we both know the feelings you just listed off relate to nearly every patient.'

He was about to answer when Rob held up his hand. 'Don't flip me off, Adam, take this supervision seriously. We are talking about what you find most challenging right now about that client's decision... the number one feeling.'

Adam read between the lines. Rob had the power to "suggest" Adam take time off as duty of care to himself and his clients. He sat back and thought about the question, gazing out the window, and then exhaled and answered: 'Helpless. I'm feeling helpless. I've spent months seeing her, made small steps of progress and now, when they've developed this course that I've been waiting for and they've agreed to accept her in it, she won't go.' His voice rose slightly, and he gave a small shake of his head. Gathering himself, he added: 'I can't keep doing this with her if she won't take the lifeline thrown her way. She'll be treading water until she sinks.'

Rob drummed his fingers on the desk for a few seconds and then asked: 'So repeat the exercise, but with Allan Sheffield.'

Adam looked at him, surprised. 'Well, I'm sure as hell not feeling helpless.'

'Not now,' Rob said. 'But you were a few days ago. What thought might have been behind that? What's changed?'

'I've flipped it around,' Adam said, understanding what Rob was asking. 'I'm taking charge, working towards putting an end to his game. I have some control back.'

'Exactly,' Rob said. 'So, what do you need to do now to

change this course of action for your patient? What can you turn around that might get a different outcome, the one that you want? That makes her feel like she can decide because she has less fear and more control?'

Adam's jaw locked while he thought about Allan Sheffield and his anorexic patient.

'Knowledge,' Adam said. 'Instead of telling her about somewhere foreign she has to go and take on a new routine she thinks she can't handle with everything else going on in her head, I could take her there.'

Rob nodded and didn't speak.

'I could take her there and show her where the course will be held. She can meet some people involved. Break it down for her, give her some control,' he said, some hope in his voice.

'And the day looks brighter,' Rob smiled. 'Better go prepare for your next client.'

Adam returned his smile and rose. 'Thanks, Rob, you're worth your weight in—'

'Beer,' Rob cut him off.

'If you insist,' Adam said and departed to prepare for his client.

Chapter 46

Then...

Nate and Adam lay on their stomachs looking into the clear water of the creek; the recent rain had flushed it out.

'There's one!' Nate said, spotting an eel as it flashed by.

'They're super ugly,' Adam frowned. 'They were swimming around us every time we were in there and we didn't know.'

'Yuk,' Nate said. 'At least they're not leeches. Remember that summer camp when the creek was full of leeches and yabbies? Oh, you weren't there, it was a school thing.'

'Yeah,' Adam agreed. 'Would have been good.'

'Where does your school go for camp?' Nate asked.

'Burleigh Beach Camp... it was good. No leeches, just sharks,' Adam said, and Nate grinned.

'If your dad comes to your cricket final, he can catch up with Uncle Allan. Is Uncle Allan his brother because my uncle is Dad's brother?' Nate said.

'Don't know, I'll ask him.'

'Dad said if my team makes the finals, he's going to come,' Nate said.

'Yeah, Dad said he'd see, depends on if they are here or away. Mum's shooting a commercial for TV in Sydney at the end of the month, that's probably when the final will be.'

'That's cool,' Nate said.

'Nuh, she's done it before. Tom might come, but he's not that into coming to anything unless Mum asks him to be there and then he's around,' Adam said. 'I'm going to invite Uncle Allan.'

'How are you going to reach him? We don't know his address or phone number,' Nate said.

'I forgot that. We might see him before the finals and I can ask him. I'll write him an invitation in case he wants to think about it,' Adam suggested.

'Or we could find him,' Nate said, 'like detectives. He drives a limousine – we could try to hire him to find out where he works. You could send the invitation there.'

'Yeah! That's great… you'd make a good detective,' Adam said. He pointed to a small school of guppies swimming by. 'Guppies! We should warn them there are eels about!'

Nate laughed. 'They'd be lunch.'

Adam thought about Uncle Allan again. 'We can use the phone at home to ring the limousine companies. No one's around.'

'Okay. We'll find him,' Nate said assuredly, 'and I'm sure he'll come.'

Now…

Danielle never took her eyes off Allan Sheffield's house except to glance at the clock now and then. A man in Hi-vis workwear had left the property an hour ago, but no one else had come or gone. She was enjoying the presence of Tom Hartigan beside her. The scent of his aftershave, the way he sat in charge, his presence strong and masculine, in the driver's seat of his car.

'Nice car,' she said. 'Sporty.'

'It has to meet two criteria,' he told her. 'It has to be the fastest car I can afford, so it moves if I put the foot down, and it has to blend in.'

'Makes sense if you're working in security, or avoiding the ladies,' Danielle teased.

Tom laughed. 'Yeah, doesn't hurt to have a fast getaway or camouflage from the hordes of women after me.'

'Poor you,' she said sympathetically. 'So, are you still training recruits at the barracks?'

'Nope. After you finished up, I couldn't go on,' he joked and she laughed.

'Yeah, I bet you say that to all the female recruits who busted your ass.'

'Trust me,' he said sincerely, 'there's not too many I've trained who were as dedicated or worked as hard as you, or could give me a run for my money, for that matter. You got it – you listened to instructions, you put your mind to it, and your body.'

'I loved it; it was a buzz. I love the challenge,' she said, smiling at the memory of her Army Reserve training time.

They both paused as they saw movement. It was the house next door, an elderly man heading down the path and over to the bus stop. Their bodies physically returned to an "at ease" posture.

'If you are still up for some challenging training, come on some of the hikes I do. There's a few of us ex-military guys and girls who conquer a climb or two on the weekend. I'd enjoy seeing your butt in front of me on the hill.'

'Careful, I'll think you like me,' she warned, pleased to have an excuse not to look at him. She heard him chuckle and then they sat in silence for a brief while.

'Come on, Mrs Tatum or Uncle Allan, go on out and enjoy this fine weather so I can leave the invitation in your letterbox,' she muttered.

'Not getting impatient, are you?' Tom asked.

She scoffed. 'Are you kidding? I could do this all day, and I have. That doesn't mean I don't find it as boring as bat shit.'

Tom laughed again and agreed. They sat again for a while without talking, both used to roles that required hours of disciplined silence.

'I hope he's in there alone,' Tom said, eventually.

'You don't think he'd have another kid in there, do you?' Danielle asked alarmed and with a glance at Tom, and then back at the house.

'No. Not yet. Never hopefully. I meant I hope it is just the two of them that live there – that guy who left earlier and Sheffield. The guy in Hi-vis is probably a relative or an ex-con helping Sheffield out.'

Danielle shrugged. 'Our plan will work regardless of who lives there. As soon as Sheffield leaves, I'll knock on the door. I'm planning on no one being home so I can leave the invitation in the letterbox unseen. If someone answers the door, I'll tell them I'm collecting for the local school – I've got a fake badge if required.'

'Well done you,' he said, impressed.

'I have several fake badges for all occasions. I could sell you biscuits for the Brownies if you prefer that to school fundraising,' she said, and he chuckled. Danielle continued: 'After I do my collector's spiel – assuming someone is home – I'll subtly drop that invitation from Adam in the letterbox on my way out, and we're out of here. Sheffield won't be able to resist the chance to meet Adam.'

'He's a sick bastard,' Tom said. 'I don't know how he got

released in the first place. People who hurt kids should have their files marked "Never to be released".

'No argument from me,' Danielle said. 'I'm surprised he survived prison and got out alive.'

'Alive and with unfinished business,' Tom said. 'Adam will never really rest until Sheffield is dead, in my opinion. The mental health system will have him back out on the street in no time.'

Danielle groaned. 'I've heard similar stories,' she agreed with a quick look at him. She saw Tom duck his head and look to the side of Sheffield's house.

'I'd love to search his room. Get all Adam and Dean's stuff back and return it to them, especially Dean's items for his family,' Tom said.

'Yeah, but that'd be a dead giveaway someone is messing with him. Might even unhinge him sooner than we hoped.'

'You're talking like Adam now, analysing Sheffield.'

'If you hang around someone long enough. Heads-up, the door has opened!' she said.

Allan Sheffield came out of the house dressed as Mrs Tatum.

'We have action,' Tom whispered.

'Holy cow, that is so creepy. Freaks me out every time I see it,' Danielle said in a whisper. She had followed Mrs Tatum home from the cemetery the time prior and also viewed the footage of Mrs Tatum pulling off her wig and becoming Uncle Allan at the *Delaney and Murphy* office.

Mrs Tatum turned, locked the door and walked down the path, pausing only to look around and then continued to the garage. In a floral dress with a hat pulled down low over her face, and a handbag over her arm, she walked in an ungainly manner, not used to a feminine walk or the heel on her shoe.

Danielle and Tom waited in the car, around the corner, out of sight, and soon an old Ford that had seen better days pulled out of the garage with Mrs Tatum at the wheel. Turning onto the street, she departed the opposite way to where they sat parked.

Both of them exhaled with relief. They waited a short while to make sure Mrs Tatum hadn't forgotten anything and came straight back. After ten minutes, Danielle reached for her bag, fished for her identification, pinned it on, and grabbed her phone and the invitation.

'Ready,' she said.

'If anything goes wrong, I'll pick you up right out the front,' Tom said.

'Roger that,' Danielle said, opened the car door and departed. Time to invite Uncle Allan to come out for a reunion that will see him never be allowed out again.

Glancing around to ensure her surroundings were safe, Danielle wandered up the path to the front door and knocked, standing back. She did not expect the door to open, but it did. Danielle turned, her eyes widened with surprise.

In the doorway stood Allan Sheffield.

Chapter 47

Now...

Tom Hartigan sat alert, watching Danielle as she made her way up the path, knocked on the door and waited. In his peripheral vision, he saw a car turning into the street. As it came closer, he sat bolt upright. It was Sheffield's car – Mrs Tatum; she was coming back.

'Christ!' he swore.

The car pulled over at the corner near the park across the road, and Tom steadied, relieved but confused.

'What the hell are you doing, Sheffield?' he muttered. He could see Danielle standing in the house's doorway.

'Damn!' Was Sheffield coming back? Why was he waiting over at the park? From where he parked, Sheffield would see Danielle put something in his letterbox if he was watching. Tom started the ignition, ready to get Danielle out of there. But no, Sheffield opened the car door, got out, and dressed as Mrs Tatum walked into the park and sat down on a bench under a tree; a playground nearby was empty.

Tom breathed out in relief but still wasn't settled. Why had he come back? He glanced back at the front door and

Danielle was gone. Tom's eyes darted around the yard, back to the house, to the mailbox.

He swore and turned the ignition off, and hurriedly exited the car. It was difficult to be stealthy when there were so few trees and obstructions at the side of the house to hide behind. He moved as close as he could towards the house, avoiding the windows, and came to the edge where he could see around the corner with a better view of the front door. Danielle was not in sight.

'Fuck!' he hissed. Tom leaned out slightly to check Mrs Tatum was still sitting in the park and she was. The pressure in his chest eased a little. He checked his phone. No message or call from Danielle.

Who was in the house and why would she enter? She knows better. He vowed to seriously kick her butt when she returned to the car.

He leaned forward again. Still not there.

He'd have to break cover; he had no choice. Just as he moved away from the side of the house, he heard movement at the front door and stepped back.

Danielle reappeared and with a smile and wave to someone inside the house, she stepped back down the path towards the letterbox. Tom ducked low, cleared the fence and the footpath, and slid back into the front seat of his car.

*****

Danielle thanked the kind man who introduced himself as Wayne King and his wife, Karen. She turned and waved again at the end of the path. When she saw Wayne turn to go back inside, she slipped the invitation into the letterbox and continued towards Tom.

Sliding into the passenger seat, she belted up as Tom turned the car, and drove away, not passing Mrs Tatum.

They were several streets away before Tom asked with a controlled but frosty voice: 'What on earth possessed you to enter that house?'

Danielle took a deep breath before answering.

'I assessed the situation. It was under control, I was in no danger, the couple made a donation, I dropped the invitation in the letterbox and here we are.'

'Mrs Tatum came back.'

'What?' Danielle wheeled around to look at him. 'Did she – he – see me?'

'No, thank Christ. She stopped in the park on the corner and sat there, near the kids' playground.'

'What's that about?' Danielle asked.

'I don't know. Maybe, given there's another couple in the house, Sheffield wanted some time out or to give them some,' he suggested. 'He should be nowhere near a playground.'

Danielle frowned and straightened in her seat as they returned to the office of *Delaney and Murphy*. 'They must have seen him going out in drag, though. That's weird.'

Tom shrugged. 'Who knows what types are living there. Probably all ex-cons, minding their own business. Maybe they are used to him dressing up. Maybe they do it themselves.'

'Strange world,' Danielle muttered. She smiled. 'And look at you getting all shitty with me.'

Tom gave her a reluctant half-smile. 'It's my job to protect you. When you disappear, it freaks me out.'

She patted his leg, pleased with the hard muscle she encountered. 'You like me.'

'You're alright,' he said and grinned when she laughed. "Okay, so he's got the invitation from Adam now. Let's hope Uncle Allan wants a reunion with his nephew.'

'Can't believe Adam is going to go through with this,' Danielle said with a shake of her head.

'Yeah, well you know how I feel about it. But Adam never did what I said when he was a kid, so I'm not expecting him to start now.'

'Well, if you'd bonded with him a little more, not dragged him into photo sessions and screwed his mother, you might have had more cooperation from him.'

Tom smirked.

'Was she worth it?' Danielle asked. 'Strictly between us, top secret and all that.'

Tom hesitated and then said in a low voice: 'Hell yeah. Winsome Keeley really is the *IT* girl in more ways than one. And trust me, age has not wearied her.'

Danielle made a horrified face at him. 'Don't tell me you are still seeing her now? Behind Adam's back?'

'No, don't be crazy,' he said, shooting her down, to Danielle's relief. 'I just meant she's still beautiful. Anyway, she's engaged to the singer.'

'Jack, he has a name and you know him,' Danielle scolded Tom as they drove into the visitor carpark at the office. 'One would think you are jealous.'

Tom sighed. 'No, just looking for a love of my own,' he said and when she glanced at him, he gave her a wink and smile.

Danielle shook her head. 'Well, I'm only interested in men who can hold their own. Best I come on one of those hikes then and see what you're made of.'

'Challenge accepted,' he said and grinned, pleased Danielle had taken up his offer.

They entered the office happy; the atmosphere would soon change.

Chapter 48

Now…

Adam pulled his Mercedes into the underground carpark, parking it next to Nate's Audi. He guessed other tenants would think their business was booming judging by the cars they drove – both presents from Winsome. Or they were both in debt up to their eyeballs.

He took the stairs two at a time, pleased with this morning's results. He had taken his patient to the clinic where the program specific to her anorexia problems would be conducted. She saw the surroundings, met some of the staff and met another patient which Adam had orchestrated. Knowing someone from day one of the course made life much easier, just like at school, he thought. She had agreed to do the course, and he agreed to keep her as a patient. It was a good morning all around and he felt like a weight had fallen off his shoulders.

Adam pinned in the number on the office door and entered; he heard rowdy talk coming from Nate's office. Through the open door, he could see Nate sitting, with Danielle draped over a chair in front of his desk, and Jessica and Tom standing. He glanced at Rob's door, which was closed. He wanted to give him the good news about his patient.

'Ah, here he is,' Danielle said seeing him through the doorway and calling out to include him. 'We have delivered your invitation to Uncle Allan.'

'No drama then?' Adam asked, remaining in the doorway of Nate's office. Seeing Tom in there did little for his mood.

'No,' Tom said. 'You need to let me know the minute you hear from him.'

'Yeah,' Adam said and turned to Jessica. 'Has Rob got someone with him?'

She nodded. 'Only for another ten minutes or so.'

He thanked her and departed. He knew he was being surly with Tom, but didn't care. Tom had no respect for his parents' marriage, or for his job, Adam doubted he had changed much. Entering his office, Adam threw his keys on his desk, with his phone and notepad, nudged off his jacket and sat down, hitting the keyboard on his laptop to start it up.

He checked his appointments, the emails from Jessica, and then his heart stopped. There was an email called uncle_allan@network.com. His and Nate's email addresses were on the website, so getting in contact wasn't hard, but this was the first time Sheffield had directly contacted him. The subject line read: 'I accept.' Adam stared at it for a few moments before opening it. It read:

Hello to my favourite nephew. Thank you, Adam, for your lovely invitation. I accept. It was good to meet your friend today. She seems like a very nice girl. See you soon, Uncle Allan.

Anger fumed in Adam and he ran a hand over his mouth

and looked away while he thought. The plan had been to put the invitation in the letterbox. Why had Allan met Danielle? How could Tom put her in danger!

He rose, walked past the windows and back while he tried to rein in his rising anger. His jaw locked; his blood boiled. Laughter met him from the other room, which just made him angrier. The job had been a stuff up and they were both completely unaware. Allan had got the better of them, again, and now Allan Sheffield knew Danielle.

Adam returned to the desk, hit on the email, printed it, and grabbing it from the printer, stormed out of his office. Rob was seeing a client out the door and glanced at Adam as he strode into Nate's office. The conversation stopped as he entered, his entrance demanding attention. Rob followed him in moments later.

'Tell me what went down this morning,' Adam said studying Danielle and Tom. He lowered himself to sit on the edge of Nate's meeting table as all eyes turned to Tom. He told of doing surveillance, observing, seeing Mrs Tatum leave, and then Danielle going in and meeting a nice couple living there. She delivered the invitation in the mailbox on the way out.

Adam listened, his eyes narrowed, jaw locked, and noticed, when they finished, they expected him to be pleased. He turned to Danielle.

'Do you know what Allan Sheffield looks like now, not in drag?'

She sobered and studied him, running her tongue over her lower lip. 'No.'

Adam looked to Nate, who leaned forward, opened his browser and searched for a recent press story and image of Sheffield on his release from prison. Sheffield's release had received plenty of publicity – Dean's family had campaigned hard and long to keep him locked up. Nate turned the laptop to show a photo to Danielle. She gasped. She turned to face Adam, eyes wide, her hand across her mouth in shock.

'What's going on?' Rob asked.

Adam could barely speak he was so angry. He spat the words out. 'Danielle just had an audience with Allan Sheffield.'

Tom interrupted, standing straighter. 'No way, hold up. That's not what happened.'

Danielle rose and pointed to the screen. 'That's the man I met – he said his name was Wayne King and he introduced me to his lady friend. They donated a few dollars to my school fundraiser.'

'You went into the house?' Nate asked.

'I wouldn't have except we knew Mrs Tatum had left, and since there was another woman in there as well, I couldn't think of an excuse not to step in while the guy said he was going to get his wallet.'

Jessica looked at Danielle with concern. 'She could have been like Myra Hindley! Assisting him.'

'For the love of God,' Rob said standing next to Adam, who said nothing.

Tom studied Danielle, confused. 'No, that can't be right. We saw Mrs Tatum leave and sit in the park. I had eyes on her the whole time you were in there.'

'You've been played,' Adam said. 'Yet again, Allan Sheffield has got the better of us.' Brandishing the email at them, he read: *Hello to my favourite nephew. Thank you, Adam, for your lovely invitation. I accept. It was good to meet your friend today. She seems like a very nice girl. See you soon, Uncle Allan.*

Danielle shuddered. 'Oh my God, my skin is crawling.'

'Holy crap,' Nate said and shook his head.

Adam looked at Tom. 'Danielle was in there with a killer and there were two people who were clearly prepared to help him.'

Danielle paced, shocked. She looked at the photo again and away. 'He was so lovely.'

'He can be, that's his power,' Adam said.

'Are you sure that's the guy you were inside with?' Tom asked, doubting Danielle. 'I had my eyes on Mrs Tatum the whole time and it looked like Sheffield, like the last time we saw him.'

She nodded. 'That is the man I spoke with. If you remember, Mrs Tatum was wearing a hat and kept her head down. Sheffield has got some helpers. Whether they are friends or he paid them off doesn't matter... he was onto to us.'

'He's a killer who meticulously planned his abductions. He's still doing it, planning something. We have to take this more seriously,' Rob said.

'Agreed. Why didn't you watch the place for longer?' Adam asked. 'Nate would have done surveillance for days to see who was coming and going. Another bang-up job, Tom,' he added.

The words barely left his mouth when Tom cracked. He was in front of Adam in a moment, his fist connecting between Adam's eye and nose. Jessica screamed, Nate was on his feet in seconds coming between them, but it was Danielle who pushed Tom away.

Blood poured from Adam's nose over his white business shirt.

'You need a girl to fight for you now?' Tom said when he didn't hit back.

'Shut up, Tom,' Nate said, standing in front of Adam.

Tom shook his head. 'Yeah, you all stick up for him since he can't stand up for himself.'

Adam gave him an eerie smile, blood covering his teeth. 'Tom, you're no different to Uncle Allan... it's always someone else's fault.'

'You're both freaking me out,' Jessica said.

'I agree,' Rob said. 'Adam go and clean up, Tom go and cool down. Everyone meet back here this afternoon at 4pm and we'll review the plan when we're all calmer.'

The men continued to glare at each other, and Nate grabbed Adam around the neck and took him from the room.

'Are you alright?' Nate asked and Adam grunted.

'Doesn't matter. Dan was in danger today.' Adam saw Danielle come out of Nate's office and she gave him a grateful look for his concern.

'Tom was outside in the car and Dan can handle herself,' Nate reminded him.

'She was outnumbered and what if Sheffield pulled a knife on her? Tom's always one step behind... next time, we might not be so lucky.'

Chapter 49

Now...

Tom Hartigan stormed out of the office and went straight to his gym. He knew he was dangerous like this; he had to let off some steam. Tom took to the punching bag like a man possessed, seeing Adam's face every time he hit it. The only satisfaction from this morning was that he got a hit in. Adam was just like his father, he thought, remembering James and the control he had over Winsome. He threw a punch for every way he thought Adam was like his father – smug, quiet, successful, handsome, reserved, powerful. He knew Adam didn't seek the limelight, but by the nature of his birth and parents, he was his father in every sense of the word. The way they all pandered to him pissed Tom off, and Audrey treated the guy like he was made of glass. He thought of Winsome. She showed no affection for Adam as a kid, even so, anything he wanted she gave to him and more, nothing had changed.

Perhaps I should just take out Sheffield, he thought. Forget about the trap and putting him in a mental home, just finish him off. The guy's screwed. He killed a kid, no one would weep for him. Just bump him off, I know how to do it without it being linked to me, then I can have nothing to do with Adam and Audrey until the wedding. He moved to the weights area to do a set, and thirty minutes later, hit the shower.

When he grabbed his gear, he saw a missed call from the *Delaney and Murphy* office. From Adam's mobile.

'What the fuck now?' he mumbled and sat down on a bench in the change room. He rang back.

'Hey Tom,' Jessica answered. 'Are you okay?'

He sighed. 'Yeah, just...' he struggled for words.

'Annoyed that Sheffield pulled that trick?' she asked.

'Amongst other things.' He had to admit he hadn't given Sheffield's actions due consideration or anger, given he was expending it all on Adam. 'I missed a call from Adam.'

'His mobile's diverted while he's with a client. Nope, wait up, he's seeing them out now. He'll call you straight back.'

'Can't wait,' Tom said drily, and Jessica laughed.

He hung up, rose and headed out to his car, climbing in and putting on the air-conditioning to cool down. The phone rang and Adam's name came up. Tom took a deep breath before answering.

'Yes, Adam,' he said, in a robotic voice.

'Tom. I need your help.'

Tom was about to snap back a retort, but the silence following checked him.

'What's happened?' he asked.

'Can you meet me in the carpark at work?' Adam asked.

'On my way,' Tom said and hung up. *What the hell was going on now!*

⁕⁕⁕⁕⁕

Adam waited downstairs. He told Jessica he'd be out for a few hours; he didn't tell her where he was going or with whom. There were too many people involved in this drama, his drama. He saw Tom's car coming around the corner at Stones Corner and he stopped him before he went into the carpark. Adam got in.

'Can we go somewhere, anywhere?'

'Have you had lunch?' Tom asked. 'I've just done a workout, I need to eat.'

'That works. There's a pub down the road that's pretty quiet most of the time.' Adam indicated the way and they drove in uncomfortable silence.

Adam thought about making some sort of small talk… asking how the wedding security plans were coming along, what gym did Tom go to, what did he think of this whole sorry mess, but he couldn't be arsed. Clearly, neither could Tom.

Tom turned into the hotel, nabbed a spot in the underground car park and they exited the car, entered the hotel and found a table in the corner. Both men ordered the burger and chips with an orange juice, without speaking a word to each other.

Handing back the menu to the waiter with a nod of thanks, Tom turned his attention to Adam.

'What's going on?'

'There are too many people involved.'

'I agree with that,' Tom said.

'This is my problem, no one else's.'

'I disagree with that.'

'You're paid to say that.'

'Regardless, I still disagree.'

They paused as the waiter delivered their juices and

Adam slipped his jacket off, putting it on the back of his chair. 'You don't like me, I don't trust you, but there are two things I need from you and then you never have to see me again, all going well.'

'Tempting,' Tom said, and both men gave each other a small smile. 'What do you need?'

'I need Kelsey protected first and foremost. '

Tom nodded. 'She's not in danger from Sheffield. His focus is on you. But I can manage that.'

'I need her guarded at the wedding,' Adam explained. 'She's had a tough past.'

'Was she your patient?' Tom asked, interrupting him.

'No, of course not, I can't do that.'

Tom gave a small shrug. His lack of discipline pissed Adam off yet again. With Tom's military background, this stuff – code of conduct – should seep from his pores. All the ex-military people he counselled were as disciplined as you get.

Adam took a breath and let it go. He said: 'Kelsey's story is not my story to tell, but just know she doesn't want media attention and she doesn't need anyone, especially unidentified men, getting in her face. Read between the lines,' Adam said and loosened his tie.

'Okay, I'm hearing you. I'm assigning Danielle to Kelsey,' Tom said.

Adam's eyes widened. 'That's perfect.'

'Yeah, I can do some things right,' he said.

'Thanks,' Adam conceded.

Their burgers arrived and Tom began hungrily. Adam picked on the chips.

'What's the second thing?' Tom asked between bites.

'I want to trap Uncle Allan, now. He's not going to show

that day that I invited him to. He knows everyone will be there. He might be delusional but he's cunning.'

Tom nodded. 'Yep, I agree with that too.'

'You're freaking me out,' Adam said.

Tom chuckled. 'I was also going to suggest we go the day before or the day after.' He became serious. 'We're not doing it just the two of us though. I need Rob to have the facility ready so they can take Sheffield straight there. I need surveillance help from Nate, since you reckon he does it best.'

Adam nodded and noted Tom's smirk.

'I wouldn't mind if your police mate, Burnsy, was around, either. If Sheffield got killed by accident, well, that wouldn't be a tragedy,' Tom said.

'That's another thing we agree on,' Adam said.

'So, it can be fewer people but not just you and me. Can you handle that?'

Adam took a few bites and thought for a while before responding. 'I can live with that. There's something else I just found out… Burnsy rang not long after you hit me and stormed out.'

Tom's shoulders slumped. He looked away and then reluctantly offered: 'Okay, I'm sorry about that.'

'Really?' Adam asked surprised and laughed. His eye and cheek had blackened slightly.

Tom shrugged. 'So you're not as pretty as usual, you'll survive.'

'It would have been nice to get a shot in though, if you wanted to fight somewhere where we couldn't be separated,' Adam said.

'Not going to happen.'

'Why? Scared you'll hurt me or I might surprise you?' Adam asked.

'Think you could take me on?' Tom asked studying him.

'Yeah. But I don't think I'd win.'

Tom nodded. 'We agree on that too. It's not going to happen. Your family has hired me to protect you and them. I'm not knocking out your lights. Besides, Nate would come after me and he worries me more than you.'

Adam smiled but looked away. There was truth in that.

'What'd Burnsy say?' Tom asked, finishing his burger and throwing his napkin on the plate. 'Are you going to eat that or look at it?'

Adam offered the plate to Tom, who took the burger, leaving the remaining chips behind. Adam continued to pick on them.

'Burnsy?' Tom asked again.

'The bones from the grave, there not Dean Beals.'

'What the fuck?' Tom froze. 'Why didn't you tell me this earlier? We've been here about forty minutes.'

'I was getting to it,' Adam said. 'They belong to Sheffield's brother. Burnsy checked the death certificate. The brother was eight when he died from leukemia, Allan was 12.'

'Holy crap,' Tom muttered. 'So, we still don't know what happened to Dean Beals.'

'No. I want to expand on our plan,' Adam said.

'I'm listening.'

'It involves me taking a drive with Uncle Allan in the original cars, if you can get close enough models.'

Tom nodded. 'Do-able. Go on.'

'Then trying to find out where Dean was buried. He's done his time for Dean, but if attempts anything with me, or we can prove he can't be let out in society, we can get Sheffield put away, maybe for good. Let's flush him out now, in the next few days, and put an end to this here and now.'

Chapter 50

Then...

Allan Sheffield liked a spot of gardening. He was house proud and even more than he loved his new house, he loved the look of pride his wife and mother's faces revealed when they looked at him, at the life he was making for his family. The mortgage was sizeable, but who didn't have a big mortgage? He could manage it with his new driving job, especially as he ingrained himself with the VIPs who paid big bonuses.

He watered the flowerbed Millie had planted and gazed at their new brick home. Three bedrooms, a rumpus room for the kids to play in, and plenty of yard to run around in. As soon as Dean's father paid up, Millie could start her IVF treatment and then he'd have a son and daughter of his own. He'd have the perfect family.

His mind strayed to Dean and his brows furrowed. His free hand clenched and unclenched. Dean had said he wanted to stay with him, just like Adam had, they were both keen. Then, when the time came, the boy wanted to go home. He'd prepared a really nice room for Dean as well.

If the boy hadn't started yelling and screaming, everything would have been fine.

Allan thought about Dean's last moments. No one would ever do that to his kids, never. He'd hunt them down if they touched his kids. His body relaxed as his thoughts returned to the family he was planning with Millie, and he smiled.

His plan was almost complete.

Now....

Adam gave a nod of agreement but wasn't happy about it – Tom had won one round; he wanted the team involved. Adam was, however, prepared to trust Tom this time. At 4pm, Jessica locked the office door and turned the "Closed" sign around. She returned to her desk to work quietly while the meeting took place.

Around the table were the people who intended to stop the stalker, Allan Sheffield, and find the body of Dean Beals for his family. It was to start with a simple hit of cricket between two friends – but by the end of the meeting, the planning that had gone behind it was detailed and scripted.

'We need to achieve a relapse,' Rob said keeping the psychological perspective of managing Allan Sheffield to the point and in layman terms. He had the attention of the group. 'Adam's presence in Sheffield's car will be more threatening now that he's grown up.'

'Rob's right,' Adam continued. 'Uncle Allan is not going to go straight back into that day, but with a few triggers, he might want to show off, or at least show what he could still do.'

'We need that to facilitate him being locked away,' Rob said.

'I can get him locked away for stalking you,' Burnsy said, 'but he'll be out in a minute and he's likely to ignore a restraining order. You'll be looking over your shoulder for the rest of your days.'

'He's a kid killer,' Tom said, putting an end to any empathy the group might have momentarily felt. 'The fact he's returning items he took shows he has little remorse. He needs to never be released.'

'It's a bit more complex than that, I suspect,' Rob said, 'But let's focus on our actions. We need reminders that might cause flashbacks and create a re-living of events. Sight, sound, smell, touch, anything to create fond recollections of your time together and his former life.'

'There's not a lot,' Adam said. 'Nate and I will wear the white cricket gear… we'll have to buy or borrow. I can talk about holidaying with him, mention fishing, Dean, his wife…'

'Did he mention her to you?' Rob asked, surprised.

Adam frowned as he thought. 'Once. But Christ…'

'What?' Tom asked suspiciously.

'He had women's clothing in the back seat of his car,' Adam recalled.

'Even then! And you just think to mention this now?' Tom demanded.

'I was ten! I didn't remember that until now,' Adam snapped at him.

'Steady up, Tom, he was a kid. Adam wouldn't have given the clothes a second thought. Besides, we don't know that Sheffield was cross-dressing. The clothes might have been a disguise if he needed to get away, like he's doing now. People are less likely to suspect a woman of abducting a boy, at least that was probably the case then,' Rob said.

Tom held up his hands and mumbled an apology.

Adam spoke directly to Rob. 'He said it was his wife's clothing and that she was messy, or had stuff all over the place, or something like that.'

Rob nodded. 'Good, then mention her as well. Her name was Millie. Did he say her name?'

'I don't know,' Adam said. 'Maybe he said Aunty Millie.' He thought for a moment and shrugged. 'I don't know. I'll leave it unless I'm desperate for triggers. I want to create lengthy flashbacks, but I'll take short ones over nothing.'

'Okay,' Nate said. 'Cars?' he asked turning to Tom.

'I've secured a near enough replica of Allan's sedan that he drove that day twenty years ago, and to my own Commodore that I chased him in. I'd like to avoid an accident because the bloody repairs will be much dearer now for those old cars,' he said with the hint of a smile.

The best he could muster at being amiable, Adam thought, studying Tom. He wondered what his mother saw in the security guard… maybe the bad boy thing got women in, maybe he was so different from his dad, James.

Tom continued. 'Nate will join me once he gets off the cricket field. He won't be seen in the passenger seat because we will not get that close this time. We'll do the chase as we did on that day when I saved Adam's butt—' he paused.

Adam ignored him, knowing Tom was expecting a reaction… they were good at baiting each other.

'—but this time, I won't catch Sheffield,' Tom finished.

Burnsy nodded. 'So, in effect, we'll let Allan Sheffield do what he intended to do twenty years ago. Take you somewhere, Adam. Except, Sheffield won't get away with it as he did with young Dean Beals.'

'That's right,' Tom said. 'I bugged the black car that

Sheffield will hopefully drive with a microphone and tracker embedded behind the dash where it can't be seen.'

'What if he insists on taking his car?' Danielle asked speaking up for the first time. Listening was one of her strengths.

'Adam will also be wearing a tracker and microphone,' Tom continued. 'Plus, Nate and I will follow, listening in on the conversation between Adam and his "Uncle Allan", so even if he goes in his car, we're onto him.'

'Next… what happens if he does go to his old house?' Nate put Burnsy in the spotlight.

'I've secured safe access to Allan Sheffield's original family home where he had planned the abductions and where he lived with his wife.'

'Brilliant,' Tom said. 'What happened to the family living there?'

'School holidays,' Burnsy said with a shrug as if they explained everything. 'The family who lived there knew its history, but that was twenty years ago and that house held no bodies. According to the detectives who were on the case, it had been searched and scoured – every inch of it. There were no hidden rooms, no dark cellars, no bodies in the ceiling. Dean Beals is not there.'

'So, the family is away?' Rob asked.

'Courtesy of a voucher to spend the week at the Gold Coast and provide the police access to the residence for the week.' Rob looked at Adam. 'Audrey was happy to pay for it.'

'Yeah?' Adam said surprised and sighed. Everyone's involved. He glanced at Tom, who read his look and spoke up.

'Also, Danielle will be on location at that house, parked nearby, watching, while the boys play cricket in the park.

We'll communicate with Dan if you and Sheffield come there. Adam, regardless of the tracker, it'd be helpful if you could give us some location hints in your dialogue.'

Adam nodded.

Burnsy added: 'As soon as I get word from Tom that you're heading that way, I'll have some boys in blue at the house, out of sight. Otherwise, let me know if the plan takes off and we'll follow the tracker and be where we need to be.'

'We're ready.' Tom concluded the meeting.

'Yep,' Nate said. 'Everyone is ready to play their part; let's hope Uncle Allan comes out to play.'

Chapter 51

Now...

Adam nicked the ball and grinned as Nate took a world-class cricket dive to catch it, but missed, the ball falling nearby. He struggled to his feet, groaning.

'Yeah, you would have caught that twenty years ago,' Adam ribbed him.

The two men wore whites they had borrowed from the local cricket club, and for the last hour had taken turns at bowling and batting. Despite their poor form, they enjoyed being out of the office for a while. The carpark had one vehicle in it – a large black sedan, identical to the one Allan Sheffield had taken Adam away in all those years ago. The keys sat in the ignition.

It was the third time this week Adam and Nate had ventured to the grounds to have a hit; at the same time of the day they did when they were boys. They hoped Allan Sheffield would remember the invitation and come, and that when he did, seeing them would begin the cycle.

Adam also hoped it would be third time lucky. Each day on their return to the office, Rob had insisted on speaking to him afterwards, reading his head like Adam was going to freak out at any moment – his cross-examination was more exhausting than freaking out. Nothing happened all those years ago, at least not to him, he'd assure Rob, but they both knew it still happened – he lived to tell.

There were also only a few days left before the family returned to the home once owned by Allan and Millie Sheffield, and Adam worried they were all losing their edge – becoming weary with the process. It was dangerous to lose your edge where Allan Sheffield was concerned.

Adam gripped the bat and prepared as Nate came in from an exaggerated long run to bowl. He tried to focus while laughing at his best friend's antics. The ball arrived with a fair bit of spin and Adam hit it to the boundary for a six. He straightened and laughed again, this time at Nate's expression.

'You can go chase that one,' Nate said, hands on hips. 'I've had it.'

Adam gave a shake of his head, threw the bat towards Nate and took off to the boundary to get it. As he neared, he saw a man move away from the clubhouse wall. He was in black pants with a white business shirt.

Uncle Allan.

Adam's heart stopped, his step slowing.

It was him, Allan Sheffield, Uncle Allan. He swallowed and remembered himself, the role he had to play. He broke out into a grin and raised his hand in a wave, trying to look excited to see the child killer and the man who had given him so many nightmares.

'Uncle Allan!' he called and Allan Sheffield grinned.

Adam arrived at the boundary, acting a little breathless. 'You made it.'

'I wouldn't miss it,' Uncle Allan said.

'Just in time, we're finished. Nate has to go, he's got his bike here,' Adam said.

'I'll give you a lift, unless…' he looked around.

'That'd be great, thanks,' Adam said and he walked beside Allan, slightly behind to be less threatening in height and presence.

At the carpark, Allan hesitated. He saw the car that was just like the one he used to drive… his pride and joy. Then, he glanced at the car he just arrived in.

Adam walked towards Uncle Allan's old car, and moments later, Allan followed.

The game had begun.

*****

Nate picked up the bat and gloves and looked at the boundary. His eyes widened.

'Christ, he's here.' He turned his back to the clubhouse where Adam was talking with Allan Sheffield and grabbing his phone, called Tom. He held it in front of him, using the microphone so Sheffield could not see him holding it to his ear.

'I've got him,' Tom said before Nate said a word. 'Hurry.'

Nate turned back to see Adam disappearing to the carpark with Allan. He raced to the opposite boundary where Tom waited in his car, Nate's thoughts racing ahead.

He's here. Unbelievable. Nate calmed himself. What happened now made all the difference to Adam, to their future safety, to Dean Beals and his family.

He dived into the passenger seat of Tom's car, noting the concentration written on Tom's face.

'I can't believe he's here, he's taken the bait,' Nate said, belting up as Tom slowly pulled their vehicle out of the carpark to not attract attention to them. 'I'll call Burnsy.'

'I've done that. He's following the tracker and is on his way with a few of his lads,' Tom said. He shook his head. 'Sheffield has taken the original car, can't believe it.'

They could see Allan's car and needed to stay a suitable distance away. Adam's voice came through their car speaker system as he got into the car with Allan Sheffield.

'It's good to see you again, Uncle Allan.'

'It's great to see you. You're still a good-looking young man.'

Adam chuckled. 'Nate's says I'd starve on the income I'd make if I tried to become a model.'

Uncle Allan laughed. 'That boy, he always was cheeky. I see you can still bat too.'

'Yeah, it's nice to have a hit. Nate's pretty good on the bowling too, but he got lazy in the end with his fielding.'

'You'll keep,' Nate said, with a snort, listening to his best friend's attempt at simple banter.

'You've been fighting,' Uncle Allan said. 'Your eye is black. Were you fighting with Nate?'

'Nuh, we don't fight. Tom did this.' Adam touched the bruising around his cheek and eye.

'That guy's a thug. I remember when he broke my nose,' Uncle Allan said, his voice rising to a thin rasp of anger.

In the car behind at a fair distance, Tom and Nate exchanged looks.

'At least my punch allows them to bond,' Tom said with a shrug.

'Yeah, still doesn't excuse it,' Nate said, not letting Tom get away with the cheap shot. 'Not to mention you're in a higher weight division.'

They hushed as Adam continued.

'That was bad that day. I was stressed out,' Adam said, truthfully. 'He shouldn't have hit you.'

'If you hadn't run and made him chase you, he probably would have finished me off,' Uncle Allan said.

There was silence for a few moments and then Adam said, 'Tom saved my life once though, I guess I owe him.'

Uncle Allan snapped back. 'If he had done his job in the first place, you wouldn't need saving.'

The reality hit everyone... Uncle Allan was back in the now, remembering Tom stopped Adam's inevitable demise.

'Oh crap, Adam's in trouble now,' Nate muttered, listening in. 'Quick, change the subject, Adam, quick!' They heard Adam clear his throat.

'You know what I'd like to do?' Adam's voice filtered through. 'I'd like to visit Dean.'

'Fuck!' Tom hit the dashboard with the flat of his hand and shook his head. 'Stick to the script, Adam, for the love of God!'

'He had to change it,' Nate said in Adam's defence, 'he was stuck between a rock and a hard place.'

'God almighty,' Tom ranted.

'Dean?' Uncle Allan asked, surprised.

'Yeah, he was a good swimmer, remember?' Adam continued.

'Nice,' Tom said and exhaled, begrudgingly. 'He might save the situation.'

'He reads people for a living, he'll be alright,' Nate said.

Allan's voice came through. 'He was a great swimmer, as good at swimming as you are at cricket. We could visit him then, he'd like that.'

'Cool,' Adam said in kid speak.

Nate and Tom exchanged quick looks.

'Game on,' Nate said. 'Well done, Adam, well done.'

'Call Burnsy again,' Tom ordered, but Nate was already on to it. Burnsy answered on the first ring.

'They're going to visit Dean,' Nate told him. 'We don't know where but we're following.'

'We're tracking him,' Burnsy assured him. 'I've got two officers on-site at the house, don't worry he won't spot them. I'll call Danielle now and tell her to give us a heads-up if she sees them first.'

Nate hung up. He saw Tom grimace.

'What?'

'I don't know whether to do the chase now or abandon it if they are going to visit Dean,' he exhaled. 'If we stick to the script, Sheffield was always going to take Adam somewhere, but was it the same place he took Dean?'

'Odds are, it was. I'll call Rob, ask him what he thinks might be going on in Sheffield's head,' Nate said.

'Hold up,' Tom said as Adam spoke and then gave them the direction they needed.

'This car is great. Does it get up to a good speed?' Adam asked.

'You bet,' Uncle Allan answered.

'He wants the chase,' Tom said and exhaled. 'Let's go.'

Chapter 52

Now…

Adam recognised the look on Allan Sheffield's face. It was pride. *Bloody unbelievable!* His next words proved it.

'You know, Adam, I could not have been prouder of you and Dean. It's great now to be catching up again. Just like old times,' he said and smiled. 'You know, I always wanted two sons just like you and Dean.'

'Yeah, you were like a dad to us,' Adam said, trying to say the words with sincerity when he wanted to do bodily harm to the man sitting next to him. He wanted to take Uncle Allan by the throat and watch the life ebb out of him, to know he was gone and to know Kelsey, Jessica and Danielle were safe. He wondered if killing Sheffield might give him peace of mind, and stop the claustrophobic panic that broke his sleep and left him sweating and feeling like Uncle Allan buried him. He had mentioned none of that to Rob this week. Probably never would.

They continued along the road they had driven on before, just like old times.

Hurry the fuck up, Adam was thinking, as he turned around and glanced back. There were no women's clothes on the back seat this time. For just a moment, he expected them to be there but remembered this wasn't really Uncle Allan's car. He was having the flashbacks he was trying to get Allan to have.

'Don't worry,' Uncle Allan said, with a glance to the rear-view mirror. 'It's just a car going too fast.'

'It's not him, is it? Tom?' Adam asked, which he knew was off-script, but it created a sense of bonding and urgency.

'Don't know,' Uncle Allan said, narrowing his eyes.

Adam felt his heartbeat increasing. Soon he would be on his own with Uncle Allan. Tom and Nate would be out of sight and relying on the tracker. His thoughts went to the people who helped Allan Sheffield trick Tom and Danielle. Where were they? Were they on hand somewhere to help Uncle Allan again?

Uncle Allan sped up. He was easily doing thirty kilometres or more over the speed limit now on the back street.

Adam hated not being in control, especially when a maniac was driving.

Uncle Allan swore under his breath. He glanced at Adam. 'Don't worry, everything is fine.'

'Okay,' Adam said and glanced over his shoulder as he did that day. This time he could see over the seat and the vision of Tom's car far enough away so as not to see Nate in the driver's seat. He could see Tom was moving along at a decent speed, putting the pressure on Sheffield.

They were coming to a bend; Adam knew this was where Tom would slow down and not reappear around the corner. Uncle Allan took the corner fast, skidding to the other side of the road before straightening.

Adam's breath hitched. Thank God no one was coming the other way. Did Burnsy ensure that? He returned his thoughts to the child murderer beside him.

'Don't worry, it's all okay,' Uncle Allan said, steering the car onto the correct side of the road. He patted Adam's knee as an uncle might before returning his hand to the steering wheel.

Adam felt Sheffield's touch burning through his cricket whites and seeping into his skin. He tried not to think about it or he'd have to brush down his knee to remove the sensation. He stole a look at Allan who was the picture of concentration – eyes narrowed, his knuckles white as they gripped the steering wheel and a few minutes later, Allan slowed down.

'All good,' Uncle Allan said, and gave Adam a grin. 'Must have been someone in a hurry to get somewhere. They've gone now.'

Adam nodded. 'Good,' he agreed. 'Are we going to Dean's place or is he on holiday at your place?'

'Dean?' Uncle Allan asked as if surprised.

Adam waited, not speaking, hoping he could get Uncle Allan back on track. He tried again.

'You were going to take us on a holiday, remember? We were going to fish. Dean could swim because he's a really good swimmer,' Adam said, talking in basic sentences.

'He's an excellent swimmer,' Uncle Allan agreed, 'as good in the pool as you are at cricket.'

Adam relaxed a little. The conversation loop had started again. He was safe for now.

'We'll go catch up with Dean then.'

'At your place with Aunty Millie?' Adam asked trying to feed information to Tom and Nate listening, and hoping he wasn't pushing Sheffield too far or too fast.

'Yes,' Uncle Allan grinned. 'My place. You two will get on famously.' He didn't mention what Millie might think.

With that, Uncle Allan headed to the home he lived in when he was a young man and his passenger was a young boy named Dean Beals.

Chapter 53

Now...

Nate grabbed his phone and called Burnsy. 'They're on their way to the house now.'

'We're ready and waiting unseen. I'll give Dan the heads-up,' Burnsy said and hung up.

Nate exhaled. They were way behind and out of sight of the vehicle – which made Nate nervous – but tracking Adam's direction to stay in pursuit.

Tom gave a shake of his head 'That guy freaks me out and that's saying something. I don't freak out easily.'

'Imagine being 10 years old and arriving home with him. Poor bloody Dean. Every parent's nightmare.' He shuddered, thinking of his little girl.

'It was a lottery alright,' Tom agreed. 'If I hadn't been hired, Adam would be underground. I'm surprised Dean's parents didn't have some kind of security for him. Kidnapping for ransom was the thing in those years. A bit like all of those plane hijacking incidents before security got tightened.'

'He's turning,' Nate said, watching the tracker and the movements of Sheffield's car. Tom nodded, slowing and following the same route.

'Was Dean Beal's father that rich, though?'

'Hell yeah,' Tom said, 'but he didn't have the celebrity value like Adam's folks who were the hottest ticket in the country at that time.'

The two men stopped talking to hear the snippets of conversation between Sheffield and Adam. They were talking cricket now.

'Why did Winsome sleep with you?' Nate asked.

'Really, now?' Tom asked, and Nate gave a small shrug.

'I'm trying to distract myself from stressing out,' Nate said his eyes never leaving the screen where Sheffield's vehicle was being tracked.

'Why wouldn't she?' Tom asked and laughed at seeing Nate's expression. 'Is this between us or are you going to tell Adam?'

'Depends what you say.'

They waited again and heard Adam ask about Uncle Allan's boat. Sheffield's answer satisfied them he didn't have one, and he was embellishing. No body was hidden there.

Tom ran a tongue over his lower lip and answered Nate's question. 'Twenty years ago, and even today, Winsome is the nation's sweetheart. Gorgeous, feminine – that husky, girlish voice and little face. Every man instinctively wants to protect her. But she's a very naughty girl. James won when he got her hand in marriage – the only man she ever considered, or so she told me. Power, money, good looks...'

'Yeah, I have the same problem,' Nate joked and Tom laughed.

'James never knew the total package that was Winsome, or if he did, he turned a blind eye to it. Winsome taught me a trick or two and I'm no boy scout.'

Nate nodded. 'Yeah, best keep that to yourself.'

'Especially where an ex-prime minister is involved. But to look at Adam, you'd swear you were looking at James.'

Adam's voice cut in with a clue. 'This is a really nice area, Uncle Allan. I like King's Park. You've done well to get a house here.'

'Been working hard, young man, that's the secret,' Uncle Allan said. 'This is my home here.'

Tom accelerated a little to arrive at Allan Sheffield's home a few minutes later. He hid his car in a spot he had earlier staked out.

'Heads-up Dan and Burnsy,' Nate mumbled, watching the scene from afar, as Adam and Uncle Allan got out of the car, and Allan opened the gate and entered as if he owned the place.

*****

Adam followed behind Uncle Allan through the gate. He knew they were being watched and he knew if Sheffield entered the house, the gig would be up. Nothing in there was familiar to him.

'My, everything's grown,' Uncle Allan said looking around.

Adam walked behind looking casual, his hands in the pockets of his cricket white pants. He studied the garden, watching Uncle Allan and where his gaze fell, hoping for a clue to Dean's whereabouts. If the house had been swept clean all those years ago, then to visit Dean, Adam believed they would have to stay in the garden. The plants were thick around the border of the property, providing privacy where no fencing existed. The smell of jasmine hit Adam as well. Sweet, fresh, an anomaly in the surreal moment of visiting with a murderer to greet the dead.

'Did you plant all these?' Adam asked, stalling Uncle Allan.

Sheffield came to stand beside him, and Adam involuntarily stiffened and removed his hands from his pockets, ready to defend himself. He forced himself to relax.

'No, Millie planted these. That's my garden over there,' he pointed to one side of the wall where a good size bottlebrush tree stood. Around it, planted recently, were a smattering of small flowering plants. The bottlebrush had enough growth to suggest it was planted twenty years ago.

They walked over together.

'This is a lemon bottlebrush,' Uncle Allan said and reached out to touch the brush-like flowers.

'Even though it's red,' Adam said trying to keep his comments innocent as a child would say and allow Sheffield to feel dominant.

Uncle Allan laughed. 'Yes, I was sure I planted a lemon one. It must have been red.'

Uncle Allan looked around, confused.

'Where's Dean, Uncle Allan?' Adam asked, standing closer to Sheffield.

'Dean...'

'Where is he?' Adam asked in a quiet voice.

Sheffield looked down at the base of the tree.

'Let's get him out and put him in the cemetery,' Adam said, hoping to get an admission from Sheffield that he'd buried Dean in the garden. 'One day, they can bury us all together.'

'Me with my boys,' Uncle Allan said, his voice sentimental.

'Yeah, the three of us,' Adam said, his jaw locking after the words left his mouth. He opened and closed his fist at his side, out of sight of Sheffield. He could hear Rob's voice telling him to keep it together; Nate would tell him they were so close now and not to blow it.

Uncle Allan turned to look Adam in the eye. 'Would you like to join him?'

Chapter 54

Now…

Nate swore, frustrated at not being with Adam, as he and Tom sat listening to the dialogue and watching Adam and Allan Sheffield from afar. They were ready to move in, but Burnsy, Dan and the two police officers were closer on location.

'He'll be having nightmares for a year after this,' Nate said.

'Who wouldn't?' Tom agreed. 'Sheffield's a creepy asshole, I'd like to slam him. I hope I get the chance.'

Nate ignored the angry ex-soldier beside him. Adam hadn't answered the question, and Sheffield repeated it.

'Adam? Would you like to join Dean?'

Nate's eyes narrowed as he watched Adam for a reaction. He knew Adam was reeling; he could see his chest heaving more than it should be, his eyes fixated on the garden bed.

'Is he alright?' Tom asked. 'He's frozen.'

'He's alright. Give him a moment,' Nate said, frowning. He tapped on the dashboard with impatience, stopping when Adam's voice came through.

'In there?' he asked with a nod to the garden bed, his voice catching in his throat. 'Is that where Dean is waiting for us?'

'No.' Uncle Allan walked away and Adam's shoulders slumped.

'He said he wanted to come and stay and then when I got him here, he wanted to go straight home to his father.' Uncle Allan shook his head. 'The father who didn't give a shit about him. He was asking for his mum in the end. I told him I was here; I was the one who was here for him.'

'Christ almighty,' Tom said, the words hissing through his teeth.

'Yeah, I'm glad you're here, Uncle Allan.' Adam said in a strange voice, gagging on the words.

Nate looked at Tom. 'He can't do this for much longer. Something has to give.'

'We can storm in,' Tom said, 'but I'd prefer we let Adam handle it, see how far he can push Sheffield.'

Nate shook his head. 'He's opening and closing his fist; he's breathing too fast. If Rob was here, he'd shut it down right now.'

Tom leaned forward in the seat to study Adam. 'He must have heard you; he's steadied himself. Come on Sheffield, fucking spit it out. Where's the kid? Take Adam there, and we can all go home.'

'What will your dad pay?' Sheffield asked.

Adam snapped to look at Uncle Allan.

'To have you back, Son, what will he pay?'

'Holy crap,' Nate muttered.

'This'll be telling. What's your payday looking like asshole?' Tom snarled at Sheffield from behind the wheel of his car.

They waited for Adam's answer and then he said: 'He'll pay nothing.'

'Here we go,' Nate said, 'he'll have to react to that… he's got a "kid" with him who is not worth a cent.'

Uncle Allan turned his back on Adam and moved a step away.

Adam fell to the ground and started digging with his bare hands.

'What the fuck is he doing?' Tom growled.

'He's bringing on the action,' Nate said leaning forward, ready to move.

'Leave it!' Uncle Allan yelled, 'Adam, get away, c'mon we're going to see Dean.'

Adam stopped. 'He's not here?'

'Why would he be there! C'mon, we'll go there if that's what you want.'

Adam sighed and stood up, swiping the dirt off the knees of his cricket whites and from his hands. He followed Uncle Allan back to the car, to a destination unknown. Nate knew the last thing in the world Adam would want to do was get back in the car with Allan Sheffield.

*****

'Belt up,' Tom ordered as he turned the ignition on, ready to follow Allan Sheffield.

'Christ, the strain of staying calm with this lunatic will send Adam over the edge,' Nate said concerned for his best friend. 'So, Dean's not at Sheffield's house, and not at the cemetery as far as we know. Where the hell are they going now?'

They waited, ready to follow safely behind Sheffield. Tom hit Burnsy's number and spoke hands-free.

'Any idea where he is off to now?' Burnsy asked.

'Not a clue,' Nate spoke up.

'Righto. I'll leave Dan here with one officer, and I'll take the other and we'll follow.'

Tom hung up and they slowly tracked behind Sheffield. There was no dialogue coming from Sheffield's car.

'Is it still working?' Nate asked, but before Tom could answer, Adam spoke up.

'It's a good car,' Adam said, 'really posh inside.'

'Adam's starting at the beginning again,' Nate said and sighed. 'Poor bastard.'

They waited and then Sheffield answered.

'Thank you, my boy, it's a very good car, and I take care of it. Not all the drivers look after their cars, mind you,' Uncle Allan said. 'My clients like to be picked up in something prestigious.'

'Makes them feel important, I guess,' Adam said.

'Exactly right, young man, exactly right.' Uncle Allan said.

'So where are we going now, Uncle Allan? Can we see Dean?' Adam asked, his voice strained but rising with an attempt at enthusiasm. 'The three of us could do something.'

'That's exactly where we are going, my boy,' Uncle Allan answered. He flicked on the car's indicator and took several turns as they approached.

Nate swore. 'I know where we are going, holy crap.' He dialled Burnsy. 'They're going to Sheffield's grandfather's house.'

Tom snapped to look at Nate before returning his attention to the road. 'What the fuck?'

'He's not Sheffield's real grandfather,' Nate said and held up a hand to calm him. 'Are you there, Burnsy?'

'I'm listening,' Sergeant Burns answered.

'When Sheffield first came to us in drag pretending to be Mrs Tatum looking for her missing son, we searched for other Tatums… we thought they might know what happened to the young guy I was paid to find,' Nate explained mainly for Tom's benefit. 'Burnsy, that address you gave us for Ron Tatum helped. He didn't know Mrs Tatum but he knew Allan Sheffield. Ron and his wife were neighbours and surrogate grandparents to Uncle Allan and his brothers when they were kids.'

'And that's where he's going now?' Burnsy asked.

'It appears that way,' Nate said. 'The photo that Mrs Tatum – Allan – gave us of her so-called son, was poor old Ron Tatum's deceased son.'

'This guy's a psycho! How the hell did he get released back on the street?' Tom asked, turning and staying well back from Sheffield's car.

'Beats me,' Nate agreed. 'Anyway, we're going to his house, to Ron Tatum's place. He is an old man now. The wife has passed, but Ron told Adam and me they loved those boys like family. Ron and his wife even visited Allan in prison.'

'Then there's every chance Dean is buried at Allan Sheffield's childhood home or next door at Allan's grandfather's house – alias the babysitter neighbour,' Tom summed it up.

Burnsy asked: 'Ex-cop to current cop, Nate, when you and Adam spoke with Ron, do you think he could have been involved, could have helped Sheffield all those years ago?'

Nate thought about the interview. In his police career, he'd met all sorts including sweet oldies who would slit your throat to save their skin.

'I couldn't rule it out,' he said.

Chapter 55

Now…

Adam realised where they were going. He confirmed it out loud for Nate's benefit, but he knew Nate would be all over it as soon as the area became familiar.

Adam took a risk and asked: 'Your granddad lives next door to you, doesn't he?'

'He does,' Uncle Allan said, 'but he's not really our grandfather. We just call him that because he's been like a grandfather to me and my brothers. He's a good man.'

Uncle Allan parked out the front and leaned over far enough to look towards the house. 'Looks like he's in.' He nudged Adam. 'Come on, we'll see Dean and say hi to my granddad.'

'Great,' Adam said and exited the car. He knew the gig would be up now, as soon as Ron Tatum saw them together and recognised him from calling earlier in the week with Nate. It would bring Allan Sheffield right back to the present, blowing all Adam's hard work to now.

Unless, of course, Ron Tatum was also involved and helped cover for Allan, then he might shut up and play dumb to see how it all played out. Adam had liked the sincere old guy – God knows Ron Tatum had his share of loss, but lots of good people did the wrong thing when they were covering for family. He was pretty sure he would as well.

The front door opened as Uncle Allan headed up the path with Adam behind him. A small, white-haired old man appeared – Ron Tatum.

'Allan, my boy, so good to see you again so soon,' Ron Tatum said grinning from ear to his ear, his arms wide to embrace Allan.

So, he had caught up with Allan, Adam thought. He had said otherwise in his interview.

Then, Ron's smile dropped on seeing Adam. He looked from Allan to Adam and back to his 'grandson.'

'I brought Adam to meet you, and we want to see Dean,' Uncle Allan said and hugged Ron Tatum.

Adam gave Ron Tatum a small nod as he glanced at him over Uncle Allan's shoulders, but didn't speak.

'We've got a place for Adam, haven't we?' Uncle Allan asked as he placed an arm around Ron Tatum's shoulder and walked into the small home. He looked back and called out, 'come on, Son, we'll go find Dean.'

Adam glanced to the street. No one was in sight. No car, no faces he knew. He hoped they were out there somewhere, but he'd never felt so alone; he had no idea what he was walking into. Adam turned and followed Uncle Allan inside, his and Dean's past playing out in front of him.

*****

In moments, Nate and Tom were out of the car running towards the house. Burnsy pulled up on the corner and with his young constable, jumped the small front fence, and fanned out. Now, they followed Tom's command as agreed. They didn't want to blow it. While they had plenty of grounds already for securing Allan Sheffield in a mental facility, they wanted to find where Dean was buried.

Nate's priorities were different. 'This stops now,' he said. 'Enough. Put Sheffield away and we'll search the premises for Dean's body.'

Tom held up his hand. 'A little longer, Nate. Keep it together, your mate is.' He was listening to Adam's audio feed in one ear. 'They are going to the backyard to catch up with Dean,' he added and motioned for Burnsy and the constable to go to one side of the house while he and Nate peeled off down the other side.

Nate could see Adam now, all three were in the backyard. He breathed a little easier with Adam in his line of vision and not in the house.

'Where's Dean?' Adam asked again, looking around.

Both Ron Tatum and Uncle Allan Sheffield looked towards the corner of the house, where a small tin water tank sat on stumps. Underneath it was dirt with a smattering of weeds. They walked towards it.

'I should have been looking after it,' Uncle Allan said.

Ron Tatum put his hand on Allan's shoulder. 'You've been away, Allan, you can't do everything. I've kept an eye on him.'

'That's it,' Burnsy agreed, overruling Tom. 'Move in.'

Not a moment too soon as Adam lost it. With one swift movement, Adam turned, his hands wrapped around Sheffield's throat pushing him hard against the tank, Sheffield's eyes were bulging. Ron Tatum thumped on Adam's back as he tried to pull them apart.

'Adam, enough, release him,' Burnsy ordered running to Adam's side and trying to break them up while restraining one of Sheffield's arms.

Ron Tatum looked around alarmed on seeing the four men, two in uniform. He stepped back.

Tom fought to pull Adam back but Adam's jaw was set in grim determination, his hands attempting to take the last breath from Sheffield's throat. Was this how a ten-year-old boy's life had ended twenty years ago?

'Adam, stand down,' Nate yelled and grabbed him around the chest separating the men.

Sheffield slumped, gasping.

'It's over,' Nate said, and Adam pulled away, straightened, and wiped his hand over his mouth.

'Call in for assistance for a dig,' Burnsy ordered his young constable while he and Tom restrained Sheffield. 'Don't go anywhere,' he barked an order to the senior Ron Tatum.

'I'll tell Dan and your other young cop to stand down,' Nate said, reaching for his phone.

'How long have you known?' Burnsy asked in his police capacity. Ron Tatum did not answer. He stood by watching, his mouth agape, then shook his head.

'Don't lie,' Nate said, pausing from making his call to hear Ron Tatum's response. 'You told us you hadn't seen Allan and clearly you had. Did you help him hide the body?'

Ron Tatum stood mute. Shocked, distressed, and not answering.

'He was my nephew!' Allan Sheffield yelled at the surrounding men. 'Dean and Adam, I've got to return them home and get the ransom, Millie needs the money!' He was looking around wildly, spluttering and drawing deep breaths in an attempt to recover.

'It's alright, Allan,' Ron Tatum spoke up, trying to calm him. 'I'll get the boys home; I'll look after Millie.' He turned to Nate and offered an answer: 'He was always such a good boy, just too much pressure. He was trying to do the right thing by his family.'

'But not by Dean or Adam's family,' Burnsy reminded the old man.

'There's clothing here, sir,' the young constable called, having only dug a few feet with the garden spade. He held up a kid-size T-shirt.

'Stop digging,' Burnsy said. 'We need to preserve it for forensics.'

'It's got to be Dean,' Tom said.

'Where's Adam?' Nate asked looking around. 'Adam!' he yelled.

Tom swore.

'You've lost him again,' Nate said accusing Tom.

'He was just behind you a moment ago! How far could he have gone? Christ, just like last time when he bloody took off then too.'

'Forget it. He's not a kid, he'll be alright,' Nate said, annoyed.

'He's my charge.' Tom swore a string of words and ran to the back of the property. Nate took the opposite direction from Tom. He returned to the car, and then the street corner. Adam was gone.

Chapter 56

Now...

Nate could see Adam sitting, leaning up against a tree – his cricket whites standing out amongst the bush and scrub. Adam was talking to someone, or himself. Nate was not sure which would be better, maybe the former. He sent a quick message to Tom and Rob – *Found him, all okay.* Then, he made his way noisily through the bush towards Adam, deliberately standing on twigs and dried leaves to alert Adam of his approach. As he got closer, Adam's head snapped around at the sound, he relaxed and smiled at Nate.

'He's here,' Adam said.

Nate dropped by his side and laughed on seeing whom Adam was talking with – a phone video call with Charlie, his old bodyguard.

'My first love!' Nate exclaimed, hand on heart, and Charlie laughed.

'Look at you, handsome! I still have that Valentine's card you gave me when you were ten.' She smiled at Nate with affection.

'Get out of here,' he said and laughed.

'Well, now that Nathaniel has arrived, I'll leave you two lads to it then,' she said. 'Call me, Adam, later, tomorrow, the next day, soon.' She blew them a kiss, Adam thanked her and disconnected. He pocketed the phone.

'She knows about it?' Nate asked.

'Yeah, Charlie's rung a few times, Audrey told her what we were doing, what was going on.'

They sat looking straight ahead. The bush was thick, the sound of cicadas filled the air and the occasional magpie joined in with a song. The nearby creek smelled earthy with its heavy reeds bordering the edges, and the insect life darted over the water's surface. In the distance, the relic of the asylum loomed.

'I'd forgotten how quiet it is here,' Nate said, looking around. 'Come here often?'

'Yeah.'

Nate looked surprised. As boys, it was once their favourite spot and a regular haunt, but he hadn't been back since looking for their friend Joe, and before that, not for years. They watched as an ibis landed near the creek. Nate turned his attention to his best friend.

'Are you okay?'

'Yeah, I'm good,' Adam said without making eye contact.

'Because if you're not and need to talk... there's Rob,' Nate said, and then smiled. Adam laughed.

'Thanks. You're a big help.'

'Or you can talk to me.'

'I'm good.'

Nate continued, looking straight ahead now, and speaking in a low voice said: 'They took him. He'll be locked away now, it's over. No more looking over your shoulder or mine for that matter.'

'Good,' Adam said again.

'They've got bones. It was pretty shallow. Burnsy has that all cordoned off, so Dean can go home.'

Adam nodded. 'Right.'

'And, the best news…' Nate waited until Adam looked at him, '… you won't need to deal with Tom again until the wedding day. But he tells me that Winsome will try to get you in a family photo.'

Adam sighed and looked back at the creek. 'That almost sounds normal after all that's gone down.'

Nate felt a rush of relief that at last, his friend had said more than a handful of words. He answered, 'That's a worry.'

Adam laughed again and, pushing himself up, walked to the creek's edge. Nate followed him. The view of the deserted asylum loomed larger, and even as grown men, they were dwarfed by the spotted gums towering above them. They saw a quick movement in the water.

'Still eels in here,' Nate said watching the creature slip away.

Adam frowned. 'They're creepy with those fang-like things… swimming snakes.'

'They probably think you're scary at the moment too with that black eye.'

Adam smiled and subconsciously touched the dark area of his face.

'Let's play hooky for the day. No more work. I propose a beer at the pub,' Nate said.

'Great idea,' Adam agreed.

Nate turned and slowly walked through the scrub back up to his car that he had left on the side of the road. He looked back to see Adam studying the water, before he also turned and, like he usually did, he followed Nate out.

Chapter 57

Now...

Adam tapped the number in the office door keypad at *Delaney and Murphy* and tried again when it failed. Nate swung the door open.

'You've been away for two weeks and you've forgotten the key code already,' he said slapping his best friend on the back as he pulled him in.

Adam, tanned and looking healthy, entered. 'Who are you?' he asked Nate and got a laugh.

'You're back!' Jessica said and came to greet him. They had an awkward hug – neither were huggers. 'You look great.'

Before Adam could respond, the keypad beeped behind them, and Danielle and Rob entered.

'He's back!' Rob said, 'and don't worry, Dan and I met in the carpark. We're not having a clandestine affair,' he said with a wink to Danielle, who laughed.

'Well, not this week,' she added and grabbed Adam for an embrace, which she did often, and he managed awkwardly as well.

Nate had versed them beforehand, not to mention Allan Sheffield or anything related to the case. Sheffield was locked away safely, Dean's remains had been returned to his family, and the autopsy – despite the length of years that had passed – indicated a hit to the skull was the cause of death, most likely when Dean was trying to escape. The case and their involvement in it, was closed.

'Vacations become you,' Rob said studying Adam. 'You look good.'

'Yeah, it was great,' Adam said with a smile, which was a rare sight of late. 'We snorkelled every day, ate our weight in shellfish, tried all their beer, wine and cocktails poolside...'

'Yeah, shut up,' Jessica said with a grin and moved back behind her desk.

'We get the picture,' Danielle said giving him a wry look. 'Meanwhile, back in the workforce...'

'Come and see me when you're ready and I'll update you on your clients,' Rob said.

'Thanks for taking them.'

'Most of them, some rescheduled,' Rob said with a wave as he re-entered his office.

The group broke apart, and Adam followed Nate into his office. He sat down in a chair in front of Nate's desk as Nate took his usual seat.

'I moved out of your family mansion and back to my place while you were away,' Nate said. 'I was going to become a squatter; I miss the pool.'

'There was no rush to move,' Adam said.

'That's what Audrey said. She didn't want me to leave. She likes having someone in the house next door to her, makes her feel safer, apparently.'

'Even when it's you?' Adam asked surprised and earned a

smirk. 'Yeah, she tried that old lady alone stunt on me, too. I'm not buying it. She's not there half the time herself and the rest of the time she'd ward anyone off. But why don't you stay?'

'Nah, it was just nice to have the pool handy and to not be in my marital home, you know the story – replacing memories. Besides, I don't want Matilda thinking that kind of life is normal. Some poor bastard will have to provide it for her,' Nate joked.

'She's five – isn't it all about being a princess and dad's her hero?'

'Yeah, it's a cute age,' he said and smiled.

'I thought Kelsey might want to stay on, too. She liked the space after living in her unit,' Adam said. 'But she was happy to go. She's moving into my place.'

Nate's eyes widened with surprise.

'I know it's only been about six months.'

'Who cares?' Nate said. 'Good on you.'

'Thanks. She's keen to live in a house and have a garden, she's going to work on mine.' He shrugged, 'I'm the cheap labourer.'

'I've seen your rates – no one would ever call you cheap,' Nate joked. 'It is kind of crazy that Winsome keeps the house with the garden maintenance alone… a big, empty, white elephant.'

'Mum doesn't like the idea of selling it. For all her faults, she's sentimental. It reminds her of Dad. Stay, it won't bother me, and Jack told us both at the BBQ that Mum wished we'd stay and someone lived in the house.'

Nate thought for a moment. 'Jack doesn't understand why you won't live there. Me either.'

Adam shrugged. 'Unlike Mum, that house does not make me sentimental, quite the opposite. I'm insisting, stay there, enjoy it for a while, save some money, keep an eye on the place. Dan can rent your house, maybe.'

'There's a thought,' Nate said.

'You'll have Jack and Mum coming and going occasionally, but they'll stay in the garden wing without the river views.'

'Weird that,' Nate said. 'Well, thanks, I'll give it some serious thought.' He tried not to look too excited at the prospect of living somewhere new with no bad memories, and for just a while, having a lifestyle he could never afford. 'Speaking of Dan renting, why doesn't Winsome rent it out? At least there would be some income to cover the rates which must be huge.'

'I don't want to do that to Audrey,' Adam answered, distracted. 'She doesn't need parties or a stack of people she doesn't know coming and going. Besides, Dad's estate income easily covers the rates and maintenance, and it means Mum and Jack can stay there anytime.'

Adam looked away, realising what he said and why Nate was silent. He hadn't been concentrating, and he had let down his guard.

'You own it, don't you?' Nate asked.

Adam swallowed and looking at Nate, nodded. 'Dad left it to me on the proviso Audrey could live there until she died, if she wanted to.'

'Why didn't you say?'

He shrugged. 'Money divides people.'

Nate laughed. 'You've always had it, so what. That wouldn't come between us.'

Adam smiled his thanks. 'I know it sounds weird, probably, but I wanted to work and get a loan, and buy a house, pay it off. Own it myself.'

'With Joe's inheritance helping,' Nate added.

'That's different. We were gifted that, both of us. Besides,

I meant what I said about the family home, it's not a home. When Audrey passes, I'll probably get rid of it.'

'Does Kelsey know you own it?'

'No. No-one knows. I want to keep it that way.'

'Okay,' Nate agreed. 'So, I won't be too noisy for Audrey?'

Adam grinned. 'Years ago, yeah, but now that you're all grown up with a child, it should be fine. Even if you team up with Jessica. Audrey likes her.'

'Hmm,' Nate said and left it at that.

'It's good to be back,' Adam said and exhaled. 'It's good this,' he said waving his arm around, 'our joint office and business.'

'It's good to have you back. It's been boring this past two weeks without you,' Nate said in a rare show of emotion. He tapped on a file in front of him. 'I've got a new case for us to work on.'

'Yeah?' Adam's face lit up. 'Great. What is it this time?'

'Ever been tempted to join a cult?'

*****

Then...

The two boys pulled into Nate's driveway on their bikes.

'Your dad's home!' Adam said, surprised. It always surprised him that other people's parents came home every day, and were both home at night.

'Yeah, he finishes early on Fridays.'

'Hello boys,' Mrs Delaney called from some distance away behind the fence where she was watering the garden.

'Hi, Mum.'

'Hi, Mrs Delaney.'

'How are you, Adam darling?' she called.

'Very good, thank you, Mrs Delaney,' he answered, and

Nate rolled his eyes. Audrey was very big on manners and enforced them in Adam's household.

'Be home for dinner in an hour, Nathaniel,' she called.

'Yes, Mrs Delaney,' he called back and made his mother laugh.

'You are welcome, of course, Adam,' she added.

'Thank you, Mrs Delaney, but Audrey is home tonight.'

'Another time then, a sleepover soon.'

Nate's father came out to the garage and seeing the boys, called out. 'Shall we go to the park and have a hit?' he said and held up the cricket bat in the garage.

'Yeah!' Nate called.

'Brilliant,' Adam grinned. They'd now have one to bat, one to catch and one to field.

While they were waiting for Nate's dad to change, Adam said: 'One day, I'm going to have a home like yours. Where people are home, and there's a garden, and normal dinner time, and I'll be a dad who comes out to play cricket too.'

'Yeah?' Nate said surprised. 'One day I'm going to have a house like yours with a huge yard and a swimming pool and tennis court. I'll have a cool car too. You can come around if you like,' he joked.

'Thanks! You can come around to my place too.'

They put their bikes in the garage and joined Nate's dad as they crossed the road to walk to the park. Nate's dad roughed up his son in an affectionate hug and looked back to where Adam walked slightly behind.

'Where's my favourite second son?' he asked and grabbed Adam in a bear hug which had both boys laughing.

'Last one there is a rotten egg,' Nate said and took off. Adam followed as fast as he could. He usually did.

THE END

By Jack Adams:

Delaney & Murphy series:
Asylum
Stalker
Cult

Stand-alone titles:
Poster Girl

Also in the *Delaney and Murphy* series by Jack Adams:

Asylum

Ten-year-old best friends, Nathan and Adam, really liked Joe. He was their friend, an artist, the man they spoke to through the wire fence of the lunatic asylum.

But something happened behind those walls, in those rooms, on the grounds, at the river.

The inmate sketched it all – fine lines, truth in the negative space, truth in the pencil strokes.

Then one day Joe was gone.

Twenty years later Nathan and Adam receive a letter.

Cult

Eleven-year-old Nate wasn't happy. There was a new kid on the block named Griffin Maxwell and he wanted Adam to be his best friend. That was Nate's job, they had sworn they were blood brothers forever. Two days after Adam's birthday party when Adam received a strange birthday present from Griffin, the Maxwell family was gone.

Twenty years later, Griffin Maxwell is back.

And he wants Adam to come out and play.

Thanks and acknowledgements:

My sincere thanks to my sister-in-law. dear friend and psychologist, **Raylene Chen**, for answering my two thousand questions (okay, maybe ten). Any errors or unorthodox deviations in this field of practice found in my book are mine alone;

Residual thanks to author, **B. Michael Radburn** who encouraged this series and took time out from his writing to read an author's work and offer words of support and encouragement;

My thanks to proof-reader, **Jessica Lucci**;

And thank you to all the **readers** and book lovers for your kind reviews and encouragement. Without you, there would be no inspiration to keep creating.

Contact Jack:

I don't hang around much on social media, but here's where you will find me:

Website: https://jackadamswrites.com/
Facebook: www.facebook.com/jackadamswrites/
Email: jackadamswrites@gmail.com

From the author:

I grew up in Toowoomba, Queensland, Australia, and had one of those wonderful childhoods spent in suburban streets with neighbourhood kids, riding my bike until the sun went down. Adam and Nate are the embodiment of those days when friendships were made because you liked the person… not because of who they were, their wealth or position. Very few of those childhood friendships last, but that doesn't mean I don't often think about my 'gang' from those days and wish we were still connected.

This book is fictional, but the fear is real. I can recall when an attempted child abduction at a school in my suburbs put everyone on alert. I remember to this day, getting out of Mum's car at the school gate and the teachers outside the gate moving us all along and ensuring we got behind the school fence safely. We were only allowed to go to the toilet in pairs, and not to leave the school grounds until we were 'claimed' or put on the bus. The bogey man was very real, we were all frightened. I love the theme of friends being family as many of us do not have the functional families we see on television. I'm sure many readers will relate to the themes of the *Delaney and Murphy* books and have their own stories to tell.

Resource:
Asad, Fariyal, Looking through the eyes of a kidnapper, *Psychologs*. 23 July 2020. Retrieved 20 September 2021 from URL: https://www.psychologs.com/article/looking-through-the-eyes-of-a-kidnapper